- Please return items before closing time
  on the last date stamped to avoid charges.

- Renew books by phoning 01305 224311 or
  online www.dorsetforyou.com/libraries

- Items may be returned to any Dorset library.

- Please note that children's books issued on
  an adult card will incur overdue charges.

Dorset County Council
Library Service

DL/2372 dd05450

Published in 2012 by FeedARead.com Publishing –
Arts Council funded

A CIP catalogue record for this title is available from
the British Library.

You're so arrogant, you might
even think this book is about you.
Well you're wrong. The deranged
Nazi, with lesbian tendencies,
could have been based on
any one of a number of
women in the village.

Acknowledgements:

Anyone with an interest in this period
should do as I did and read Alistair Horne's
masterly book; 'To Lose a Battle: France 1940'.
It is both informative and fascinating.
Also consulted were;
'Outwitting the Gestapo' by Lucie Aubrac
'Fleeing Hitler' by Hanna Diamond
'That Woman' by Anna Sebba
And finally my thanks to Margaret, Sarah
and Cate, for their welcome assistance.

Chapter 1

Doktor Theo Leibniz
Berlin, Monday April 29th. 1940

I had hardly sat at my desk before Gerd came bustling into the office. She's normally a rather placid young lady, but this morning there was clearly 'Something Important' to say, and she was going to say it. The flimsy sheet of teleprinter roll that she was waving like a flag seemed to be a part of the process.

"Herr Doktor, there is an urgent message for you, from Gruppenfuhrer Vogel; it's only just come in." She thrust the paper towards me.

Taking the paper, I asked what seemed the obvious and reasonable question. "And who exactly is Gruppenfuhrer Vogel, do we know him?" The question seemed to surprise her.

"Well, no, I don't think so."

"Then I shall delay my excitement until I've read his message. A cup of coffee would be most welcome."

"But he's with the SS at the Reich Security Office." Her voice had risen a pitch, denoting an eagerness to explore the subject.

I'm a methodical man, it's how I do my work, and I have a very low tolerance for this sort of nonsense. I tapped the desk, quite sharply. "Gerd, go away and get me a cup of coffee - if you would be so kind." She went, and I looked at the paper.

It was brief and to the point. It requested the presence of Herr Doktor Theo Leibniz, myself, at SS headquarters at 11.30 to see the aforementioned Gruppenfuhrer Georg Vogel. No reason was given, and there was a marked lack of enquiry as to how convenient this might be, but that was unsurprising.

Working for Himmler does tend to give his senior staff the impression that they can walk on water and that all doors will be open to them, and certainly in the second case they're usually right. He might not be the Fuhrer's official deputy, that honour belongs to Reichsleiter Rudolf Hess, but he is surely, in reality, the second most powerful man in the country. And though personally charming, Himmler is not a man noted for his tolerance of opposing views. But then in a country at war, strong men are called for; as Goethe wrote, cometh the hour, cometh the man.

If there is anyone who still needs a lesson in the results of unfettered political opportunism and racial inbreeding, they need look no further than France. There are blacks on every street corner, Jews in the parliament and defeatism in the army. Any rational man comparing that with out own concept of 'Ein Reich, ein Volk, ein Fuhrer', and then preferring the French model has probably just produced a technical definition of the word insanity. In the surrounding moral chaos that is present day Europe, a somewhat rigorous approach to public policy, in defence of national self respect and decency, is a small and worthwhile price to pay.

Whilst my work frequently takes me out on site for field tests, at naval bases and Luftwaffe stations, my main place of work is at the Institute in Berlin, one of the world's leading centres of research into radio frequency generation and oscilloscopes. When it was founded in 1928, it was called the Heinrich Hertz Institute, in honour of the famous German scientist, the man after whom the Hertz unit of frequency is named.

6

It rapidly became the established leader in its field, attracting the attention of the international scientific community.

However, in the early thirties disturbing news came to light about the Hertz family's background, and especially the fact that there was Jewish blood in the line. It was felt it would be more discreet if the name were changed to the H.H. Institute, and the marble lettering over the entrance was altered to reflect that fact. More recently still, the lettering has undergone a further small but subtle change, and it now reads the A.H. Institute. Most of us accept such realpolitik as a fact of life and just call it The Institute.

April in Berlin is often a month with two distinct parts, the dark grey grip of winter still making itself felt in the first half, and the occasional promise of spring in the second. Monday April 29th. should have fallen into the second half, it was late enough in the month. But it was clearly a first half sort of day, with ice cold gusts of wind shaking the trees in the park, and what might have been either rain or sleet rattling against the windows.

I could have walked to Prinz-Albrecht-Strasse, it wasn't far, but in view of the conditions I had Curt drive me. The headquarters building of the RSHA, which includes the Gestapo and the SS, is a rather gloomy grey five story pile of a place. Someone told me that it had once been a hotel, if that was truly the case, then they must have had a lot of flowers around the doorway.

The black clad, rifle carrying, guards at the top of the entrance steps presented arms as I approached; the slap of their hands against the rifle stocks perfectly in time. The politeness of the gesture impressed me. I'm a respected man in my own field, but little known outside that fairly narrow discipline, and yet somehow they had recognised me. That sort of thing indicates a reassuring level of attention to detail. An adjutant greeted me in the foyer and led me to the lift; this was not a place for unsupervised wandering.

I was unfamiliar with Vogel's name, and his rank gave little away. If it could be said that the SS had a fault, it is perhaps summed up in the amusing American expression; 'Too many chiefs and not enough Indians'. I once spent a year with the University of Chicago Physics Department, and some small vestiges of their culture remain with me.

It sometimes seems as if half the SS officers one meets socially are introduced as Gruppenfuhrer, what the regular army would call a Major General, or perhaps it is simply that I have finally started to move in the right circles. Vogel's office gave me the first clue; it was extremely large, and the German culture, more than most, equates size with importance. Vogel was clearly no run of the mill Gruppenfuhrer. However, what set the seal on the man's status was the presence in an armchair of the Director of the RSHA, Reinhard Heydrich. If someone like that comes to visit you in your own office, instead of summoning you to his, it marks you as special.

Despite the importance of his position he was still a comparatively young man, thirty six or seven I think, and although widely known as Himmler's personal protégé he is also widely known to be extremely determined and efficient; two prized German virtues.

He stood as I entered the room, not, I suspect, from any respect for me, rather because his conversation with Vogel had been ended by my arrival. His immaculate uniform must have been newly pressed that morning, as it probably was every morning. He is rumoured to have a colourful past, including, almost unbelievably, a reported discharge from the Kriegsmarine for 'conduct unbecoming'. Even if true, this in no way detracts from his air of complete authority.

Everyone remarks on his personal appearance, his sheer presence, and having met him I can see why. At the risk of sounding like a lady novelist, my own view was that his swept back hair, his piercing gaze and his prominent nose made it quite impossible to avoid the term 'hawk like'.

I acknowledged him politely and waited for him to conclude his business with Vogel. Instead, however, he turned his attention on me. It was like being caught in a searchlight beam.

"Herr Doktor, you are to be honoured with a most special assignment. Please remember at all times that Reichsfuhrer Himmler and myself will be paying the closest attention to your progress, success in this matter is absolutely essential. Heil Hitler." Then with the briefest nod of the head he turned and was gone, leaving me wondering if I should return the Heil Hitler, or even make the salute. But the moment had passed and I found myself looking helplessly at Vogel.

He smiled. "Don't worry Leibniz; he has that effect on most people. Take a seat - coffee?" I relaxed, accepted the offer of coffee and sat in the recently vacated armchair. After the briefest discussion of the weather, as the coffee was brought in, we found ourselves alone and he came immediately to the point.

"You're an intelligent man so I won't insult you with warnings about the need for secrecy, but sometime in the second week of May, we shall be going into France and the Low Countries."

"We?"

"That's right, you and me - and if it's a nice day then I imagine the army and the air force will probably come with us." He smiled. "The Allies have been calling this the Phony War; well we're about to warm things up for them."

"But what possible use can I be in such an operation? My place is at the Institute, driving our work on Radio Location forward with the utmost urgency." Vogel leaned back in his chair, still smiling slightly.

"Tell me Herr Doktor, in simple layman's terms, exactly what you're trying to do."

I hesitated for a moment trying to find a starting point. "Well basically, the principle underlying my work is so simple a child could understand it. Heinrich Hertz discovered back in the eighteen eighties that radio waves are reflected back from metallic objects, and that this return wave can be detected on an oscilloscope. That laid the starting point for the current hunt to produce a workable Radio Location Finder, a simple but effective device to locate the position of enemy units."

"And where have you reached in this hunt?"

I sighed. "We have repeatedly demonstrated the long distance detection of both ships and aircraft; the trouble is that in order to do this we're currently using very long wave lengths, typically around fifteen metres. But radio waves of that size are badly distorted by ground reflections, and require huge aerials. What we need is some method of producing high power, extremely short radio waves, less than a metre, that would solve most of the problems. A lot of research funding at the moment is being spent on a type of electronic valve called a magnetron, but the frequencies generated are wildly unstable."

"Would you like me to tell you where you can find an efficiently functioning version of such a device?"

"I would walk on broken glass to find it."

"An excellent sentiment, my dear Leibniz, but I don't think we need to be quite so dramatic. As I understand it, the latest version of this device is the so called cavity magnetron, is that correct?"

"Yes, but any advance they offer in terms of power output or ultra short wave length is, so far, more theoretical than real. There are several other, more promising, areas of enquiry, my own team is attempting to refine an alternative device called the klystron."

"Be that as it may, our information is that a small team of French scientists have just conducted a series of highly successful experiments near Paris, on what we understand to be a development of the cavity magnetron. Our contact on the team assures us that when the news of German troop movements reaches them, they will attempt to surrender their device to the British, in order to prevent it falling into our hands."

"Which scientist is leading this team? It's possible I might know them."

"Maurice Ponte from the CSF laboratory in Paris."

"Yes, I know Ponte, and I wouldn't trust him across a crowded room, he's rabidly anti German. Anyone attempting to secure the device would need to assume his opposition; he would have to be taken completely by surprise."

"And there you have it in a nutshell, Herr Doktor, you are the only person we know who would both recognise Ponte and be able to tell if the equipment we were seizing was genuine. It would a great shame to deploy a team of crack troops only to find that they'd seized a central heating valve, or some such."

I was silent for a moment, staring out of the window across the shiny wet rooftops of central Berlin. The scenario was astonishing but utterly fascinating.

"I take it that you would want me, and this team of yours, to go in with the very first wave of troops to cross the border, and race directly for Paris."

"Good Lord no, when the starting pistol goes for this particular race, I expect you to be on site and waiting in position."

"But we're at war with the French; I can't just drive over there and book into a local hotel."

Vogel laughed at my naivety. "On the contrary, my good Doktor, that is exactly what you're going to do."

Sir Freddy Villiers
London, Friday May 3rd. 1940

I'm not sure there is any such thing as a good funeral, surely the whole idea is that they're supposed to be awful, the public display of a raw wound. All that personality and fun stuffed into a wooden box, and then buried. The idea would seem to be that once such a huge wave of emotion has washed through you, then there should be some chance of dealing with life again. Yet Mary's death had been so long anticipated that all feeling was exhausted, it felt more like passing the finishing post in a gruelling race.

So much so, that it seems to be no more than a statement of the obvious to say that since that day I've been at a bit of a loose end - or should that be a dead end? My life has a semi detached, unfocussed quality to it, as if I'm looking at myself from a distance and wondering; *why is he doing that?* The natural order of things is now so different that I'm not sure if I have sufficient energy or interest for the adjustment.

There had been an almost audible sigh of relief from our friends as we left the cemetery; the relief in knowing that they could gradually stop speaking to me in hushed tones, that they would no longer have to phrase everything to allow for my recently bereaved sensibilities. I have no grounds for complaint, the only reason I can recognise the feeling in others is because I share it so fully myself. Friends and colleagues were genuinely sympathetic and helpful during the illness; in Mary's case it was leukaemia, which for some reason is one of the few forms of cancer that can be discussed openly.

In the immediate aftermath of Mary's death, I was buoyed up by a wave of real warmth and helpfulness. Cassie even wanted me to move up to Scotland to live near her and John and the boys. But the point about Cassie is that, quite apart from being her own woman, she is now the boy's mother and John's wife, much more than she is my daughter. I love her and the boys dearly, but their lives should be pointing to their future and not my past. Her major concern must be about this war dragging on and John being dragged into it. He should be past the age of conscription, but if things turn nasty, and I think they will - then you never know.

That had been three months ago, and for the first time in my life I ducked a challenge, I failed to cope. I feel that I've wasted all that sympathy and good will by failing to keep my side of the bargain, and allowing myself to drift aimlessly.

There was the normal cascade of differing emotions, from why is this happening to me? Through to, how dare she go and leave me like this? Feelings, which despite being so utterly irrational, are still very real. It isn't as if bereavement is something peculiar to me, it's happening to men and women everywhere, all the time. But most of them probably cope better than me. I don't think it was a case of me lacking the ability to take a grip of myself, and overcoming the inertia that swamped me, I simply couldn't see the point.

But life continues, whether or not I join in. The newspapers are all talking about this as the 'Phony War', on the grounds that, apart from the Royal Oak being sunk at Scapa Flow and our revenge on the Graff Spee, nothing much seems to be happening. You can see what they mean, but I still feel that such talk is akin to poking a large sleeping dog with a sharp stick. Not to be recommended.

I hope that I'm not being sorry for myself, I don't think I am. There was plenty of time, during the debilitating and awful progress of the disease, for me to grieve over what we all knew was coming. But now, after three months of metaphorically pulling the sheets over my head, the time has come when I should either take an overdose, or get on with things. Mary would never have put up with this level of wallowing, and Cassie is spending too much of her time worrying about me, instead of the hundred and one other things she has to do. The knowledge that there are not likely to be any further achievements in my life is just another of the adjustments of old age. You can look on it as a tax for not dying young.

This sounds more mournful than it feels; at the age of sixty six I hope to have a few more useful years left in me. The problem is that, at my age, even if I were to summon the energy for some new project, no one would be interested in having me. It goes without saying that I'm far too old to play any part in the services, I had to make a fuss to be allowed to join up in the last lot, and even then, I never saw any serious action. Still, it is rather humiliating to find that I am also too old to be considered as an ARP Warden or a member of the Observer Corps. Perhaps my only use will be if some organisation wishes to quote my title on its notepaper. It would seem that my ending will be - Not with a bang, but with a whimper.

The fact that I don't feel like an old age Pensioner is irrelevant, my age puts me into a certain category and the sooner I get used to that fact the better. I don't mind playing bridge and gardening, but they were always part time amusements, rather than full time occupations.

Perhaps I should take to growing prize leeks and go round sabotaging the gardens of my opponents at dead of night. Perhaps I should join the church choir and have an affair with the vicar's wife, that would give Mary a laugh, wherever she is now. But, as I said, it has all seemed rather pointless.

A more realistic assessment of my future would involve getting used to cooking meals for one and a cold bed every night. Life can seem cruel, it's true, but even if this is all there is for me, I still have no excuse for moaning. Thirty eight, mostly happy, years with Mary, a lovely daughter and a reasonably worthwhile and interesting career; it's more than most people get. I won't be in any position to ask Saint Peter for a refund.

But just before sinking into torpor and senility I need to sort out my formal retirement from the Ministry. In view of my position both as an electronics engineer and the ministry liaison with the continuing Radio Direction Finding tests, being conducted by Watson Watt, I had been allowed to remain in post beyond my normal retiring date in 1934.

It was only because of Mary's illness that the axe hadn't fallen on my sixty fifth birthday, last year. That, and my friendship with the then Air Minister, Sir Kingsley Wood, had meant there had been a collective reluctance to give me yet another piece of bad news.

Accordingly, and perhaps somewhat unfairly, I had been allowed to remain on the Ministry payroll, despite taking significant amounts of time off, both before and after her death. An honest assessment of my behaviour since then would have to conclude that I have outstayed my welcome, that I have become little more than a time serving pen pusher - exactly the sort of person that I have always looked down on.

Even if I don't know what I'm going to do next, the first step to regaining my self respect is going to be to acknowledge that the music has ended and the carousel stopped, it's time for me to do the decent thing and go quietly. It would be unfair to embarrass them by making them push me out.

Then I shall come home alone, to our rather attractive house in Putney, with its garden leading down to the river, home to so many shared and happy memories. And then for the very last time, I shall pause by the hat stand in the hall to hang up my civil service badges of office; my bowler hat and rolled umbrella. After which I shall give careful consideration to the position of Sir Freddy Villiers, the recently widowed man who was at the very forefront of scientific progress on one day, and a candidate for carpet slippers the next. Don't get morbid Freddy, don't get morbid.

Chapter 2

Doktor Theo Leibniz
Basel, Switzerland, Wednesday May 8th. 1940

I had to wear my overcoat, although it was not as cold as Berlin, there was still a cool breeze from the river. But it was worth it, to sit at an outdoor cafe, a stein of beer in my hand; overlooking the broad sweep of the Rhine as it curved around the city centre. The historic Mittlere Brŭcke river crossing in the foreground provided an endless source of casual interest, with the cars and trams passing over it, and the deep laden Rhine barges beneath.

The difference between Berlin and Basel wasn't simply a matter of three degrees of temperature, it was also one of atmosphere. It's true that Berlin is every bit as safe as Switzerland, the Luftwaffe will see to that. It was only last year that Herman Goering himself said that if enemy aircraft bombed Germany you could call him Meyer. Yet there is still a subtle difference of public mood between the two cities; one is at war, bold and confident and the other, rather smugly at peace.

Despite their Germanic background the Swiss are a terribly dull people, they don't have our sense of vitality and are almost Jewish in their lack of principle. They will suffer any indignity and kiss any arse if they think there's money to be made. I suspect that if the burghers of this German speaking city were to be told of our plans, most would publicly express loud and wholehearted approval, but I could never imagine them actually volunteering to help us. When we have finally dealt with the Jews and the communists, agreed a peace with the British and fobbed off the Americans, the Swiss will still be there with their hands out for German gold, saying 'Remember, we were always your friends in the war'. Perhaps something a little more concrete than friendship would occasionally be useful.

Heidi Fuchs arrived at the cafe, scanning impatiently around until she spotted me, then she came and sat with me. It had been decided by the security services that the cover story for a group of fit young men and one noticeably older one, me, going to Chalons, near Reims was that they were the Binningen Athletic Club's Football Team, and that I was their coach. For what I thought were fairly flimsy reasons, Vogel had said that he wanted a woman to come with us, pretending to be the wife of the team captain, either that or the team masseuse. He didn't seem to mind what we called her, just as long as she was included. He assured me that the presence of a woman in the party, especially as half of a married couple, would make everything look more normal, more relaxed.

Frankly, I reckoned that anyone with a brain in the Swiss Security Services would think that twelve fit young men, and me, pretending to go to an away match near Paris at a time like this would give grounds for concern, with or without Heidi Fuchs flaunting her wares. But the fact that no such alarm seemed to have been raised, suggested that whatever suspicions might have occurred, the people they occurred to weren't interested in pursuing them.

I waved her to a seat and offered to buy a drink, but she declined, quite curtly. I hadn't been told where they got her from, probably an out of work actress, or someone seconded from the female services. Her

18

appearance was, in my opinion, rather vulgar. She possessed that very obvious and rather tarty look that young men always seem to find so magnetic, and wore tight fitting jumpers to emphasise the fact.

My first reaction on meeting her had been to wish that they could have found a slightly more intelligent soul, and one with rather less lipstick, but on reflection her looks were entirely appropriate for a woman supposedly married to footballer. Heidi Fuchs provided ample confirmation of my own choice to remain unmarried.

It had never been a single conscious decision, that my love of music and my obsession with my work, would provide all the fulfilment I wanted in life. Somehow, it had been more a series of individual small decisions, that this girl or the other was never quite interesting enough for me to sacrifice my very comfortable and self sufficient life for one of conventional wedded bliss. Anyway, I would have been a terrible father, regarding the Institute as far more interesting than the demands of sticky fingered children.

"It's time you went back to the hotel, Herr Doktor." She said. "We were especially warned to stay together and not to move about individually."

"All in good time my dear." I smiled at her, determined not to be annoyed by this impertinence. Perhaps my own position had not been fully explained to her, unfortunately she was not deterred by my politeness.

"Herr Doktor, there are experts in this group, specialists who know how to organise these things, and they say that we should keep out of sight in the hotel, and not go wandering round the city like tourists."

I had the impression that even her minimal politeness was only skin deep, that she would like nothing more than to address me as an equal.

"Fraulein Fuchs it might be helpful for you to remember that I am the senior person in this party, and do not need to be reminded of my duties."

She had pulled a substantial gold medallion from the neck of her blouse and was twisting it round in the fingers of her right hand as I talked, she seemed to be indicating that it was of more interest than me. I had the clear impression that Fraulein Fuchs had ideas above her station. For an unemployed actress, or whatever she was, she was going to need to be kept firmly in her place.

"Please don't play with your jewellery whilst I'm talking to you."

"This isn't jewellery." She said, swinging it on its gold chain. "This is a party eagle and swastika. It's the old pattern, with the narrower wing span. I think it's so much neater than the new ones, do you like it?"

I leaned forward to get a better look, and was astonished to see the swastika, held in the eagle's claws, gleaming in the Swiss sunshine.

"It doesn't matter if I like it," I hissed. "We're supposed to be under cover. Take it off immediately."

She dropped it back down the neck of her blouse, and smirked unpleasantly at me. "Come and get it, I'll wrestle you for it."

The girl was insufferable, and I could feel myself getting hot, but I was determined not to give her the satisfaction of joining her game and so ignored the taunt. I had, in all honesty, been ready to leave the cafe when she arrived but would now need to delay that move.

"You will return to the hotel yourself, Fraulein Fuchs." I said in stern tones, to emphasise the difference in our positions. "And I shall join you when I'm ready." She left, clearly disappointed that I was unwilling to descend to her level. Two days with this young lady was going to be more than enough for me.

I remained long enough for her to clear the immediate area and then, leaving a few Swiss Francs on the table, began to walk along the pavement overlooking the river. My previous visits to Switzerland have usually been to scientific conferences, and whilst there is often a spare day at the end, this rarely leaves time for anything more than a look around the immediate locality of whichever town we happen to be in. I keep on promising myself that one day, whenever the work at the Institute has quietened down, I shall spend a week here, just admiring the scenery. Though with the current situation, that seems to be an increasingly distant prospect.

*****

During the 1938 re-occupation of the German part of Czechoslovakia, known as the Sudetenland, Heydrich had adopted the brilliant scheme of employing flying columns of specially selected personnel to achieve particular goals. He had formed small units made up of experts, drawn variously from the SS, the Gestapo, the SD and even the Kriminalpolizei - whatever suited the job in hand.

He called them Einsatzgruppen, or Special Action Teams, and they operated independently of the regular military. The idea was that they should move at high speed and seize specific government archives, bank reserves, and even nominated prominent people; the sort of things that might so easily and conveniently disappear in the confusion of a more general military action. They had achieved great success on that occasion and had been used again last year, when it had been found necessary to occupy the remaining portion of Czechoslovakia, in order to prevent civil unrest.

It is exactly this sort of original thinking that marks the difference between the forces of the Reich and those of France and the British Expeditionary Force. Those two relics of a former age which are, even now, sitting calmly in north eastern France and expecting to re-fight the Battle of the Somme. Even though some French units have modern equipment, it is all to no avail, as they have politically weak leaders. Which brings us back to the very heart of the difference between us.

Our own particular Einsatzgruppe was, as I mentioned, travelling as a football team, and had all the requisite documents to prove that. Early tomorrow morning, Thursday the 9th of May, we would set off, with our group split between a small team bus and a car, to drive the 480 kilometres from Basel to Chalons, a small town to the south of Reims. Once there most of us would check into our pre booked team hotel, whilst myself and two others would take the car for a final reconnoitre of the area. At roughly breakfast time on the Friday morning, our supposed football opponents, along with the rest of the world, would hear the radio news telling them of events that made our match unlikely.

At that time we would cease all pretence and begin to operate as a military unit. Because of my childhood asthma, I had been found unfit for active service in the Great War, a fact that has always caused me to think less of myself. If there is any fighting to be done on Friday I acknowledge that my young companions will have to deal with most of it, it's what they're trained for. But at least on an occasion like this, which calls for my specific expertise, I hope to acquit myself sufficiently well to recover at least a part of my military self respect.

The leader of our special action team, Sturmbannfuhrer Gunther von Strenglen, was one of that hereditary class of Prussian landowners that we call Junkers, and was a particularly fearsome example of the type. They are usually portrayed wearing a spiked helmet, the pickelhaube, with rigidly waxed and pointed moustaches below that; in the manner of the former Kaiser. And though von Strenglen sported neither of these items he was still, by his bearing, every inch the old school Prussian.

He had, however, an even more distinctive adornment, his right hand had been replaced by a wooden prosthesis. As he wore a black leather glove on it, I only discovered the substitution when I first shook hands with him, an unnerving experience. The reason for this state of affairs was never explained, perhaps an accident, or an injury in the Great War. This casual assumption that the possession of a wooden hand was such a routine event it required no comment, showed the sort of aristocratic disdain for common politeness that one expects from such people. I was visited by the most unfortunate notion of him making an over enthusiastic Fuhrer salute and the wretched thing flying off and hitting someone.

I had no valid grounds to object to the man and was sure of his abilities, but his sort, even without trying, still made me feel inadequate. I would have to ensure that I maintained my own position and allowed no sense of diffidence to appear in my manner. He represented a last vestige of the outdated class structure that National Socialism was now getting rid of.

But when I did arrive back at the hotel, there was some most unexpected news waiting for me. Von Strenglen told me that he had just received word from Berlin that our target, the man around whom this whole raid was planned, had disappeared. Professor Maurice Ponte, together with his magnetron was believed to have boarded a light aircraft early this morning, and had not been seen since. No one had any idea of his current location, our instructions were to remain exactly where we were, until further orders.

Sir Freddy Villiers
London, Wednesday May 8th. 1940

Before finally clearing my desk at the Ministry, I decided to pay a last visit to the Bawdsey Research Station, out on the coast near Ipswich. This was the headquarters of our national effort to perfect Radio Direction Finding, or RDF as it was more commonly called, and it was here that the Chain Home aircraft location stations were developed. The Superintendant was Albert Rowe, a brilliant physicist, generally known to his friends as Jimmy. He has a reputation for being a rather prickly character, and one or two highly qualified new recruits to his team have failed to fit in, blaming his moodiness and curt manner for their departure.

I have never had any problems with the man myself, and found that we enjoyed an excellent working relationship. People who don't like his manner should try dealing with the pressure of his position, and the sheer volume of complex technical work he's responsible for.

The Manor itself is a sprawling Victorian heap, standing on a bluff overlooking the mouth of the River Deben. In more peaceful times it would be an excellent spot from which to explore an interesting stretch of coast. But these aren't more peaceful times, and now it's home to a dedicated collection of scientists and engineers, with ballrooms turned into laboratories and drawing rooms into offices.

Jimmy seems to have understood my recent lack of interest in the work that had once fascinated me. He had followed the course of Mary's illness through the last year with sympathy and understanding. The fact that his own wife is also called Mary seemed to make it more real to him. Another connection between us being the fact that we both, at different times, studied at the Royal College of Science, later to become part of what is now Imperial College.

Jimmy took me for a walk along the shingle beach, as the only place he could avoid the constant demands of telephones and colleagues. The wind was whipping smartly in across the water and we turned our coat collars up, lighting a cigarette was almost more trouble than it was worth.

"Has any intelligence come in yet about German troop movements?" He asked. We shared a certainty that Hitler was planning something, The Fuhrer's statement that he had 'No further territorial ambitions' was obvious nonsense, recent history giving all the proof one needed of that point.

"Nothing that I know of, but then when they do move it will probably take us all by surprise. The latest thinking at the Ministry is that he might move into the Low Countries; Holland and Belgium, it would avoid an outright battle with the French and would give the Luftwaffe useful forward bases for attacks on south east

England. You saw how easily he annexed Denmark and Norway."

"Well if they do, we've got East Anglia and the Thames Estuary fairly well covered with the Chain Home stations, but at such short range even if we pick them up as soon as they're airborne, they can be over here in fifteen minutes, it's not much notice. But what do you know about this latest nonsense from London, about them wanting one of my boys on secondment for some operation, the details of which they won't even discuss with me?"

I frowned in concentration. "Which department do they want to move your man into?"

"That's what I don't know. They've just asked for a short list of three of four names of physically fit young men, who are completely up to date with the latest RDF developments. They won't tell me anything beyond that. But it's rank idiocy, and I've told them as much; I'm not going to stand for it. I'm already desperate for properly qualified staff, I have a standing order with Oxford, Cambridge and Imperial for details of all graduates with a first in physics or electronics. But I'm just one of a dozen departments all making the same request. There simply aren't any spare people down here to be detached onto some Air Ministry wild goose chase."

I was less annoyed than him, but every bit as puzzled. "Why would they specify physical fitness? The whole point about your people is that they use their brains not their muscles."

"Who cares. I'm just starting work on a centimetric system for airborne interception, with the detector set actually built into the plane. It will revolutionise air combat, and they think I have time for this damn nonsense? I'll resign first."

We walked along the shingle beach in silence for a while, neither of us having any answers to offer, until I raised the other obvious point about the present situation.

"When the Germans do make their move, wherever that is, it will make Chamberlain's position quite untenable, he will go down in history as the man who thought he could deal with Hitler. I wouldn't be surprised to see him lose a Vote of Confidence, and if that happens we'll end up with Lord Halifax in Number 10, and he's a complete wet fish. That will be an even bigger disaster than the Germans moving into Denmark."

Jimmy stopped and turned to look at me. "Is that the official view at the Ministry?"

I nodded. "The new Minister, Sam Hoare, is one of Chamberlain's friends and even he agrees. Halifax will press for some sort of accommodation with Hitler, some agreement that leaves him in power with all his present territory. Then in another year's time, he'll rip that agreement up, like all the others, and move against us."

"You're not usually this pessimistic Freddy, don't be offended, but is Mary's death affecting your judgement?"

"I'm probably not the best person to say - but what are the choices? The only possible alternative as PM would be Winston, and he's trodden on too many toes to make that a realistic possibility. Even the King thinks he's a wild card and little better than a war monger."

Jimmy looked thoughtful. "As we seem to be at war with an unstable madman, then perhaps a wild card and a war monger is what we need."

I picked up a stone and threw it angrily at the grey water, then we turned and trudged back the way we'd come.

*****

As a Deputy Secretary, which in Civil Service terms is a fairly senior position, I had ready access to the new Air Minister. Sir Samuel Hoare, he'd only been with us for three weeks but I'd already spoken to him a couple of times and liked the man. The fact that we were both hereditary Baronets, hence the 'Sir', might have been thought by others to form some connection, but I don't think either of us ever considered the matter.

He was eminently well qualified for the post, having previously served as Air Minister for most of the nineteen twenties, but was best known for having been a very able Foreign Secretary and for forging the Hoare-Laval Pact with the French. However, his position as a known and unashamed Chamberlain loyalist put his cabinet future in serious doubt with either of the possible replacements as Prime Minister.

As I entered his office, he stood to shake my hand; "Good to see you again Villiers." Was all he said, acknowledging that I'd probably had as much sympathy as a man can take, which I thought a nice touch. There were two other men sat to one side, neither man was in uniform but they weren't civil service, they weren't the type. Neither spoke, nor seemed interested in me.

I explained that I had simply come to give my thanks for the Ministry's forbearance throughout the last year, and to say how very much I had enjoyed my time and appreciated my colleagues. These were all routine expressions, almost clichés, but none the less genuine for that. He thanked me and said how valuable my work

28

had been, and how grateful the Ministry must have been to have someone of my calibre coordinating the RDF work for the last six years. He even looked as though he meant most of it.

I had already declined the offer of a departmental get to together to mark my departure, the bogus sentiment of such occasions is usually enough to turn your stomach. Besides which, the rest of the department had better things to do, but I was still grateful for his comments, and pleased to be wrapping things up in such a civilised fashion. It was the sort of moment the English instinctively cope with quite well, with a bare minimum of surface emotion. But as I finished shaking his hand, and was turning to leave, he stopped me.

"Do you have a moment, Freddy?" The informal address came naturally, now that I was retired and we were equals, though he sounded uncharacteristically hesitant.

"Moments are what I'm about to have lots of, and I'm happy to share them."

He smiled at being put at his ease. "Take a seat." He gestured to the remaining unoccupied chair, next to the two men. I did so.

"These gentlemen work for a certain government department, which has an interest in the work at Bawdsey Manor. And the fact of the matter is, they need someone to accompany them on a particular mission, someone who has a working knowledge of the technology involved."

"If I could speculate Sir Samuel," we were heading back into formality. "You put them in touch with Mr. Rowe at Bawdsey, they told him what they wanted, and he told them to get on their bicycles."

Sir Samuel simply looked surprised, but the two silent men swung round in my direction very sharply. The one nearest spoke.

"This is a Top Secret matter, Sir Frederick, and not for discussion in the Civil Service canteen. How exactly did you come to be aware of this?"

"Well certainly not in the canteen. I was at Bawdsey Manor this morning, talking to Jimmy Rowe, the Superintendant, wrapping things up before my departure. Your requirements came up in conversation, a perfectly legitimate conversation as both he and I share the necessary level of security clearance. The salient point is that your suggested secondment of any of his top scientists would significantly hinder vital war work. The question would seem to be what exactly your own security clearance is, and why you're prepared to risk damaging the work of that establishment?"

"We're not impressed by the old palls act Villiers, nor how important your supposed friends are. You're here to answer questions, not ask them."

That annoyed me, the use of my surname without a prefix. One might as well come straight out and say it, these things are not difficult; English culture is perfectly clear on the point. My superior or anyone else I take a shine to may, strictly upon invitation, call me Freddy, or simply Villiers, and even accompany it with a geniality such as, Villiers my dear fellow. But without such an invitation a person of lower rank is expected to adopt a more formal usage; in my case, Sir Frederick. Whatever their position in the shadow world of Military Intelligence, from their lack of manners, these two sounded rather less than top drawer.

"If you please, gentlemen." Sir Samuel was not about to surrender control of his own office to a couple of security service upstarts. "You seem to forget yourself. Sir Frederick is one of the most trusted and reliable people in the Air Ministry. You asked my permission to solicit his opinion, not to abuse him."

Swallowing rebukes was clearly not their customary fare, and there was a moment's angry silence before one of them managed. "I apologise Sir Samuel, but this is an extremely important matter." Hoare nodded his head for them to continue, and they swung back to me.

"The lack of cooperation at Bawdsey Manor has been noted and will be dealt with in due course, for the time being we have more important matters to deal with."

Even as he spoke I was considering what a thin lipped and nasty piece of work he was, just the sort who would try to take his revenge on Jimmy in some way - well he'd need to get out of bed very early to manage that. Meanwhile he droned on. "We need, as a matter of considerable urgency, someone who is familiar with the appearance and function of modern magnetrons and who is in reasonable physical condition. What we require from you Sir Frederick is a list of possible names."

I thought about it, and rude though they were, if Sir Samuel accepted their bona fides then that was good enough for me. But thinking about their request did nothing to change the obvious facts.

"Gentlemen, what you're asking for simply doesn't exist; no matter how desperate the need. There are some people in university physics departments who might have a familiarity with older magnetrons, but anyone who knows anything worth knowing about the latest developments in that area works at Bawdsey. That is a simple fact of life."

But the small thin lipped one wasn't giving up. "There must be someone, someone who used to work there but has now left."

"I'll grant he's a demanding taskmaster, but if he doesn't get on with people he gets rid of them in their first week, before they get anywhere near the interesting stuff. Anyone he keeps past then stays with him."

They looked baffled and angry, this was not going they way they wanted. After a while it seemed that nothing further was likely to happen, so I looked enquiringly at Sir Samuel, and he looked at the two men. But they'd clearly drawn a blank on the only thing they wanted.

"Thank you Freddy, I'm sorry to have delayed you, and my very best wishes for your future." He stood to shake my hand once more, and I turned to leave. But then I paused, with my hand resting on the door knob. With Hoare's mention of my future echoing in my mind, something had occurred to me.

"There is one man who fits your description." I said, still facing the door, and almost to myself.

As I turned back into the room, its three other occupants all turned in my direction.

"And who is that?"

"Well, me - of course."

The two men took a moment to assimilate the comment and then burst out laughing, Sir Samuel looked slightly embarrassed. I resumed my departure and left.

The journey home was accompanied by a rueful sense that I had rather set myself up for their sneering derision. A man nearer seventy than sixty has no business passing himself off as some sort of prime physical specimen, whatever it was they meant by that.

Mrs. Jackson, Mary's daily, or more correctly now, my daily, had repeatedly offered to come in and cook my evening meals, and no doubt I would eventually come round to the idea. However, I'd told her to leave it for a while. I needed to settle my own feelings, without the distraction of her well meaning fussiness. Basic cooking is something I'm perfectly comfortable with, I might not be running up a Victoria sponge anytime soon, but meat, potatoes and two veg. were well within my capabilities.

I had just finished, it was slightly earlier than normal, and I was still sat at the dining room table, even eating alone I like to do things properly. My plate was pushed to one side and in its place was the Times, folded to the crossword. Five Across: A Journey Home Needs Divine Approval, seven letters. As I waved the end of the pencil in the air, to count out the letters in various possibilities, I heard the crunch of car tyres on the gravel drive. I waited, there were footsteps, more than one set, followed by a slight pause and then the front door bell rang. I looked at my watch, it was a quarter past seven. I carried my plate through to the kitchen, leaving it on the draining board and went to answer the summons.

The two men from Sir Samuel's office were standing side by side, they looked like a pair of song and dance men ready to start their routine.

"Good evening." I said, and then waited for them to pick up the conversational baton.

"This is an official visit Sir Frederick," said one, "we're here to interview you about your suggestion, but we couldn't let Sir Samuel know that we were interested."

"Ah yes, my suggestion." Did they mean the fact I'd put my own name forward for whatever contortions they had in mind for their physically fit scientist. I waited, they were going to have to do at least some of the work.

"We need to come inside and talk to you."

"About what?"

They both seemed uncomfortable, and the small one actually looked round, as if checking my front garden for eavesdroppers. "It's confidential, it can only be discussed in private." He looked meaningfully at the open front door behind me. I'm not an unreasonable man, and they were by all accounts public servants, so, with a sigh, I took them into the drawing room and sat them down. Offering them tea, or anything stronger, seemed a step too far.

"I'll take it on face value that you're in the security services, you wouldn't have got into Sir Samuel's office without your identity being checked, but that's all, you're going to have to explain yourselves from that point on."

The taller of the two took up the running. "I must formally caution you Sir Frederick, that what we are about to discuss is subject to the Official Secrets Act and any repetition of our conversation would be subject to . . ."

"Look, I know you're just doing your job and I honestly don't want to be rude, but I've had a Top Secret security clearance for the last thirty five years. I would suggest that you get to the nuts and bolts of whatever it is, before I really do die of old age."

"It concerns a French scientist, a Monsieur Ponte."

"If it's Maurice, he's a Professeur." I corrected him.

"So you do know him?" He asked, almost accusingly.

"We're hardly personal friends, but I've met him three or four times, at conferences."

" He and his team have been testing a new pulsed Radio Location system, and are claiming ranges in excess of 80 miles. We warned him a week ago of the imminence of a German attack on France, but he wouldn't believe us. We were going to ask you to accompany a team of ours to France in order to meet Professor Ponte and request that he provide you with his new and apparently more powerful magnetron, before the Germans got it."

"You *were* going to ask me, what's changed?"

"What's changed is that he turned up in London, this afternoon, complete with his magnetron. Nobody even knew he was in the country, and then he just walks into the GEC office in Wembley this afternoon, cool as you like, and hands them this device in a cardboard box."

"Well that's splendid, so now we can send it to Bawdsey Manor for them to work on, and the Germans can't get at it. That would seem to conclude the matter most satisfactorily."

"Not quite, when he left France it was his view that, despite our repeated warnings, there would be no German invasion in the near future. He was of the opinion that even if they did invade, the French army was more than a match for any German force, and that there would be plenty of time to move any vital equipment out of harm's way."

"That would seem to be irrelevant now, the new magnetron and its developer are both safely in London, whatever happens."

"There were two of them."

"Two of the new magnetrons?"

"Precisely, and he left the other one with his deputy, Claude Roland, at an undisclosed location in France. We understand that you've also met Monsieur Roland?"

"Yes, I have, but all you have to do is tell Ponte to call Roland and tell him to hand over the unit to any British forces in the area, or simply destroy it."

"Unfortunately it's not quite that simple. He has repeatedly refused to tell us where Roland is, and says that whilst he is prepared to share it, he has no intention of surrendering French possession of this technology. Apparently his team are continuing to test and develop this device, independently of our own work. He is confident that Roland can outwit the German army; we're not."

"How reliable is your information of a German attack on France?"

"All I can tell you is that our superiors believe implicitly that such an attack will take place in the next week, perhaps even the next day or two, and that when it does it will make rapid advances. There are serious concerns about the quality of the French army and its leadership. A simple numerical comparison between French and German troop numbers doesn't reflect the markedly different reliabilities of the two armies. There are even high level concerns about the advisability of leaving the British Expeditionary Force on that side of the Channel."

"You can't seriously tell me that there is a possibility of withdrawing our troops and leaving the French to go it alone."

"I don't think it's got to that yet, but if the French army either withdraws or collapses, then the BEF alone will be massively outnumbered and outgunned. We can't afford to lose that army, and it's beginning to strike some of our senior people as a real possibility. It could turn into a very turbulent and fast moving situation, the orderly evacuation of our forces might prove extremely difficult."

I was shocked, Jimmy Rowe and I had been discussing this as a theoretical situation, this made it very real, and very immediate. The whole idea of the Phony War was about to go up in smoke.

"What exactly are you proposing?"

"We can't do anything until we get some indication of Roland's whereabouts, and there are people working on that now. Then as soon as we have an address, we shall have to go in as if we were in enemy territory. It's absolutely vital that the Germans should be prevented from getting their hands on this. We plan to take the bull by the horns and make an assault using a small team of crack troops to simply seize the equipment and whatever drawings or other details we can. But in order to make such a seizure, we would need someone to go in with that team and direct exactly what it is that we should be taking. Someone who is fully up to date with the latest developments."

He stopped talking and the two of them looked at me appraisingly, and then at each other. They looked doubtful.

"The trouble is that with you being so old, even if you could identify the equipment, you'd be a real drag on the rest of the team when they were making their escape."

"I can scarcely imagine you're planning to walk there, and if not, then why do I need to be so fit?"

"We intend that the team should go in by plane and, if possible, leave the same way. But the fact of the matter is that if the situation deteriorates as rapidly as it might, you could be required to go in by parachute and leave on foot." He stared at me, I'm not sure if a stare can be arrogant - but his seemed to be. "That's where the fitness comes in, old men don't generally jump out of aeroplanes."

"Have either of you made a parachute jump?"

"He hasn't, but I have." Said the tall one.

"Stand up." I said; he looked at me blankly.

Leaning forward, I repeated myself, more clearly. "Stand up." Looking puzzled, he complied.

"Turn to face the window." Looking even more puzzled he did so. I surveyed his body in profile, and was unimpressed.

"You can sit down again now."

"What was that supposed to be about?"

"You have bad posture and a protruding belly, you're in worse shape than my dog, before we put him down, and he only had three legs."

"Who the hell d'you think you are, talking to me like that?"

"I think I'm the person your superiors told you to go out and find, and I don't think that you want to go back empty handed. That's who."

"So you reckon that if it comes to it, you can jump out of a plane, do you?"

"If this is something that you've managed, then I shouldn't have any trouble at all. As for me hindering the team's escape - the answer's simple. If an aircraft departure is impossible, then the rest of the team can take the equipment and leave me behind. I shall make my own way home. Now there's a talk due to start shortly on the radio, which I wish to listen to, so do either of you have any further questions?"

"You mean that you're prepared for us just to abandon you in enemy territory - how would you expect to get out of there?"

I looked at him for a moment. "Do you really care?"

He looked back at me, a long impertinent stare and then he smirked. "Not in the slightest. My sole interest lies in getting you to France in one piece to do your stuff, after which you can go to hell in a bucket for all I care." The two of them stood and turned to leave, but then at the front door the tall one looked back and said.

"Pack a bag and make a will, you can expect to be contacted at short notice, any time in the next day or two."

Chapter 3

Doktor Theo Leibniz
Basel, Switzerland, Saturday May 11th. 1940

Yesterday's news, although anticipated by us all, was still thrilling. The Fuhrer is righting a historic wrong and fulfilling his pledge to the German people. It had been difficult to conceal our pride in front of others, even the experienced and hard bitten men who made up my team had almost permanent smiles on their faces.

The early morning announcement on the Reich's Broadcasting Service; 'Armed forces of the Reich are today taking up defensive positions in Belgium, along the French border, to counter threats to our national territory posed by continuing French mobilisation and the British Expeditionary Force'. It was followed by a stirring rendition of the national anthem. We all knew that, despite the truth of the reports, this could well mark the opening phase of a major advance - if the Allies had any sense at all they would be able to read between the lines as well as we could. There was a feeling that at last we were rolling up our sleeves to get on with a long overdue task, a task that had been waiting for twenty years.

Throughout the day, more and more bulletins had been issued, giving details of Belgian perfidy in granting French and British forces access to their territory. It seemed as though there had been little choice left for us, but to take decisive action and, unlike the so called democracies, we were capable of doing so.

As the day wore on, it seemed that even the local Swiss were listening to German radio, as the most authoritative source of reliable information. You had only to walk down the street to hear it in all the cafes. The French radio stations were slow to broadcast their version of events, no doubt having been taken by surprise, and when they did it was the most childish and unbelievable nonsense. Stories about German forces being 'Thrown Back' were the most common. Even the BBC ran a story, which claimed that French forces were advancing further into Belgium and stemming German troop movements.

The difficulty with this sort of self denial is that, whatever your propaganda might be claiming, sooner or later people will see with their own eyes and the truth will become evident. There can be little doubt that every national broadcasting service will favour their own version of events, but such a complete departure from reality is not the sort of mistake one can imagine Doctor Goebbels making.

The Armistice we had been forced to sign at Compiegne in 1918 had not been the end of the matter. It had merely been the end of the first chapter, today marked the opening of chapter two, and this time the job would be done properly.

One astonishing piece of news, that none of us is sure what to think of, is the report from London that Prime Minister Chamberlain has been replaced by that poisonous anti German demagogue, Winston Churchill. At first we thought this to be no more than some idle rumour that would soon be denied, instead of which it has been confirmed on all the radio stations. The man had a disastrous record in the Great War, with his mad scheme at Gallipoli, and has been in the wilderness ever since.

The BBC freely admit that he is sixty six years old, the man is a Pensioner and widely known to be a drunkard. The idea that they should have replaced a man like Chamberlain, with whom the Fuhrer has an established relationship and with whom we could have agreed terms, with someone like this, is a sign of either madness or panic at the very heart of the British establishment. First their King runs away with his foreign mistress, and now they appoint a drooling geriatric as Prime Minister, it is simply astonishing.

Returning to more immediate matters - Sturmbannfuhrer von Strenglen, though an excellent officer, has found this delay in Basel to be a serious trial to his patience. Being by nature a man of action, and accustomed to wearing his uniform with pride, our stay in Switzerland has represented everything he dislikes. We are still posing as the members of a football team, and still pretending to be civilians; yet this disguise, which had only ever been intended as temporary, has now gone on for three days. Even I am beginning to agree, there must soon be a limit to how long we can stay here. The wilful blindness of the Swiss security services cannot be counted on indefinitely.

There is no problem with the men's morale, the continuing developments in the north are a sufficient tonic to hold everyone's attention. However, it has to be said that if our delay here is prolonged much further, the disruptive presence of Heidi Fuchs could become a problem. She is the very opposite of a team player, that is if she is any sort of player at all. I shall do my best to rise to the occasion, my management skills have always been excellent in the past and I shall regard her as a special challenge.

Even without any formal military rank, I am clearly the senior member of our group, by virtue of age, academic rank and my Party Membership number. One of the minor pieces of snobbery that we Germans can be held guilty of, is the discreet mentioning of one's Nazi Party Membership number. The lower the number, the longer you have been a member, the earlier you had the sense to recognise historical inevitability. Not that I wish to make too much of these things, but they are perhaps worth mentioning in passing. The Fuhrer himself is number seven, Himmler is, I think, 14300, and Heydrich's number is somewhere in the five hundred thousands. Today of course, now that everyone wishes to hang onto the Fuhrer's coat tails, the membership numbers are in the millions. I take a degree of quiet pleasure from the fact that my own membership dates back almost ten years and my number is 375,015, it is surprisingly uncommon to encounter a lower number.

Despite this seniority, and the fact that the mission would be impossible without me, immediate control of the 'troops' is handled by SS Sturmbannfuhrer von Strenglen. I have taken my courage in my hands and made it my business to let him know that, despite the difference in our positions, I am more than happy with the idea that he should handle logistics and be responsible for any military action. Once we have achieved our aim of securing the French technicians, and their equipment, I will then decide which of them can be safely released and which must accompany us back to Germany. It's an efficient division of authority and caters to our differing skills.

*****

Finally at three o'clock yesterday afternoon word came by telephone, from our local contact, that the operation was back on track, and that we were to depart this morning. No trace has yet been found of the missing French scientist, Professor Ponte, but it has been decided that we should go ahead anyway and undertake our own investigation, starting at the site of his last known location. The news went through the men like a crackle of electricity, coming on top of yesterday morning's radio announcements it made for a very cheering day.

The various people in our group had travelled in twos and threes to Basel by train on Wednesday, and then taken buses or taxis to the hotel. Our onward transport arrangements were all laid on and waiting for us, and had been for the last three days. A sixteen seat Renault bus, only about five years old, and with the name of some holiday company on the side, was delivered to our hotel last night along with a Citroen saloon car.

Both vehicles seemed to be in good condition and had full fuel tanks, the arrangements for this operation were completely professional, everything had been taken care of, including a supply of weapons. Von Strenglen has now sent two of the men to make the final checks on tyre pressures and oil levels, and whatever else one does to a motor vehicle. Nothing was left to chance, which might have delayed our departure this morning.

The driver who had come in to give us the keys explained that there were twelve large sports bags, one for each man, already packed and locked in the back of the bus. The two men spoke quietly for a few moments about their contents, presumably guns, I didn't feel it necessary to join in, after all this was von Strenglen's area of responsibility.

Leaving Basel this morning had been a prolonged affair, the southern end of the Maginot Line starts just to the north of here, and all the French side of the border near Basel is a militarised zone. I had assumed, especially since yesterday's news, that this would result in a much higher level of security than normal, with individual spot checks and vehicle searches, but apparently not.

The delay was simply down to the high volume of traffic waiting to be processed through the Swiss and French border posts. That and a couple of overheated cars in the queue ahead of us, which had to be pushed to one side. The actual border checks themselves were relatively relaxed for those leaving Switzerland, though from the length of the queues that could be seen waiting to come in, travelling the other way was a different story. Still, as we weren't planning to come back this way that wouldn't be a problem for us.

Once the red and white barrier was lifted at the French check point, and we drove through onto a French road, and saw French road signs, it all seemed a lot more real. Until then I had been treating it as something of a theoretical exercise, but now the troops we passed on the road were enemy troops. As the Panzers were storming into northern France we were, if not exactly storming, at least driving into the south. We were committed, worse than that, we were in civilian clothes with false documents and could be shot as spies if caught. I shifted uncomfortably in my seat at the prospect.

I was sitting in the front passenger seat of the Citroen car and Fraulein Fuchs was sitting in the back, claiming that the bus wasn't comfortable enough for her. Like a shark sensing blood in the water she had obviously spotted my brief unease.

"Don't worry, Herr Doktor, as long as you remember not to lift your right arm above shoulder level - you'll be fine." Then she cackled loudly at her own subversive comment. I glanced at the driver, unobtrusively, from the corner of my eye, but he wasn't sharing the laughter. For some reason I was relieved at that.

This stretch of countryside lay beyond the end of the main section of the Maginot Line, nonetheless, clearly visible from the road we could see the occasional gun casement. There was usually a dull steel dome set low in the ground, with a levelled concrete area around it. I recognised them from pictures I'd seen in the newspapers, but hadn't expected them to be on such public display. However, the most surprising thing was the slovenly attitude of the French troops. Groups of them could be seen at crossroads or gathered in villages, and there wasn't a smartly turned out man amongst them. Tunic buttons were undone, they slouched about with hands in pockets, they were smoking on duty. They were a rabble, everything I'd been told about the state of this country was true. If these men were representative of the rest, then this place was a house of cards, and the German army a lot more than a strong wind.

"Have you seen them?" I asked the driver, needing someone else to confirm my own astonishment. This time he did smile.

"I've already been here twice in the last three months, and it's got worse each time. A decent German Sergeant would rip the balls off any one of his men that looked like that."

"Twice in the last three months?" I queried in surprise, I had imagined our own expedition to be an isolated event.

"I'm from Alsace, I can pass as local and I know the area. Aerial reconnaissance is all very well, but what you need is a man on the ground, someone who can tell the difference between an operational tank and derelict junk just left around to look good. As for their army, if they don't mutiny - they'll desert."

"Surely not in the face of an attack on their homeland?"

"*Particularly* in the face of an attack, if the troops are bad, the officers are worse. They must have some good units somewhere, but I haven't found them yet."

I relaxed slightly, this man was a professional, these people knew their jobs just as I knew mine.

"I read in the paper that some of their tank factories are on strike, is that true?" I might as well learn what I could from the man.

"Not at the moment, but they were earlier this year, and so were a couple of their aircraft factories. They should have learned a lesson from us, having communists working in your factories is as bad as having Jews owning them, and they've got both here." He laughed. "What do you expect from a country where they think that taking two hours for lunch and then washing it down with a bottle of wine constitutes reasonable behaviour?" His tone made it clear what his own views were, and I shared them.

"What about you Fraulein Fuchs, what do you think?" As team leader I felt it my duty to include her, no matter how pointless I believed her presence to be.

"Who exactly gives a damn? We're going to invade them, we're going roll all over them and we're going to rub their faces in the dirt. You think I care about their lunch breaks? The Slavs and the Latin types are naturally subject races, and that includes them."

"But what about Il Duce and the Italians?"

"The fat little eyetie will fall in line with whoever he thinks is winning, and that's going to be us." The driver nodded, "I agree with her, he'll be desperate to climb onboard when he sees which way the wind's blowing, and Franco won't be far behind - take my word for it. These little Generalissimos are all the same."

It was interesting to hear these views from the ranks, in my position, at the top of an organisation, it is sometimes possible to miss out on the strength of public opinion. It was exactly this sort of feeling that the Fuhrer managed to grasp and then articulate so clearly as national policy.

Fuchs prodded the back of my seat with her foot. "I need a pee, so why don't you be a good Doktor and prescribe us all a nice cup of coffee, heh?"

I'm not the sort of doctor who prescribes things."

"Oh for God's sake."

I told the driver to take no notice, she should have gone before we started. Though I suspect that, as much as anything, her request was no more than the disruptive behaviour one expects from small children. Had there been any way of sending her home I would have taken it, but it rather looked as though we were stuck with her for the duration.

We drove steadily north west through the rest of the morning, and despite being in enemy territory it became rather boring. An unending succession of wooded hills and valleys, with never a decent view to be seen. Perhaps tomorrow would be more interesting.

Sir Freddy Villiers
London, Saturday May 11th 1940

Since the departure of the two ill mannered intelligence agents, on Wednesday evening, I had kept a light bag packed with a bare minimum of clothing, sufficient for about four days; if I'm away any longer then it won't be the first time I've washed clothes in a hotel washbasin. Of course that thought rather assumes there will in fact be a hotel, which on my present knowledge is distinctly uncertain.

Other than that, my life had been as low key as one might expect for an old age Pensioner. On Thursday, my first complete day of retirement, I had tried to stay in bed - to have a lie in, as people say. But at eight thirty I was wide awake, and had been for some time. It felt vaguely ridiculous to make myself lie in bed, just because other people seemed to think it a luxury. I eventually got up, if only to listen to the news, after which I went for a walk and contemplated the possibility of buying another dog - if nothing else it would give me someone to talk to. I would have loved to have been back at the office, if only to find out what had been going on with Maurice Ponte.

I wasn't sure what to make of the news about Winston becoming PM. It was clear on Thursday night that Chamberlain was going to lose the Vote of Confidence, and quite properly so, considering the bungled operation in Norway, but it took some hours before we learned who was to be his replacement.

Like so many other people, who had taken it for granted that Lord Halifax would receive the call, I was somewhat shocked at the news. But on reflection, I think that it might turn out to be an extremely shrewd move. Halifax would have done all the routine sorts of things that people expected of him, he was a man of the lowest common denominator. He was a man who would always settle for slightly less than he should. He is, in the words of the day, an appeaser. Winston, on the other hand, will always demand more and I think that might be just what we need at a desperate time like this. I was heartened to read that in his first speech to the Commons, he stated the government's policy would be to wage war by sea, land and air, with all our might and all our strength. Exactly the sort of intellectual clarity and directness this country needs.

One strange thought is, that as I have been ushered out of office at the age of sixty six, at exactly the same age, Churchill has been ushered in. One could never call the times boring.

On Thursday, most of my day was spent to listening to regular radio reports about the German attack through Belgium and Holland. Like many people, I had an atlas open on the table to follow the names of the places mentioned. But my predominant feeling was one of apprehension about the relentless optimism on offer, it was only last year that Neville Chamberlain had talked of Hitler having 'Missed the Bus'. And now the BBC was giving the impression that large scale movements of German armoured units, supported by their air force, were some sort of inconvenience that would soon be sorted out. Trying to discern the German's true intentions from the various reports, it sounded like more than just the annexation of Holland and Belgium, it sounded like the prelude to something much bigger.

By the middle of this morning I was beginning to wonder if I would hear from my two friends again, but no sooner had the thought occurred, than they materialised on my doorstep once more. Their car was parked in the driveway, both its front doors and one of the back doors were open, the summons was clear. I left a note for Mrs. Jackson, on the kitchen table, to say that I would be away for a few days, and then collecting my bag, joined them in the car.

Instead of taking me, as I had rather expected, to some army camp or airfield, I was deposited at the Metropole Hotel in central London. In normal times this was the sort of establishment at which a commercial traveller might stay, or a middle aged man might arrange to meet a floozy. As I had never been a commercial traveller or engaged with floozies, this was my first visit.

Like several other mid ranking hotels, or under used office blocks, it had been requisitioned by a government department; that much was obvious from the sandbagged doorway, the taped windows and the uniformed sentries. What was less obvious was which department. Despite it being a Saturday morning, the increased tempo of the war meant that the place was teeming with people, and all of them looked busy.

The ground floor was a warren of newly constructed partition walls, dividing the space up into small crowded offices. A pleasant young lady, wearing some kind of military uniform that I probably should have recognised, but didn't, led me past all these and down a set of stone steps into the cellars. Empty wine racks lined the walls and anonymous boxes were stacked wherever space allowed. We squeezed past, and into a small room with a brick vaulted ceiling, lit by bare bulbs. My first thought was that if this was MI6 then they should have a quiet word with their estate agent.

A military officer rose from one of the two desks, extending his hand.

"Sir Frederick?"

"Yes."

"I'm Major Grand, but we're very informal round here, call me Lawrence."

"Thank you, and please call me Freddy."

A elderly lady in civilian clothes at the other desk, interrupted us. "Sugar?" She asked, looking enquiringly at me.

"Just the one, thank you."

My second thought was that if this was MI6, it was nothing like I'd expected. But then in the Intelligence community I'd imagine that's considered to be a good thing.

"Are you MI6?"

"Lord no, we're Section D." He said, with a brief laugh, as if that explained anything. "I'm sorry if Smith and Jones were getting a bit above themselves the other day."

"Smith and Jones?"

"Yes, the two who came to pick you up. That's not their real names of course, in fact to be honest I can't say I'm too sure what their real names are. We've got them on loan from Colonel Baker for this operation, but you can take my word for it - they're very good at this sort of thing." He smiled at me reassuringly, but then realising that I was still looking puzzled he continued.

"Sorry, that was silly of me, you don't actually know much about this yet do you?"

"Only that I'm supposed to go to France, where I will jump out of an aeroplane to meet someone called Claude Roland and somehow or other take the remaining magnetron off him. But I know nothing about the operational details yet."

He pursed his lips, and made a reflective sort of *mmm* sound. "That's not totally inaccurate, as far as it goes, but there have been one or two changes in the details." He paused for another moment, looking into space above my head, before re-focussing on me.

"It seems that Monsieur Roland has developed a taste for private enterprise. He is what our Gallic chums would term, an entrepreneur."

"Is this a good thing, or a bad thing?"

"To be honest, we're not completely sure about that. We've received information that he's trying to sell the device, and that would be a bad thing."

"I can't see a problem with that, just give him what he's asking for, it would be worth almost any reasonable amount."

"Would that we could, old chap, would that we could. The trouble is, he seems to think that as we've already got one, we won't offer him much for another. You see it's not us he's trying to sell it to, we've just got word that he's opened up communication with the Krauts. So it's not so simple as just paying the little bugger, we've got to find him first - and do so before they do. You see the problem."

This time it was me that made an *mmm* sound, then slowly. "Yes. And we've got no idea where to find him?"

"Nothing concrete, just an address for where he was."

In the end it was agreed that Smith and Jones and myself, with a small team of what he called specialists would go to the laboratory where Roland and Ponte had been until four days ago, and begin our search there.

He looked at me, with some concern. "Are you quite sure you're up to this? It could be quite hairy you know; we wouldn't want to pressure you in any way."

"You just lay on the transport and I'll remember to pack a walking stick and my prescription glasses." For a moment he looked worried at this evidence of my frailty, but finally laughed, hesitantly.

"Well that's fine. As far as the operational details of jobs like this are concerned, Smith and Jones have done all this a dozen times before. All you have to do is stick with them, and then when the time comes you can verify that we're picking up the right bit of kit. Oh and one piece of good news, you can forget about the parachute, the area you're going to is a long way from any likely action, so you'll be going in and out by plane. Get yourself a couple of bottles of Cognac while you're over there, it'll make the trip worth while."

After some further desultory chat, most of which was just to reinforce the fact that I would be nothing more than a passenger, and have no responsibility for anything but the scientific verification, we parted.

The same car that had collected me this morning drove me out along the A4 to Heston Aerodrome, and dropped me at a small hangar, to the side of which was attached an office bearing the name 'No.1 Photographic Unit'. There was no further explanation of their chosen subject matter, but I supposed it was more likely to be enemy troop movements than weddings. The tall one out of the Smith and Jones pair emerged from the office to meet me.

"Sorry if we got off on the wrong foot yesterday, but Larry was running us ragged, and then when we discovered that our only hope was an old age Pensioner. No offence meant. Well the fact is I suppose I over reacted a bit - I mean you don't really look *that* old."

"So in a bad light I might pass for sixty five, you think?"

"Oh yeah, easy."

"That's very kind of you."

"That's alright chum. Anyway come with me and we'll get you kitted out."

As is so often the way in the forces, the simple task of supplying me with a military uniform, of which one might imagine they had thousands, took hours. I had originally turned down the idea of going in uniform, but was told that it was absolutely essential that our whole party were seen as being an official contingent of the British Army, as it was the only way the French authorities, and perhaps Monsieur Roland, would take us seriously. I was unconvinced, I speak French quite well and am perfectly familiar with their routines, I didn't think that Roland would be either more or less cooperative on account of how I was dressed - in fact I had the clear impression that if ever we found him, our conversation would be at gunpoint.

Eventually at about five o'clock in the afternoon Smith, or possibly Jones, turned up with the promised clothing. I took one look at it and handed it back.

"I'm not wearing this, it's a Sergeant's uniform."

"Sorry chum, but that's all we've got, and it is your size."

"I'm not your chum, and I'm not wearing it. My rank at the Air Ministry is Deputy Secretary, which in the army would be the equivalent of a Lieutenant General. I won't even consider anything less than a Brigadier."

He tried to respond with a laugh, but then saw that I was serious and so became annoyed instead. "Now you're just being ridiculous, this isn't bloody Moss Bros, we don't keep a selection Staff Officer's uniforms lying around on the off chance."

"Well that settles the matter, I shall travel in my own clothes, which is what I said in the first place."

He started to object, but I simply wagged a finger at him, and said. "No." I've found that relatively junior military officers tend use this war as an excuse to get awfully self important, this can become tiresome unless firmly checked.

As my next scheduled appointment with the military hierarchy was not until a briefing at seven thirty, I occupied some of the intervening period by taking a walk along the airfield perimeter. I was delighted to find that, despite the comings and goings of the aircraft, they had some resident woodlarks, not a showy bird to look at, but it does have a delightful song.

At least the briefing was completely professional. Eight of us were gathered into a mess room, with a blackboard on the wall at one end, covered by a sheet. Once the blackout curtains had been drawn and the door locked, the sheet was removed, showing a map of the area south of Reims. A large red X had been marked on the road between Epernay and Chalons. The officer used his pointer to tap the spot.

"This is a temporary RAF base at a small airfield called Condé-Vraux, we've got a squadron of Blenheims there. They're supposed to be for the defence of Paris, but they'd be useless for that, what would be needed is fighters and anyway as far as we know Paris isn't under any immediate threat. Putting them here is a completely political act, their Prime Minister, Reynaud, has requested that we demonstrate out commitment to the mutual defence pact by stationing forces deeper inside France. There's a feeling that we've deliberately kept the British Expeditionary Force close to the Channel, so that we can get them out of there when the Nazis break through."

"And have we?"

"Yes of course we have, but we can hardly come right out and say that. So the compromise is that we put some light bombers down here, and then as and when the Germans break through, if we've got any sense, we pull them back to the Channel with the rest of the Expeditionary Force. But the point about Vraux is that it's very near to the research centre where your chum Roland was working. We can land you there, first thing in the morning. Then the RAF will provide you and the team with transport out to the research station and you can see what there is to be found."

"What happens if we find Roland and he won't cooperate?"

"That's why we're here." Said either Smith or Jones, with a cold smile. He and his thuggish looking colleagues all stared at me as if I were the village idiot, and frankly that's rather what I felt like, for having asked such a stupid question.

Chapter 4

Doktor Theo Leibniz
Chalons, France, early Monday morning,
May 13th. 1940

The town itself is not bad, indistinguishable from lots of other provincial centres, but as I say, not bad. A big town hall sitting on a large open square, some pleasant black and white buildings, a cathedral that looks too big for the population, and the River Marne curling round the edge. Neither the towns of this region nor the countryside itself can compare with Bavaria or Baden-Wurttemberg, but by French standards it is, shall we say, acceptable.

The most serious disappointment is the hotel, it's south of the river, in one of the side streets near the station. It's called the Commercial Hotel and is dirty and extremely shabby. French haut cuisine has made no impact on its kitchens, and on rising this morning I was astonished not to have flea bites.

When we arrived von Strenglen had stood aside to leave me to deal with the owner, but I am unsure if this was a recognition of my seniority, or a demonstration that he was too grand to deal with cheap hoteliers. Our party occupied the entire hotel last night, sharing their only two bathrooms, and despite it being an embarrassing subject to raise, I feel it worth mentioning that both the lavatories were of the stand up variety. I complained immediately to the owner, a fat man wearing a vest, he simply shrugged and said that even he did not possess a water closet.

However, as a serving soldier in the field of battle, I must expect to make sacrifices, no doubt our front line troops have it worse. The man regarded my description of our group as a football team with unconcealed scepticism, but then astonished me even further by doing nothing about it. Imagine if the situations were reversed, and a German inn keeper was visited by a group of fit young men, carrying large heavy bags and speaking the language of the country with whom you are at war. He would have called the Gestapo before you could say Gruss Gott.

Fraulein Fuchs made a complete fool of herself after the evening meal, going round the men and stroking their faces as if she were some sort of French tart, then asking in childishly bad French which of them wanted to share her room. The men pretended to be amused and join in with the charade, but I don't think any of them regard her as more than an inconvenience. As von Strenglen took no interest in her behaviour, it fell to me to make sure that she eventually retired to her own room, alone.

With my agreement, the Sturmbannfuhrer took over the final briefing last night, and arranged that we should leave the hotel at six o'clock this morning, in order to take any scientists still at the site completely by surprise. The grumbling owner had appeared with weak coffee and what tasted like yesterday's croissants, but it was enough to ward off our hunger. The anticipation of forthcoming action had given me stomach ache, but I took the greatest care not to let this be seen. The men would not appreciate their commander showing any sign of weakness, and von Strenglen would see it as an opportunity to extend his own authority.

Unfortunately, our careful planning didn't even last long enough for the men to get in the bus. As we left the hotel, I heard the sound of aircraft overhead, and casually looked up. Two black shapes were turning overhead, their engines sounding high pitched, as if at full power.

"Shit, shit, shit. Who the hell authorised this?" Von Strenglen was loudly outraged, and didn't care how many Frenchmen he woke up with that fact, but I wasn't sure what he was outraged about, and looked at him for an explanation.

He swept his black gloved wooden hand angrily skywards. "They're Dorniers, DO17s, they're ours and they're not supposed to be here."

I looked back at the planes, now that he'd said what they were, I recognised the slim fuselage and bulbous nose of the famous Flying Pencil. The bomber that was faster than most fighters, that had been used so successfully in Spain, to flatten towns like Guernica.

"Is this going to cause a problem for us?" I asked, as he hustled the men into the bus, pushing Heidi in with them. Apparently her comfort no longer mattered.

"The people we're after are based near an airfield at a village called Vraux, which just happens to be the home to a squadron RAF fighter bombers, it's about twenty kilometres east of here. Now work out which direction those planes were going. My whole plan depended on taking these arseholes by surprise, and not having them given a friendly wake up call by our own people."

I have often found that a readiness to use vulgarities, such as 'arseholes', is as common amongst the aristocracy as it is amongst the working men. They share the same lack of inhibition and manners. I tolerated none of it at the Institute.

He grabbed my arm and steered me towards the car. "You're coming with me, Carl's driving the bus, he knows the way."

By any rational calculation a one handed man should not drive a car, but he managed it. It seemed there was a gap between his wooden hand and its matching wooden thumb, whenever he needed to change gear he simply wedged that slot around the gear lever and rattled it around with gusto. If ever it failed to move as he wished, he cursed loudly and rammed it into place even more firmly. The overall effect was very frightening.

The Citroen is a powerful car and he used every bit of its speed. We were too early for there to be much traffic, but he used the headlights and horn to clear away what little there was. As we emerged from the edge of town, and had a clearer view of the countryside, columns of smoke could be seen ahead of us. And over the smoke were the shapes of about ten Dorniers, wheeling, banking and diving. The attack was still going on.

"This is Goering and his fly boys, desperate for any bit of glory they can get, catching the RAF with their pants down. I was promised this place would stay untouched, at least until I'd finished with it. Whoever authorised this lot's going to be on bloody traffic duty for the rest of the war."

As we came closer the sound of explosions could be heard, even above the revving of our own engine. All our aircraft had left by the time we passed the airfield entrance, but there were fires burning all over the place, and smouldering heaps of scrap metal littered the field, presumably the remains of the British planes.

We continued along the road for another two kilometres, and then swung left along a track between two fields, towards an isolated house with a large modern steel barn next to it. I recognised it from the briefing pictures, this was Ponte's field test centre, it was from here that he'd disappeared. Behind the house I saw two wooden aerial towers, with wires stretched between them, this certainly looked like a radio location finding station. He skidded the car to a halt by the front door and jumped out, but even I knew that it was pointless. There were no cars parked there, and the front door was open, like a soldier once told the English King when he arrived too late to arrest some people - 'The birds have flown'.

Less than two minutes later the Renault bus pulled in behind us, and everyone climbed out, ready for an action that had already taken place. Von Strenglen emerged from the house.

"Herr Doktor, take two men and search that building I want to know if the equipment you're looking for is in there. Carl, you take the rest of them and split them up room by room - I want all technical looking papers in boxes and on the bus, and I want every other bit of paper examined for any clue about what sort of vehicle they might be driving and any mention of another location they could use."

The equipment in the steel building was familiar; the commercial strength radio transmitter, the amplifiers, the oscilloscopes, it wasn't identical to our own and the differences would need to be examined, but there was no doubt about what it was. There was also no doubt that the magnetron, and its base tray had been removed. On reflection, I agreed with von Strenglen; shit, shit, shit.

One of his men came back from the house. "The coffee can is still warm, they've been gone less than twenty minutes, we might even have passed them on the road."

Then the Sturmbannfuhrer showed me the difference between a civilian, like myself, and military officer. He joined me at the work bench and picked up some spare radio valves, that were of no particular significance, and packed them into a small cardboard box. Then telling the rest of them to continue searching for documents, he told me to get in the car and hold the box carefully on my knee as we drove back to the airfield.

Although, as far as I was concerned, all need for speed had now evaporated, he drove the last few hundred metres to the airfield entrance gate at high speed, skidding to a halt in a cloud of dust and gravel. Beyond the fence the fires still burned, confusion and destruction were all around, and the smell of burning fuel filled our nostrils.

Two edgy sentries pointed their rifles at us as we stopped at the barrier. I considered telling them they should have been pointing at the Luftwaffe if they'd wanted to achieve anything, but like their gun pointing, the advice would have been too late.

Von Strenglen already had his window down, and was shouting at the men. "We have the missing equipment for Professor Ponte's team, we must get it to them immediately." He gestured towards me and the box I was holding, I silently lifted it in their direction, like an offering. But he had spoken to the men in French, and they were English, with all the command of the local language that arrogant island race normally possess.

"What did you say?" Asked one, in English.

Von Strenglen repeated himself, in slow but perfectly good English.

The two sentries looked at each other, across the roof of the car. Genuine puzzlement was written all over their faces.

"They're not here."

"Yes, they must be, we were all working together at the radio station only half an hour ago. They said they were coming here and told me to follow them. They need these valves urgently." Once again I half lifted the box.

"Listen chum, you can take my bloody word for it nobody's come in here in the last hour." He looked over his shoulder at the chaos behind him, and then back at us. "You'd need to be bleedin' mad trying to get in here half an hour ago. The entire friggin' Luftwaffe was droppin' bombs on us."

"But if they didn't come here, where can they have gone? They're waiting for these valves, the entire experiment depends on it."

"Can't help you chum, none of your lot's been in 'ere this mornin', and there's not much point now, is there?"

We drove back to join the others with no idea where our quarry might have gone, all we had established for certain was that they weren't at the airfield. But as we walked into the house, Carl met us with a smile on his face.

"I used the time to report back on the radio, boss, and they had a message waiting for us." He handed von Strenglen a piece of paper. He read it silently and then handed it to me, it was a transcription of a Morse code signal, and like all such messages was brief and to the point.

'Ponte believed travelled to England with device, senior remaining technician Claude Roland has a duplicate and is offering it for sale direct to us. He wishes to conceal his location until money agreed and paid. Suspect he may be at their storage location at Hangar number three Barberey airport Troyes. We will try to agree terms with him - but in unwelcome event of

there being alternative bidder - report from there soon as possible. Cheaper and faster if you seize initiative. Vogel.'

Sir Freddy Villiers
London, early Monday morning, May 13th. 1940

In order to allow the maximum possible time on the ground in France, it had been decided that we should be airborne at the cock crow hour of 5.00 a.m. At least the military know the meaning of an early start. Apparently our flight time was due to be slightly less than two hours, and very sensibly the planners had allowed for us to use every possible hour of daylight.

Before leaving the mess hall, where I had gone for an early cup of tea, I was disappointed to hear a BBC report of the situation, Apparently, a government spokesman had said that that the Germans were only interested in Holland and Belgium, and that massive French forces were reinforcing the Belgian border to contain matters. My own view was that such remarks were comparable to government statements in 1914, to the effect that it would all be over by Christmas. I didn't believe them that time, and I still didn't this time.

Having made my small stand over the issue of clothing, I relented as far as a coat was concerned and had borrowed an army greatcoat. My seven companions and I, together with the two crew members, gathered in the first flush of dawn outside one of the hangars.

Our aircraft was an American model called a Lockheed Electra, the same sort that Amelia Earhart was flying when she disappeared on her recent round the world flight; I hoped that we were going to be more successful. I'm happy to fly when my work requires it, and over the years have logged up a great many hours in a wide variety of aircraft, yet even so, I'm not a great enthusiast for air travel. It's not the danger that bothers me half as much as the fact that they're noisy, cramped and cold, one can normally reckon on having a headache on arrival.

However, as aircraft go, this machine was exceptionally sleek and good looking, if light aircraft could be compared to cars, this would be a sports car, an MG or an Aston Martin. There were five rows of two seats for the passengers, with a central aisle between them, the low ceiling made it impossible to stand fully upright, but otherwise it looked rather plush.

The pilot said that our route was just over 300 miles, and that with a cruising speed of 190 miles an hour that would put us on the ground at just after six thirty. The forecast promised good weather all day, it seemed as though we had covered all the eventualities we could. Five minutes later we were airborne and heading south for the Channel, with the dawn sunshine streaming in through our port side windows.

In deference, either to my seniority, or my incredibly advanced age, they had insisted that I should occupy the seat immediately behind the pilots, it was said to have more room than the rest. Then once I was seated several bags of 'equipment', by which I assume they meant guns, were strapped onto the seat across the aisle from mine. The rest of the men, filling all but one of the remaining seats, behind me.

The Captain, in the left hand pilot's seat, had offered me a head set and boom mike, on which to listen to the radio traffic and talk to the crew. As I reckoned the ear phones would help deaden the relentless din of the engines I accepted, I have always found the technicalities of flying to be more interesting than the fact of doing it.

We crossed the south coast near Eastbourne, on a heading which I noted from the instrument panel was 135 degrees, and twenty minutes later we crossed the French coast just south of Le Touquet, a resort that Mary and I had often visited in more agreeable times. I was, for once in an aircraft, both warm and at least semi comfortable, so much so that I was in danger of nodding off.

The area controller came on the radio to assure us that there were no reports of enemy aircraft activity in the Amiens to Reims sector, the next portion of our route, but that if we wished we could divert onto a more westerly track. The pilot looked over his shoulder at me and said. "It's up to you, we've got enough fuel."

"Hang on, I'll check with El Supremo." I still hadn't sorted their names out and the pilot smiled at my disrespectful description. I turned round and beckoned the tall one forward.

He and the pilot and I huddled together in the aisle, talking loudly at each other to be heard. The pilot showed us his folded map, with the line of our course marked in thick pencil. He tapped his finger on the line.

"We're just here, we'll have passed to the north of Amiens in the next couple of minutes, after that the next position check is Reims. It should be safe enough to continue on course, any enemy aircraft action will be in support of their ground troops and they will have to be north of the Ardennes, because that's impassable to tanks." He tapped his finger on the area in question.

"As far as I'm concerned we stick to track, otherwise we're just wasting time." I said, the other two nodded their agreement.

"The only change I'll make will be to go in at low level, less conspicuous." Said the pilot. "Then whenever we make the return trip you can decide if you want to go round to the west of Paris, or not."

"Tell Air Traffic what we're doing." He nodded and swung himself back into his seat.

The ground rose to meet us, unrolling rapidly under our nose, as we settled at our new and lower level. Houses, washing hung on lines, cows in fields, cars on the road and even individual people, all came clearly into focus, most of them just about to have their breakfast on a beautiful sunny morning. It could have been a nice day, if it weren't for the fact that for the second time this century their homeland was about to be invaded and fought over.

Now that we were actually over France, the two pilots were making regular scans of the surrounding sky, to the sides, above, behind. For the lack of anything better to do, I found myself following suit, peering at the section of sky visible from my window. After almost half an hour spent earnestly searching the skies, we were passing Reims, and the only other aircraft we'd seen had been well above us. They either hadn't noticed us against the visual clutter of the ground below, or just weren't interested. I had become slightly bored.

Then with sickening speed and brutality our safe little world was torn apart. An inarticulate shout of alarm from one of the crew, blasted through the headset. The pilot pulled the control column sharply back, and with his right hand pushed the power and mixture levers fully forward. The engines howled and I felt suddenly much heavier as we went up like a rocket. As we did so, two black shapes hurtled past us - only yards away, their wakes banged us around as if we were driving over cobbles on flat tyres.

"ME one oh nines." Was the pilot's only comment, as he flung us hard over to the right, our wings completely vertical against the earth below. The view from my window changed from sky to fields and trees. Moments later he turned us the other way, then we slewed sideways as he stood on one of the rudder pedals to change our direction without banking. As he ran through his repertoire of evasive manoeuvres both pilots kept twisting their heads round in an attempt to see where the Messerschmitts had gone.

From my work at the Air Ministry I knew exactly what the German fighters were capable of, almost 400 miles an hour, twice as fast as our own plane. Even more significantly, they had guns and we didn't. No matter what our pilot did, this could only end in one way, to the Germans it must look as if we were moving in slow motion.

I looked out to my left, over the pile of equipment bags on the seat across the aisle, and through that window saw what should have been the last sight of my life. The perfect head on outline of an ME 109, exactly like the black silhouette shape on an aircraft recognition chart, but this one had twinkling lights in front of its cockpit. The two machine guns on its engine cowling were firing through the propeller disc, at us - at me.

The aircraft around me exploded with a staggering series of blows, windows shattered and various pieces of debris flew violently in all directions. The equipment bags across the aisle from me were thrown about, as bullets hit their solid contents. Our whole airframe bucked and jerked. Men must have screamed, but I didn't hear them.

It can only have lasted two or three seconds, and then there was a horrible pause, horrible because I knew there was more to come. And then it came, another storm of hammer blows swept across us, but from which direction I have no idea. And then it was all over.

I looked down at my arms and legs, but could see no damage. then I looked back, there were bullet holes in the cabin walls and whole windows were missing, but even more obvious was the deadly effect of the attack on the passengers. There was not as much blood as I would have expected from such an attack, but the seven men behind me were twisted and slumped into unmistakable shapes of death. The engine noise faltered, coughed and died. There was an unnatural and unwelcome quiet, with only the noise of the airflow whistling across and through the holes in the fuselage. On each side plumes of black oily smoke emerged from the silent engines.

At last I realised where I ought to direct my attention, and swung myself round to look at the pilots. This time there was every bit as much blood as I would have expected, if anything, rather more. I grasped their seat backs and pulled forward to get between them, I had to make sure, but there was no room for doubt. I was the only survivor, no doubt courtesy of the piled equipment next to my seat.

As I crouched there it began to seem as if I was tipping forward, I looked up, through the cracked but still intact screen and saw that we were entering a dive. The temptation was to pull the control column back, but I had the presence of mind to roll back the elevator trim wheel instead. This reduced our rate of descent while I dragged and manhandled the pilot's mortal remains upwards and backwards from his seat. The involuntary grunting noises this exertion caused me to utter were a

71

reminder of my advancing years. Fortunately the Lockheed's control columns came in from each side of the cockpit, rather than emerging vertically from the floor, and this enabled me to move his dead weight without the legs becoming tangled round the column.

As I dumped his body roughly in the aisle, the head banged noisily and unceremoniously on the aluminium floor. I realised with a guilty start that, despite being introduced to him last night, his was another name I couldn't remember. Dismissing the thought as irrelevant, I slid myself into his ripped and bloodstained, but still warm, seat.

At last I had my hands on the control wheel, the only question now was what to do with it. A great deal of familiarity with light and medium sized aircraft as a passenger, and a considerable knowledge of their technical specifications does not qualify one to fly them; but I'm an intelligent man and given the choice between learning quickly and dying I decided to learn.

Using the external horizon as my reference, I levelled the wings and settled the nose into a slight descent, the last thing I needed was to enter a spin, then I looked for the Airspeed Indicator. I knew that the different coloured arcs around the edge represented safe speeds for different modes of flight, what I needed was to know the stall speed.

This one had white, green and yellow arcs overlapping each other. It seemed a reasonable guess that the lower end of the white line, which was the slowest of the three ranges, would be the stalling speed with the flaps down, which ought to be slower than with them up. The figure it showed was just under seventy miles an hour, and we were now doing almost ninety. I found what I thought was the flap lever between the seats and pulled it up a notch, sure enough the nose tipped slightly down. I pulled the column back to reduce our speed to eighty, everything seemed to be stable so I rolled the elevator trim wheel until it took the back pressure off the controls.

The altimeter said one thousand feet, only a minute or so before we hit the ground. I looked at the approaching terrain, there were two big fields that looked more than long enough, but which one? I had no idea of the wind direction, where can you find a smoking chimney when you need one?

To hell with it, I picked the nearest and swung the nose round to line up. The speed had dropped to less than eighty and I was sure that we were close enough to make it, so I pulled the flap lever all the way up. This time the aircraft nose tilted quite sharply down and the speed dropped a little further. I now had both hands on the control wheel but was squeezing it far too tightly, I made myself relax my iron grip a little.

Keep your wings level, watch your speed, about seventy five, should be alright. The ground was getting frighteningly close, I couldn't image anyone choosing to do this for a living. The wheels! I'd forgotten to put the bloody wheels down. I leaned forward in desperate attempt to locate the undercarriage control. Forget it - you're too late - just watch the speed and keep your wings level.

We cleared the boundary hedge and I eased gently back again, trying to get rid of as much speed as possible. The plane floated on, and on. We were ten feet off the ground and staying there, the damn thing had no intention of landing. The field sped past beneath me, and the far hedge came closer and closer. At last, it settled itself reluctantly to earth. Even without wheels it was nowhere near as bad as I'd feared, and we slid quite smoothly across the short grass.

The far hedge had trees in it, and without any steering I had no option but to watch as my starboard wing hit one and was neatly removed, just beyond that engine. There was a brief flicker of yellow flame. We were now spinning slowly to a standstill in the next field, the hedge and tree having provided the required braking effort, but the small flame was now a large one.

Even before we were fully stopped, I scrambled out of the seat, stepping awkwardly on the pilot's leg as I did so, and made my way as quickly as I could through the carnage of the cabin to reach the only door. By good luck that door was at the port side rear, and the explosion on the starboard side. I was only four or five paces from the aircraft when it went up. I was vividly aware of flying through the air, and then I landed for the second time.

Chapter 5

Doktor Theo Leibniz
Troyes, France, Monday midday, May 13th. 1940

As we were loading our men back into the vehicles, a black saloon car came nosing slowly down the track from the road, it wasn't marked as a police car but von Strenglen said that it smelled like trouble. This was another area where I suspected that his previous experience might be more useful than my own.

There were only von Strenglen, myself, one of his men and Heidi Fuchs who had yet to board the bus. He called through the open bus door for the rest of them to stay where they were, then sending Fuchs and the man round the back of the bus, he and I stood by the house door to meet the newcomers.

The car drew slowly to a halt, the occupants taking everything in. Now that they were this close I could understand what Gunther had meant about them being trouble. They acted like Gestapo officers, openly suspicious of whatever it was they were looking at. The difference was that the Gestapo were there to protect my interests, these two weren't. The Sturmbannfuhrer stepped forwards, raising his gloved hand in greeting.

Can we help you?" He asked in French. The driver got out, while the other stayed where he was, he was looking down at something inside the car. The driver was a tall prematurely bald man in a grey suit, he was every inch police or security. He had a black leather identity folder in his hand, he held it up, so that the cover fell to one side revealing whatever it was that confirmed his identity. In his other hand he held a revolver.

"Police, who are you and what are doing here?"

As he was saying this Heidi Fuchs had emerged from behind the back of the bus, beside the car's front passenger door. She paused and looked at von Strenglen, they nodded to each other. Then without uttering a word she took a small pistol from her pocket, pulled open the car door and shot the occupant twice, he slumped sideways out of the car, his head resting on the ground. Now that the car door was open we could hear a voice talking on a radio. "Say again fourteen, say again."

As Fuchs was dealing with the passenger, von Strenglen calmly shot the driver, his lack of a right hand doing nothing to cramp his style with the left.

I didn't know if I was more horrified at this escalation, or astonished at the slick and professional speed of it. The driver was, briefly, as surprised as I was, he hadn't even been seriously aiming his gun, more showing it as a symbol of authority. There had been no shouting and no sudden drama, it had all been very contained and matter of fact, as if it happened every day.

Insofar as I had imagined such a thing at all, I had imagined the act of shooting the enemy to be something which occurred at long distance, and between uniformed soldiers. This was the first real action I had ever seen, and the change from casually talking to someone, to killing them as they stood next to you was shocking, but I would learn to cope. Now that I had seen it done, I would learn to do it myself.

Even more surprising than the circumstances of the action, was the revelation that Heidi Fuchs was no longer acting like a tart, but more like a soldier. There was perhaps more to her than I had thought, and just as surprising was the fact the von Strenglen seemed to be happier to work with her than with me. Another example of the affinity between the opposite ends of the social spectrum.

He had the two bodies dragged around the back of the steel building, at least they would be less obvious there. Then he assembled the men and told them that they would be taking the bus back to Basel. I stepped forward to interrupt.

"Sturmbannfuhrer, this incident with the two police officers is no reason for us to abandon our task, Reinhard Heydrich himself entrusted this mission to me personally." I would have continued but he responded immediately.

He spoke soothingly, as if I were a child with some irrational objection. "Calm yourself Herr Doktor, there is no question of us abandoning the mission. These men were required for a surprise attack on what might have been a defended position, that is no longer the case. The man Roland is in hiding, it is our job to find him, and the presence of such a large group would result in nothing but unwelcome attention. From this point on there will only be four of us, a much less suspicious group."

He turned back to the men to complete his instructions, and Fuchs strode over to me, a hard and arrogant look on her face. She stood close and spoke quietly. "I don't know why he's so polite to you Leibniz, you know nothing about these things, you should learn to keep your mouth shut."

As von Strenglen was still addressing the men, only two or three metres away, any correction of her impertinence was going to have to wait for a more suitable occasion. So, for the moment, I was obliged to bite my tongue and walk away.

We left the police car, carefully locked, in a side street on the outskirts of Chalons and dropped the keys down a grid. Then the Sturmbannfuhrer, Fuchs, Carl and myself went on our way in the Citroen.

The fact that Roland, one of Ponte's own men, was offering to sell his chief's secrets for his own advantage was a grubby business, I couldn't believe it possible that any of my own team would have stooped so low. He must be an extremely stupid man not to realise that, once we had our hands on the device, we would treat him with the contempt his sort deserved. I was confident that von Strenglen, or even Fuchs would see to it.

The trip to Troyes took us just over an hour, during which the other three were discussing various means of breaching the airport perimeter. Should we steal a French commercial vehicle and pretend to be making a delivery? Or rely on finding an unobserved portion of the fence and cut the wire? To the great surprise of all of us, no such subterfuge was required.

On arrival we found that, unlike the situation in Germany, there simply wasn't a security gate at all, and nothing to stop us driving straight up to the hangar. Is such a casual attitude the result of Jewish or communist influence? One can't be sure, but one indication was shown on the town plan we had for Troyes. The largest square in the middle town was labelled Place Alexandre-Israel, which seems a fairly explicit statement of local loyalties. Changes would clearly need to be made in this, as in so many other areas, of French life.

Despite the speed of our reactions and the accuracy of our intelligence, there was no sign of Ponte's men.

Hangar number three had a padlock on the door, there was nobody home. An old man, who looked like a caretaker, turned up shortly after we arrived.

"Are you looking for Gaston?"

Fraulein Fuchs held up a warning finger for the rest of us to be silent, and got out of the car to speak to him herself. She was not only charming and friendly, she also spoke excellent French, which is more than she ever had previously in my hearing.

"I don't know about Gaston, we've just come down from Vraux and were hoping to catch up with Monsieur Roland. He told us to meet him here, have you seen him?"

The old man shook his head. "No, Gaston said he'd been here earlier, but I didn't see him."

"Where did he go from here, do you know?"

The old man took down the half smoked cigarette from behind his ear, and started to pat his pockets for matches, Fraulein Fuchs remained calm and patient.

"No, Roland's far too grand to talk to the likes of me, just like his boss, but Gaston will know."

"Where can we find Gaston?"

"God knows, he lives in a world of his own that man, he just said that he had some errand in town. But he's got to be back here this afternoon, I do know that. I'll tell him you're asking after him shall I?"

"It doesn't matter, we'll wait for him in the hangar, and talk to him when he gets back."

He hawked and spat on the ground. "You'll be lucky, he's got the only keys. I'll go and talk to them in the office - tell them someone's here for Gaston - perhaps they'll know something."

The old man was still patting vaguely around for matches, Fuchs looked casually round, but there was no one else in sight. She put an arm on his shoulder."Come over to the car, we've got some matches there."

As they started towards us she nodded to von Strenglen, he got out of the car and stood waiting for them. He was standing between the car and the side of the hangar as the old man approached, with Fuchs following closely. As they came together, Fuchs and von Strenglen stood right up to him in a tight little group, and then, as I watched, the old man staggered and collapsed. He was dead, and even though I'd been looking, I still didn't know which of them had done it, or even how. It was very professional, I was thrilled to be leading such a truly elite team.

We broke the lock off the door of the hangar and drove the car in, dragging the old man with us. Then we settled down to wait for the wandering Gaston.

Sir Freddy Villiers
Vraux, France, Monday midday, May 13th 1940

There was no amnesia, I was aware of my situation even before I opened my eyes. I was lying face down in a French field. I remembered everything about the attack and the crash. The fact that I was conscious argued against me being dead, but I was probably injured, perhaps seriously.

As I moved my arms and legs slightly, to confirm they were still there, I could hear the crackling of flames, which meant that I hadn't been here for too long or the fuel fire would have burnt itself out. At length I opened my eyes and slowly rolled over, in order to get myself laboriously into a seated position, at which point I paused to catch my breath and take stock. As any reasonable person would have expected, I felt terrible.

I had been thoroughly bashed about, so many parts of me felt kicked and bruised it wasn't worth trying to identify individual problem areas. My trousers were torn, my jacket was ripped, and yet, despite the fact that I had blood all over me I somehow didn't think that it was mine, and. . . and that was about it, as far as I could tell. I started to try and organise my arms and legs into suitable positions for achieving verticality; standing up was going to take a while, but it would be a good next step.

"Freeze - don't you move a bloody muscle - you German bastard."

I froze and looked round, there were two nervous looking young soldiers, pointing rifles at me. The one in front was so excited to be catching a Nazi that his rifle was shaking, considering that his finger was on the trigger I thought this a bad idea.

"Stand up, but keep your hands in the air, where I can see them."

"I can't, I need my hands to help me get up."

He took another step towards me, pointing the rifle even more emphatically. "Stand up, Now." He was close to hysteria. Reckoning that sudden moves were more dangerous than staying still, I just sat there, but put my hands up to shoulder level to show that I was complying.

"Why do you think I sound as though I'm English?"

"Because you learn it at school, that's why - now if you don't shut it I'll shoot. I mean it."

After a minute or two of sitting there with my hands up, a Sergeant appeared, he looked questioningly at the two soldiers.

"We caught him trying to escape, but I think he's the only one that got out. He speaks English."

The Sergeant looked at me. "On your feet sunshine - you're coming with us."

"I'm English, not German."

"Then if you're English, what the 'ell are you doing climbing out of a friggin' Dornier?"

I turned my head to look at the wreckage and saw what he meant. A narrow fuselage, twin engines and the distinctive twin rudder tailplane. But he didn't know as much about aircraft specifications as I did.

"The DO 17 has its wing attached to the top of the fuselage, if you look at what's left of that, it has the wing attached to the bottom of the fuselage. That's because it's an American aircraft called a Lockheed Electra. It's a ten seater passenger aircraft and we were en route from Heston to somewhere called Condé-Vraux when we were jumped by a pair of ME one oh nines."

"Condé-Vraux?"

"Yes, it's an airfield near Chalons, south of Reims. There's a British squadron based there, it can't be all that far from here."

"About a mile that way." He said, jerking his thumb over his shoulder. "That's where we're from." He came over to me, stretching out a hand. "Here you go, I'll help you up."

The airfield was in a complete mess, they had just been attacked by a flight of Dorniers, which accounted for the soldiers' less than friendly welcome. Fortunately, the bulk of the damage was materiel, with very few actual fatalities, and eventually one of their medics patched up my cuts and bruises.

It seems extremely selfish to say so, but as I didn't really know any of the dead men, the saddest aspect for me was the realisation that I wouldn't be able to tell Mary about my brush with death. One grows accustomed, down the years, to having an alter ego with whom to share all of life's adventures. The whole affair seemed to reinforce my solitary state.

They sent out a recovery team to the wreckage, but there wasn't going to be much left to bury. We'd still had half tanks of fuel, it had been a fierce fire, more of a cremation than a burial. The C.O, though obviously preoccupied with the state of his command was, in his own way, a decent enough fellow and his adjutant got me kitted out in spare civilian clothing. There was even a new pair of shoes to replace my own, which had, without me realising it, had the sole neatly removed from one by a large calibre machine gun bullet.

"It could be a couple of days before we've got anything going north from here, but we should be able to get you back to the UK within three or four days."

I was shocked. "There can be no question of me returning to the UK, not until I've dealt with the matter I came down here for in the first place."

"My dear fellow you're suffering from shock, your whole team has been killed, and all your equipment lost - continuing alone would be out of the question. I don't wish to be rude, but surely this sort of work is a job for younger men."

"Nonsense, a decent meal and a stiff drink and I'll be right as rain. I'd appreciate the loan of a vehicle, but as for the 'equipment' you refer to, as far as I was aware it was just a load of guns. I'll admit they saved my life on the plane, but I have no intention of carrying one around with me, I'd look like an old age version of Al Capone."

"I'm sorry Sir Frederick, but I'm afraid you don't understand, I'm the base commander and if I say that you stay on this base until I can send you home - then that is exactly what will happen. There happens to be a war on, and to be blunt about it, you're far too old to be gallivanting about the French countryside without an escort. I'm afraid that's the end of the matter, so if you'll excuse me I have more pressing matters to deal with."

He eventually relented sufficiently to allow me out under escort, with the same Sergeant who'd brought me in earlier, to examine Ponte's experimental station which was just down the road.

The CSF team was based near the airfield in order to use their aircraft in the radio location experiments, and they had sometimes set up equipment at the field. The Sergeant had been there before, and drove me the mile or two down the road. As soon as we walked in it was obvious that everything of importance had been cleared out of the place, but as I stood there, surveying the debris, the scene didn't ring true.

"Norman," the Sergeant and I were on first name terms by now, "If you were abandoning your base in a hurry, and needed to take any secret paperwork, or bits of kit with you, is this what it would look like when you'd finished?"

He looked around. "If I was taking my own stuff, then I'd know where it was. What's happened here is that Ponte's lads have loaded their own stuff in the van and scarpered. If you'd heard what it was like round here earlier - you'd have done the same. They must have thought Jerry would be bombing them next. Then separately, someone else has come in after them to try and find the same stuff. If you look you can see things have been pulled out of drawers and out of cupboards, that's somebody looking for stuff when they don't know where it is."

He was right, but we split up for a last look round anyway. As I was still sorting through the radio transmitter parts, he called me from round the back.

"Freddy, come and take a look at this."

There were two bodies, lying together against the back wall of the steel shed, with a wheelbarrow turned upside down on top of them for partial concealment. They had both been shot. Norman was emptying their pockets onto the ground, it looked as if he'd done this sort of thing before. This one's a local copper, here's his ID, from the look of those suits I reckon they're both coppers, but they were shot somewhere else and dragged here." As he pointed I could see the marks in the ground, it looked as they had been brought round from the front.

He lifted one of the arms, then let it fall. "No rigor mortis yet, so take a rough guess it's happened within the last four hours, or less." We both instinctively looked around.

"This means that whoever was ransacking this place for Ponte's stuff was caught in the act by these two, and let them have it." I said, thinking aloud.

"So the guys doing the shooting weren't either French or British, that doesn't exactly leave a lot of options. Watch out there's a Kraut about."

He was right, I had competition. They were hours ahead of me, they were armed and they were extremely dangerous, perhaps it was time to re think the Al Capone look.

Back at the airfield, the police were called and the front gatehouse staff questioned. This revealed the visit by two men in a dark green Citroen Avant saloon car, trying to get information on the whereabouts of the Ponte team. The two men on the gate had no idea whether the men had been French or not, only that they had initially spoken in that language. As closely as we could estimate, this had been approximately three hours earlier.

Norman remembered Ponte, or his men, driving a black Renault, and thought they also had a small flat bed truck, but wasn't sure what make it was. I was collecting useful information, but it wasn't enough to indicate a next step. Then the French police arrived, and Norman and I were required to go and make statements.

French policing is divided between two principal bodies; the Police Nationale, a civil organisation who are responsible mainly for towns and urban areas, and the Gendarmerie Nationale. The Gendarmerie are a branch of the armed forces, complete with military style ranks, though they are used as the civil police force in rural areas and around French borders. They also act in major criminal investigations where the case might spread beyond one particular area. In this case we found ourselves talking to the Gendarmerie.

In terms of legal jurisdiction there might have been a clash over them entering an RAF base, but Squadron Leader Jackson, the commanding officer, didn't seem to wish to make an issue of it. Whichever was the fastest way to settle the matter seemed to be his very sensible preference.

The first surprise was that the investigating officer was a female, Capitaine Martine Dumont, accompanied by a junior ranking person whose name escaped me. The Squadron Leader followed me into the office which Capitaine Dumont was using as an interview room and, despite the fact that the two Gendarmes and I had made our introductions in French, he made a point of using English. Whether he was linguistically limited or simply emphasising his position, I was unaware.

He called the Capitaine, Miss Dumont, and whilst she showed no displeasure I felt this to be slightly discourteous. Were he to have spoken French, it would have been more polite either to use her title or, in view of her rank, simply address her as Madame. But then as a Civil Servant I do have a nose for the finer degrees of protocol.

"The point is," said the Squadron Leader, not bothering to sit down, "That none of this nonsense actually occurred on the base, and although this gentleman," he gestured at me, "Had plans to visit the remaining members of the Ponte team, that's all gone by the board now. He'll be going back to England on the first available flight - I've got injured men and wrecked aircraft to deal with. So I'm afraid that the statements from this gentleman and my Sergeant are all we can offer."

"That's very kind of you Squadron Leader." She replied in English, but he was already leaving the office as she spoke. In fairness to the man he did have a moderately full schedule.

As the door closed behind him, I asked. "Would you prefer English or French?"

"If you're comfortable in French it would be more convenient for my colleague." I nodded my agreement and her colleague, who was apparently a Sergeant Barnier, mouthed *Merci*.

We discussed the circumstances of discovering the dead police officers, and my companion's deductions about the time and place of their deaths. During all of which she nodded politely, and her Sergeant made notes.

"I understand that you are a senior *fonctionnaire* with the Air Ministry in London?" Her slightly raised eyebrows made this a question.

"To be honest I finally retired last week, to leave with some dignity before they kicked me out. But then I was approached by our intelligence people, don't ask me the department because I don't know, they wanted me to make this trip because of my familiarity with some of the people involved, and the particulars of their work."

It was a leap in the dark to have been quite this open with someone I had only just met, but there wasn't the time for lengthy pussy footing around. If she was going to be helpful I needed to be frank about my aims and intentions, then she might do me some good, and if she was going to be a pain in the arse then the sooner she got on with it the better.

"Thank you for your honesty, that was as helpful as it was unusual. But first, tell me how are you after your dreadful crash this morning? It must have been terrifying."

"It was, and I'm a lot better than I ought to be at my age, I was very lucky."

"And the gentlemen with you, who perished, were they also with the intelligence services?"

"Yes, but they were the professionals, I was the amateur who was just dragged along for my small area of specialist knowledge. In their eyes I was very much a passenger."

"But I understood that you made the forced landing yourself, although you are not a pilot."

"Wouldn't you, if everyone else was dead and your only alternative was to go nose first into a field at two hundred miles an hour?"

"I suppose. And now your Squadron Leader imagines that you will go home, like a good boy, and stop causing him all these unnecessary problems." This time it wasn't a question, but a statement.

"That would seem to sum things up."

"But you have no intention of going home, not until you've done what you came here for - have you?"

My eyes widened before I could control the reaction. "What a remarkably observant Gendarme you are." Then we both smiled. "Are my intentions really that obvious?"

"Only to those who pay attention, and that officer is extremely busy at the moment."

She paused, leaning forward, her elbows on the table, hands clasped together by her chin, her two forefingers resting together on her lips. For a while the two of us regarded each other, while her Sergeant leaned back in his chair and regarded the pair of us. A random thought emerged unbidden, it had taken an interview with a police officer to make me smile. My first smile in a very long time. What a strange world this is, and what a very pleasant personality she had. Then she spoke again.

"I think, Sir Freddy, that I agree with your Squadron Leader, he has too many important things on his mind to deal also with you. It would be better if you removed yourself and allowed him to attend to his other duties."

"I think that you are an extremely devious woman, and quite probably dangerous with it."

Her Sergeant almost concealed a smile, while she shrugged delicately.

"Perhaps."

Chapter 6

Doktor Theo Leibniz
Troyes, late Monday afternoon, May 13th 1940

It was five o'clock before Gaston finally returned to the hangar. We had used the wait to search the crates and boxes they had stored there. It was the same story as at the radio station, there was no sign of a magnetron, not an old one, not a new one, not any sort. We were still chasing.

The man who had to be Gaston slid the hangar door to one side, its small steel wheels squealing as it moved. Then he peered round to see if there was any reason for the lock having disappeared. Carl emerged behind him and pushed him in, pulling the door across, behind them both. They tied him to a chair and Heidi Fuchs stood in front of him, staring down at him, not an ounce of pity in her face. I realised that my earlier view of this woman had been wrong, she was prepared to get her hands dirty in pursuit of the Reich's interests. Her lack of social graces now seemed irrelevant.

"You're going to tell me where Roland is, and you're going to tell me in the next few minutes. If you tell me, then I'll leave you tied up and if you're lucky someone will find you before you die - but we will leave you unharmed."

"I don't know where Roland is."

"I'm afraid you interrupted me before I'd finished - what I was saying was - otherwise I will personally drag the information out of you, and I'm not only good at that, I enjoy it."

"Boche whore!" He said, then spat on the ground.

He tensed himself for the expected blow. Instead of which she laughed.

"Boche? Certainly, that's exactly what I am. And whore - why not? I did a couple of years on the Reeperbahn, I would even screw a Frenchman for money, that's how low I sank. But then I found the Fuhrer. He saved me." She pulled the gold eagle and swastika medallion from the top of her blouse and held it up to him." See that - belief in that man turned my life from solid shit to pure gold. I was a nobody, scum, like you - but now I'm a somebody. Now tell me, which of us is the fool?"

This silenced the man and he sat there looking sullen and defiant.

She reached inside his jacket pocket and pulled out his wallet, and then opened the identity card, pursing her lips in thought as she read it.

"48 Rue Bertrand, what's that, about five minutes away? It says here that you have a wife, Yvonne, that's interesting. What's even more interesting is that I know exactly where she is right now, she's at home getting your meal ready." She lifted her attention from the card to look him in the eye. "I'm right aren't I?"

His defeated look and downcast eyes gave the answer.

"Good, now we've got that sorted out, perhaps I should be more honest with you. We both know that I was lying when I said we might leave you alive. That isn't going to happen is it? What is going to happen is that I'm going to ask you a few questions, that's all. They're going to be easy questions, and I already know the answers to some of them, but you'll never know which. If you tell me the truth then we'll shoot you through the head and go, we won't have time for anything else."

She waited, as he digested her words. Then she gave him the rest of it, the bit he'd known was coming. "But if you lie to me, I will know, and then Carl there will go and pick up Yvonne and anyone else he can find at your house - your child, your mother, your dog, anyone, and he will bring them back here." There was another pause, a long one, before she added. "You do know what we'll do to them, right in front of your eyes, don't you? Then you'll talk."

It seems that he had a very good idea of where Roland might have gone. He talked freely and fully, and Fraulein Fuchs had never so much as raised her voice. It was an astonishing display of control. I had seriously misjudged the woman, there was a good deal I could learn from her.

Eventually he paused, he had said every possible thing he could think of about the movements and possible location of Claude Roland. He had been looking at the ground, as he struggled to remember, but having finished he now he looked up, a glimmer of hope in his eyes. Would his cooperation dispose his captors to mercy. Unfortunately not, at a signal from Fuchs, Carl drew his pistol and shot him, just once, in the head. Gaston, and the chair he was tied to, tipped sideways and fell to the ground.

But nobody was interested in Gaston's end, even as the body fell, Gunther von Strenglen was unfolding a map on the the table.

"Paris, that has to be the worst possible answer." Was his immediate comment.

"Why is that so bad?" I asked. The three of them looked at me, impatiently.

"If the easiest place to hide a tree is in a forest, then tell me Herr Doktor, where is the easiest place to hide a man?"

"A city." I lamely agreed

He switched on the portable Telefunken radio set that we carried, and although I didn't know what he was tuning in to, I didn't want to risk another foolish question, and so remained silent as if I knew what was going on. The power light glowed and the set made that low warble which indicates the valves warming up. He switched frequency and turned the central tuning wheel. After a succession of hisses, whistles and snatches of music, the familiar tones of the Reich's Broadcasting announcer came on. At first he was detailing Luftwaffe victory figures, and they were astonishing. A figure of 148 allied aircraft shot down for the loss of six of our own. It had long been recognised that the Luftwaffe enjoyed an advantage in both the quality of our pilots and the machines they flew, but these figures far exceeded even the most optimistic pre war estimates.

Then came the news of our ground forces. Following a massive and unopposed aerial bombardment this morning, Guderian's 10th. Panzers had crossed the Meuse at Sedan and reinforcements were pouring across the river in their wake. Not only that, but further north, near Dinant, a little known Major General called Rommel had forced another bridgehead with the 7th. Panzers. This was a textbook operation, a very high speed textbook operation, this was history in the making.

"That gives us very little time." Said von Strenglen. "The French stations will be pumping out their usual deluded nonsense; 'Ils ne passeront pas' and that sort of thing. But give it another twenty four hours and even they will have to start telling some of the truth."

"Which means that . . . ?"

He looked at me and spoke slowly. "Which means that there could be mass panic at any time, with the roads blocked by refugees. People pushing their belongings in prams and on carts, anything to escape our advance. Movement could rapidly become impossible. We have to find him before the whole place grinds to a standstill. Once we've got him and his machine it will be a different calculation. But first, we have to find him."

Within minutes we were back in the car and heading for Paris. There was no hint of panic, as such, on the roads, but even out here in the country, there were the early signs of civilian fear. Every so often amongst the other traffic we would see an overloaded car staggering along with furniture and suitcases tied to the roof rack, and always heading south. French radio stations might be slow to grasp reality, but some of the public were already starting to pick up the hints.

Sir Freddy Villiers
Chalons, late Monday afternoon, May 13th. 1940

After a hesitant start, during which we had politely stepped around each other's sensibilities, and addressed one another as Capitaine and Sir Frederick, we settled, with some relief, into Martine and Freddy. We both seemed to find in the other, a person who could be worked with, rather than against. She was also a remarkably attractive and engaging woman.

After finishing her formal interviews Martine had left, taking my bag in her car, and I had made my own unauthorised departure from the airfield by simply turning up at the gate, and saying that I was going for a walk. On the basis that there was so clearly nowhere else for this elderly gentleman to go, in wartime France, no orders had been given to stop me. I walked, not briskly, because my leg still hurt from this morning's crash, but purposefully along the road. Now that I was clear of the base it was no longer necessary to pretend that my leg didn't hurt, at some point I should have to find myself a walking stick. Once round the first corner I came, as planned, on Martine's car.

From the moment I rounded that corner I was on my own, my Military Intelligence supervisors in London were beyond any means that I had of contacting them, and even had we spoken, they could well have taken the Squadron Leader's view of matters; that I should return immediately. The one point on which all were in agreement was that this was a young man's war. Well, all except me, and perhaps the lady Gendarme? As it had been so firmly established in London that there was no meaningful role for me in current events, perhaps I could be useful in some small way down here. There's no fool like an old fool.

Sergeant Barnier drove us the ten or twelve miles down the road, to the Gendarmerie in the small town of Chalons. Or as the town sign more helpfully said 'Chalons sur Marne' and that helped me to locate the place. After the scenes of death and destruction at the airfield, it came as a surprise to find most of French provincial life continuing in its usual unhurried way, the shops were just putting up the shutters and closing after an uneventful day, and people were making their perfectly routine way home. It felt like another country rather than just down the road.

She explained in the car that there had already been a notification of suspicious strangers in the area, with a report coming in from the Commercial Hotel, near the station that a group of twelve, mostly young men, and one young woman had stayed there last night. Apparently the owner had waited until after they left, and had presumably paid their bill, before realising just how suspicious they were.

Following the murder of the two detectives this morning, the hotel owner had been visited by some of their colleagues, to express their 'disappointment' at the speed of his report. Alerts had been put out to watch for a small Renault coach and a dark green Citroen Avant, but so far unsuccessfully.

"How eager will one or two Gendarmes be to pull over a group of twelve armed men, particularly now, with the Germans on their way?"

The question embarrassed her, with it's joint suggestion of French military collapse and police cowardice. I hadn't intended either slur, but didn't know how else to phrase it.

"We shall just have to cope as best we can." Was her reply, but accompanied by a slight flush of agitation that I should have asked.

"I'm sorry, I don't make any suggestion that we could have coped any better, and we have the enormous good fortune to have the English Channel between us and them. Anyway, who knows what the next few months will bring for both of us."

"Thank you, but I agree that we should look at matters realistically. Reports coming in from the Ardennes Departement, north east of Reims indicate significant numbers of army deserters on the roads, growing in number during the course of today." She gave a regretful shake of the head. "I think that might give a more accurate view of the situation than the radio reports."

"Were there any clues left by the men at the hotel?"

"Only that one of them, older than the rest, was referred to as Herr Doktor. They pretended to be Swiss but in retrospect were obviously German."

"Yes, of course." I said, as a part of the puzzle fell into place. "The Herr Doktor is the German's equivalent of me. He's the scientist who's going to verify that they're collecting the right piece of equipment, he's going to tell them when they've found the magnetron. All the rest of them are just the muscle, to knock down anyone who gets in the way."

"Then it would seem that we are all pursuing the same people, even if for different reasons,"

"Ponte's company, CSF, had offices in various places, Roland could be using one of them as a hideout. Is it possible to get a list of addresses and then have your people on the spot call in and take a look?"

"I rang them from the airfield and told them to get straight on with it. We've had answers from Le Havre and Toulon - deserted and locked up, we're just waiting for Paris."

"What about his home address?"

"Already checked, and his parents house." She waved a sheaf of papers from her desk. "All blank,"

We both sat and stared at the paperwork. Then we looked up at each other. Whenever you come to a dead end, you should go back and start from the beginning, we must have missed a side turning somewhere.

"What sort of a man is Claude Roland? Do you have his personal record?"

She rifled through the papers, and then extracted one and holding it up, she read from it.

"Claude Eustace Roland, secondary education at Marmande, in Lot et Garonne, and then onto university in Bordeaux. He read Physics and came out with a First

Class Degree, then he went to study in America for two years."

"Any political affiliations?"

Her eyes ran down the paper. "Nothing listed. In other respects it seems to be a very full report, but it says specifically that he has no known hobbies, nor are there any obvious vices, no gambling, drinking or women of ill repute."

"That's a pity."

"Why?"

"They're the best sort."

She declined to laugh at my small joke. "This is not the time for your second childhood."

"Does it say where he studied in America?"

She went back to the paper. "New York University for his doctorate, he was there in 1936 and 1937, under a Professor Paul Schmitz."

"I know they've got all sorts over there, but Schmitz sounds like a Hun to me."

A uniformed young man knocked and came into the office, handing Martine yet another sheet of paper. She looked, but there wasn't much on it, then she dropped it onto the desk with all the others.

"That was from Paris, the CSF office there is closed up and locked, and has been for days."

I was still considering the New York connection. Roland had been there at an important and formative time in his life, and the report saying that nothing was known of his activities wasn't good enough. He hadn't spent every evening staring at the wallpaper. I looked at my watch it was almost seven o'clock in the evening, in other words mid morning in New York.

She was dismissive at first, saying that we would never get through, but I said that if her rank counted for anything she should damn well try. Eventually she agreed, and picked up the telephone.

"No, tomorrow morning will be no use, because that will be the middle of the night in New York." - "This is a national emergency, you will connect me to your supervisor immediately, or you will be arrested." - "No, I do not know the number, but when you speak to the New York operator they will have the number." - "Very well, you have a maximum of thirty minutes, if I have not been connected at the end of that time you will be charged with wilful sabotage in the face of the enemy."

She replaced the receiver, and I asked. "Is there such a charge?"

She made that moue face that only the French seem able to manage, turned her hands palm upwards and shrugged. And then to my delight, smiled conspiratorially.

In fact it only took twenty minutes before the return call came back, she handed me the receiver. It never fails to amaze me when making such long distance calls, the fact that I am speaking to someone thousands of miles away, when only a hundred years ago it would have taken weeks to cover that distance.

However, the person at the other end was not the Professor, but his secretary, who said her name was Ethel. She apologised for his absence, saying that he was on a lecture tour in Canada, and wouldn't be back for another week. She then commented on how bad the line was, and without thinking I replied that would be because I was calling from France.

"From France, well ain't that the damndest thing, you're actually in France right now, while we're talking. Can you see the Eiffel Tower from where you're at?"

"Absolutely, it's just down the road, it looks lovely in the evening sun."

"I can't wait to tell him, the Professor's wife's is French, she comes from Paris too. They were over there only last summer, they've got this sweet little apartment somewhere or other in Montmartre - where all the artists live - I've seen pictures of it. Let me make a note of your name, what did you say it was?"

"Monsieur Blanc, from the Sorbonne, I will speak to him again in a week or so. Many thanks madame, au revoir."

"Au revoir, monsieur." She responded, and then giggled at having found herself speaking French.

The uncertainty of the connection, and our awareness of the distance, meant that we had conducted the conversation at the level of a medium bellow, so it had all been audible across the desk. Martine stared at me disbelievingly.

"Monsieur Blanc? That is a very stupid name, no one will believe that."

"Ethel did."

She waved her hand in dismissal, she was a very self assured woman, a most attractive quality. She pressed on, regardless of my opinion of her qualities. "Her information settles it, we're going to Paris, we shall stop the night at a Pension I know, and then visit the Hotel de Ville as soon as they open tomorrow morning, to find the address of this apartment."

With a brief stop for Martine to collect an overnight bag we set off along Route Nationale 933 to Paris, which the signpost said was just 180 kilometres away. For some reason, as I sat waiting in the car, I noted the fact that when Martine went to her apartment, there was no light on before she arrived, and it returned to darkness as she left.

I was slightly surprised that I so much as registered this point. Even if I was in my second childhood, the fact that a woman almost young enough to be my daughter lived alone, was of absolutely no interest to me. None whatsoever.

Chapter 7

Doktor Theo Leibniz
Paris, Tuesday morning, May 14th. 1940

The road into Paris last night had been almost empty going in our direction, the vehicles we saw were all leaving Paris. As we came closer, passing through Creteil, before crossing the Seine to enter the city itself, there were more and more of them, cars and vans loaded down with people and furniture. Most of the heavily laden vehicles had Belgian or Dutch plates, these were refugees who just happened to have passed through Paris on their way to somewhere safer. But even the sophisticated and cynical Parisians must be having second thoughts about their future, with such a daily procession of refugees on the roads.

Although there would have been some small numbers of people genuinely forced from their homes by our army's progress, I still thought that a lot of these people were fleeing needlessly. For years French propaganda has portrayed us as brutal oppressors and yet nobody seems to blame them for spreading panic. This misperception of the German character, which is so widespread in France, this willingness to view us as barbarians, is the root cause of so much of the trouble in modern Europe. The truth of the matter is far more likely to be that an honest government of decent Frenchmen, running their own affairs with German support, will bring about dramatic improvements in all their lives. Even the French themselves have lost count of the number of corrupt and self serving administrations there have been in the last twenty years. It is ever the burden of the liberator to be misunderstood.

Von Strenglen emphasised that this was just a trickle, once the army came anywhere near here it would turn into a tidal wave he said. I understood more clearly his desire for speed, it wouldn't take a great increase in refugee movements to block the roads altogether.

We spent last night in a private hotel whose Austrian owner, a friend of von Strenglen's, greeted us warmly and incuriously, a useful combination in our present circumstances. This morning I directed that we should use the radio to ask Berlin if there was any Parisian connection known about the man Roland, all that we had learned last night was that he had an apartment somewhere in the north of the city, perhaps near Montmartre. Even giving his maximum cooperation the man Gaston had known no more.

Now that there are just the four of us, the rest of the men having returned to Basel, I have found that Fraulein Fuchs no longer behaves so outrageously. I always had the feeling that she was playing to the gallery when there was a bigger audience, perhaps in compensation for her unfortunate background. As long as she continues with her present attention to detail, I shall be happy to write a decent appraisal of her conduct when we return.

It took an hour before we received a reply from Berlin, and when it came it was not entirely helpful. It said that the offer to sell the magnetron had been passed on via a junior functionary at the Spanish embassy in Paris, a cultural attaché. I took it on myself to ring him in order to arrange a meeting, only to find that he would not be available until this afternoon. I insisted on speaking to his superior, a man named Castole, and it was not a helpful conversation.

It was clear that the Embassy staff felt themselves to be somewhat under siege, pending the arrival of German forces. Castole went to great pains to say that under no circumstances must we imperil their neutrality by approaching them directly, saying that there were already strong feelings of distrust being expressed about their Fascist views and Nazi sympathies. He believed that as the German army approached the city there would be a break down of public order, and that this could well involve an enraged mob storming what was widely seen as a pro German embassy. His best advice was that we should leave the city as soon as possible, to avoid mob rule or being bombed by our own forces.

Although this left me unsure of our next move, our Prussian Sturmbannfuhrer decided that we should examine the CSF Paris office, despite having been repeatedly assured that it was completely deserted. It seemed to me to be a waste of time, but having no alternative of my own to suggest, I chose to keep that opinion to myself. At least, when we eventually find the search to have been pointless, it will not have been at my suggestion.

The CSF premises turned out to be a small warehouse with two stories of offices at the front, on a Zone Industrielle near the Porte de Clichy. It gave no sign of being at the forefront of scientific development, and could not be remotely compared to my own Institute in Berlin. As none of the nearby units appeared to be occupied there was no need for discretion, and with a complete lack of subtlety Carl simply jemmied open a lavatory window. There would no doubt be door keys somewhere inside.

The ground floor of the offices contained a reception area, men's and women's toilets, an open plan typing office and small kitchen. We moved upstairs, which was much more promising; two locked offices and a large open laboratory area. Despite this visit being von Strenglen's idea, he decided to go and look round the warehouse, leaving the rest of us to undertake the actual work. Carl and I started in one office, while Heidi Fuchs went to the other.

Opening the filing cabinets and desk drawers revealed just how much paper an office can hold - a great deal. We looked first through Roland's personnel file, which we found without difficulty, but it was no use. His only listed address was in Amiens, and given the present circumstances that was due to be a battle zone in the next few days, he wouldn't be there. I then moved on to other employees to see if any had an apartment in Montmartre, but none seemed to. I widened the search to the general files, simply trawling through to see if anything caught our attention.

After almost an hour of this I walked through to the next office to see if Fraulein Fuchs was having any more luck. I found her sitting in a chair with her feet up on the desk.

"If this is your idea of a useful contribution, Fuchs, then I can only say that I am most disappointed. Get out of that chair and start going through those filing cabinets, drawer by drawer, file by file. Now if you please."

"The speed you and Carl are moving it's going to take all day to read even half the papers, and that relies on you recognising what you're looking at - if you ever see it."

106

"Do you have some faster method of checking the documents?"

"Yeah, don't bother. Ninety nine per cent of them will be a complete waste of time."

"Of course they will you stupid girl," I said irritably, "That's obvious. But how, exactly, do you find the one per cent?"

"Think about Roland, he's a cheap little crook, ready to sell his mates out to us. People like that aren't just dishonest in one way, they're dishonest in all ways."

"And where exactly is that supposed to lead us?"

"What I know of Montmartre is that there's not likely to be any easy car parking round there, the streets are too narrow and crowded, and I didn't see any Metro station near here. If he's a crook he'd be milking the expenses for all he could get. So if you can't get a Metro at this end and you can't park a car at the other end, I bet he used a taxi to get to work." She paused and smiled at me, delighted with her own cleverness. "And furthermore, I bet he kept the receipts to claim against them."

Then, with her feet still on the desk, she felt around in her bag for a cigarette and took her time lighting it. I silently turned and went back to the next office, there had indeed been an expenses file, we just hadn't examined it yet.

There were dozens of taxi receipts, to addresses all over the city, but at least seven of them were between a Rue Cortot and the CSF office. The street directory showed that Rue Cortot was in the heart of Montmartre, and while most of the receipts simply gave the street name, one of them also gave the number. My anger at not having worked this out for myself was almost as great as my dislike of Heidi Fuchs. When Von Strenglen finally condescended to reappear he congratulated her effusively, holding out his left hand for her to shake. On meeting him I had been offered his right hand, the wooden one. The sooner we completed this job and I was back at my proper work in Berlin, rather than taking part in this travelling circus, the happier I would be

There were only six apartments in the building, and it seemed the place was too small to merit a concierge. None of the postbox names in the foyer were for Roland, and so von Strenglen sent Fuchs round, door to door, simply asking after him as if she was a girlfriend. Or, considering her appearance, some tart looking for work. He was in number six, on the top floor, under the name of Paul Schmitz - or at least he would have been, if he'd been at home.

Carl managed to prise the door open without leaving obvious external marks, and leaving him to watch the door the rest of us began to search for the magnetron, I described what it could look like, and its likely size. If nothing else this should be a lot easier than reading every piece of paper in his office.

It was ridiculously easy, it was in a box at the bottom of his wardrobe, the only concealment being the fact that there was a lid on the box. I sat at the kitchen table examining it as best I could, naturally without connecting it up to a radio frequency generator and an oscilloscope, there could be no indication of its range or effectiveness. Even so, I had no doubts that this was a magnetron, and it was a sort that I hadn't seen before.

Unfortunately, that wasn't enough. There are probably scores of magnetrons whose exact details are unknown to me, but my position here was as the Expert, the man who would know the answer, uncertainty wasn't an option. Once I stopped being the Expert, then I was nothing. I pretended to examine it more closely, all the while considering that if it was the genuine article there would be no problem and if it wasn't then I would simply say that the French had been lying. I looked up at von Strenglen.

"This is it."

"Are you sure?"

"Well obviously I can't test its capabilities here and now, but you can take it from me that this is the one they've been talking about. Once I get it back to Berlin then we can see if it's as good as they think."

Sir Freddy Villiers
Paris, Tuesday morning, May 14th. 1940

We began our first morning in Paris listening to radio reports with the owner of the small Pension we were staying at, the old lady was some sort of relative, Martine referred to her as Tante Mimi and treated the place as if she owned it. But to be honest, Capitaine Dumont is not a woman who lacks self confidence, and to observe her acting as though she owned the place looked more like her natural behaviour than any result of kinship.

From the reports we heard, it is now clear that the entire three day opening section of this campaign in the Low Countries, with German forces pushing through Belgium and Holland, was never at the top of their agenda. It would be an exaggeration to call it a feint, or a diversion, because they undoubtedly intend the annexation of both those countries. However, with the news of the armoured breakthrough from the Ardennes, and their multiple bridgeheads across the Meuse, it has become clear that this is at the heart of the matter.

The Germans now have a dagger stuck deep into French territory, having successfully moved their armour through the hilly and heavily forested Ardennes, which all conventional wisdom had said was impossible. The new word Blitzkrieg is being used repeatedly to describe this sort of lightning thrust, with fast moving armour supported by air power, typically with Stuka dive bombers replacing the more traditional artillery. The three of us sat at the Pension dining table, plotting place names on the map. The only question remaining seems to be; will they continue the thrust westwards to Paris, or curve north to trap the British Expeditionary Force against the Channel?

Local news bulletins are reporting that the French Prime Minister, Paul Reynaud, has requested urgent reinforcements of British fighter aircraft. I can't believe that Churchill would agree to this, the idea that we should strip our own defences to reinforce what is already obvious as a defeat would be madness.

The Paris newspapers are filled with references to the Battle of the Marne in 1914, when the French successfully halted a German advance in the very suburbs of Paris, as if history might be repeated. What this ignores is the unfortunate fact that the French plan on this occasion has been the defence of a series of fixed lines along the Belgian and German borders, and the sad truth is that now those lines have been penetrated, there is nothing behind them. Nothing that is, except a terrified civilian population and an unguarded capital city.

Martine is as deeply depressed by all this as I would be if it were happening in England. Political recriminations are already flying, but they're futile, there'll be plenty of time to apportion blame later. For the time being it is enough to try and assimilate the almost unbelievable fact that with one huge gamble, Hitler looks set to capture as much of France as he wants to take.

The latest news from the queue at the boulangerie this morning, is that all the Parisian main line stations are completely blocked with refugees. At first they were mainly Belgians, but now it seems there are thousands of French people fleeing from the affected departments. Apparently the government are trying desperately to balance the packed incoming trains with an equal number moving people on to outlying departments in the south and west, and at the moment they aren't managing. It's an unstable situation, and the fact that the news has to be spread through bread shop queues, because local newspapers and radio stations aren't reporting it, won't make the problem go away.

Although we were both up early this morning, we had been obliged to loiter, with the radio and the newspapers, until such time as public offices began to open for the day, nine o'clock at the earliest. Martine has released Sergeant Barnier to return to Chalons, on the basis that if we need any backup we can call on local staff.

Finally it was time, and as we left the the old lady hugged Martine, kissing her on both cheeks and calling her 'Marti'. She rolled her eyes helplessly at me from across the old lady's shoulder, and I agreed. Martine is a delightful name, but Marti sounded more like a Cuban gigolo. Extricating ourselves, we took the Metro to the Place de l'Hôtel de Ville.

The Town Hall itself is a huge and imposing structure, standing sideways on to the river, opposite the end of the Ile de la Cité, with the towers of Notre Dame rising above the intervening low rooftops. The historic interest and beauty of our surroundings and the

111

warmth of the spring sunshine were glaringly at odds with the grim reality of our pursuit.

While I had seen the building itself on previous visits to Paris, I had never actually been in, fortunately Martine knew her way around. We were there as they opened the doors, and went straight to our destination, an enormous two story library on the third floor, reached by a wide stone staircase that could have come from a gothic castle. Even the name of this palatial repository of public records was suitably impressive; La Bibliothèque Administrative de la Ville de Paris. Absolutely nothing about this establishment suggested a place for casual browsing.

Acquiring the services of two of their staff to assist us, using the full weight of her Gendarmerie rank and possessing the name of the probable property owner should have made our search straightforward, and it might well have made it faster than otherwise. Even so, it still took us more than two hours to locate the address; Rue Cortot in the XVIII Arrondissement, which is just another way of saying Montmartre. We looked at each other, our anticipation, once vague and unspecific, had suddenly become focussed. We now had an address where Roland and his German friends might be found.

The library staff had assured Martine that nobody else had been making the same enquiries for this address, but did the Germans have other sources of information? Were the Germans and Roland already in direct communication? Were they already making the purchase while we were two miles away?

Without even discussing it, the two of us were already running down the stairs

"Are you going to request back up?" I asked.

"There isn't time. Roland is a traitor and the Germans killed two of my colleagues. If we miss them at this address we have no idea where they could go next. We have to get there as quickly as possible."

As she was saying this, she had increased her speed, her footsteps ringing sharply on the stone steps. I was trying to keep up, but was frightened that my walking stick would skid out from under me as I hobbled down behind her. She was making no allowances whatsoever for me, and that was the way I liked it.

There was sweat on my forehead by the bottom of the stairs and my chest was heaving. Her lithe and smartly uniformed figure was fifty yards in front of me, and she was already flagging down a taxi, whilst I still limped to catch up. As I fell into the back seat alongside her, it was already moving forwards.

With Martine encouraging him to greater efforts the driver took us up the Boulevard de Sébastopol, and then swung left to take us past the main line stations; the Gare de l'Est and the Gare du Nord. As they had predicted in the bread shop queue, large crowds could be seen blocking the immediate approaches to both stations.

Things are bad, and are quite certainly going to get worse. I reflected that, whatever I might have thought earlier, retirement in Putney was beginning to look like an attractive option.

Leaning forward, the better to see through the windscreen, I could see the garish and rather vulgar white bulk of the Sacré Coeur sat atop its hill, blocking our view. With the exception of a few notable cathedrals, French ecclesiastical architecture is so often a disappointment. But Montmartre seems to please the tourists, so perhaps I should keep my views to myself.

The driver changed down a gear, and we began the slow climb up a narrow and winding street. Martine took out her pistol and worked the action, confirming it was ready for use, before returning it to the holster. We were almost there.

Chapter 8

Doktor Theo Leibniz
Paris, Tuesday morning, May 14th. 1940

The rest of the morning wore on, and there was nothing for us to do except wait. Carl had been stationed in the street, in case Roland managed to bolt when he saw us, the remaining three of us made ourselves comfortable in his flat and wondered how long this could take. Indeed, was he coming back here at all?

It became apparent from our inspection of the papers we found, that the owners of the apartment were an American university professor with a German sounding name, Paul Schmitz, and his French wife. In reflection of its joint French American owners, the books on the living room shelves were split almost equally between the two languages, and there were one or two tourist guides of the sort that a native would be unlikely to possess. We had guessed that Schmitz and his wife had probably used Roland as an emergency local key holder, which would have given him access. His temporary occupation of the premises was marked by the dirty dishes in the kitchen, the unmade bed in the bedroom, shoes and clothes lying about, and a box full of empty wine bottles standing in the hall. It struck me as wholly consistent that someone who was planning to sell out his friends should also have slovenly personal habits.

At a little after twelve o'clock there was the sound of a key in the front door lock, and we all came to our feet, ready for action. Fuchs took the prime position, by the living room door, her gun held ready for use. There was a pause from the front door, as whoever it was, presumably Roland, tried to work out just why the front door lock didn't seem to be working properly.

Fuchs jammed the pistol into the waistband at the back of her skirt, and stepped into the hall, her hands visibly empty to each side of her.

"Monsieur Roland." She said in her warmest and most welcoming voice. "I've come from the Spanish Embassy, in response to your call. Please come in, there seems to be some sort of problem with your front door lock."

"How did you get this address, who gave it to you?"

From the sound of his voice, he was still stood by the front door, he was obviously being very cautious at finding this unexpected visitor, no matter how pleasant she might be.

Fuchs gave a small laugh. "Oh don't ask me to explain the workings of our bureaucracy, I would imagine that they were talking to Professor Schmitz. All I can tell you is that the embassy told me to call round and make whatever arrangements you wanted about the sale of your device." She laughed again. "Their exact instructions to me were to make sure that you got what you wanted. It seems that you can pretty much write your own cheque."

"What are you talking about - who are you?" The man at the door was completely un-persuaded and sounded both puzzled and panicked.

I could see her in the hall, she had been standing relaxed and unconcerned, this woman should be an actress, but as he failed to take the bite she looked suitably concerned and began to move towards him and out of my line of sight. Then there was a different sound, a slight grunting noise and some scuffling, and the man cried out in alarm. This would be Carl, who was supposed to have followed the man upstairs and would now be trying to push him in, through the front door. There was the sound of a serious fight developing, with various French and German expletives, this wasn't going to be as easy as we'd thought. Then Von Strenglen elbowed his way roughly past me, in his usual arrogant way, a pistol in his hand.

"Shut him up." He hissed, but the man continued with his noisy protest. As I followed them into the hall I was just in time to see von Strenglen deliver a savage downward blow to the side of the newcomer's head, with the steel but of his pistol. At last the noise stopped and Carl pushed the inert body forwards, to fall on the hall floor, kicking the front door shut behind him. Phew. For a moment we all just breathed deeply, staring at the fallen man.

Fuchs was the first to recover and went to kneel beside the body, she felt the side of his neck, looking for a pulse, Carl and Gunther stood watching her, nobody took the slightest notice of me.

After several moments of examination she stood up and looked up at Gunther. "He's dead, you've killed him." I was astonished by her tone, it was an accusation rather than a statement. The idea that this woman, whoever she was, should speak to an officer in this fashion was contrary to all my ideas of military discipline. Von Strenglen recognised it as a charge of incompetence, and didn't look happy to be accused by his junior.

"It makes no difference, he was always going to be killed anyway. He would never have fitted into the

Fieseler, those things have only got room for two passengers, and Carl can hide in Paris until the army gets here."

But Fuchs wouldn't let go. "That's not the point, we don't even know if he actually was Roland."

"Well how many people d'you imagine have keys to this place? Apart from the owner's stuff, there's only evidence for one man living here."

Instead of answering Fuchs leaned over to get a better look at the corpse's shoes, then she silently turned and went into the bedroom, emerging shortly with one of the shoes that had been left carelessly lying around. She knelt back beside the body and held it against the foot; even I could see that it was much too small for the dead man.

She looked steadily at von Strenglen, her lips pursed and the shoe still held by the foot, to demonstrate the error.

"Heidi, my dear girl, just put the shoe away and stop showing off. They told me you were smart and I believed them. Whether it was Roland himself, or one of his grubby little gang of blackmailers doesn't matter. He was making too much noise and needed killing, and so I killed him. The only thing that matters is the magnetron, now that our little friend here has positively indentified it, all that's left is to get it back to Berlin."

Fuchs seemed mollified by this most uncharacteristic burst of Prussian bonhomie, but I was still troubled by something.

"When you mentioned about how many people would fit into the Fieseler," I said. "I assume you mean the light aircraft of that name."

Von Strenglen looked as if he was surprised to hear from me, and held his finger up to indicate that I should wait my turn. Then still addressing Fuchs he continued.

"Give Carl the device and tell him to take it down to the car, then he's to come round to the front and wait there, we shall be leaving very shortly."

Satisfied with his other arrangements he turned back to me, his eyebrows raised, as if he couldn't remember my question.

"The aircraft you mentioned," I reminded him. "Is it supposed to pick us up?"

"Yes, a lightweight short take off aircraft will be landing in the Bois de Boulogne sometime tomorrow to take the magnetron back to Germany."

"And who will be coming with me, yourself or Fraulein Fuchs?"

I'm afraid that you'll be staying here Leibniz, Fraulein Fuchs and myself shall ensure the magnetron reaches the Institute as soon as possible. Doktor Anton Gebhart is, even now, standing by to start work on it."

I was astonished. "Gebhart! What do you mean Gebhart is standing by? That man is my assistant, I am the head of the Radio Location Unit and it is my place to work on the magnetron."

"Yes, I can see your confusion here Leibniz, but the fact is that Gebhart was promoted to your old position last week, whilst we were in Basel. The party think very highly of him. Your sole connection with this affair was to verify the device itself, we would never have risked the life of such a senior scientist on an escapade like this. Surely you can understand that?"

For a moment I was incapable of coherent speech, but even as I struggled to phrase my next question an icy dread had gripped me.

"What is happening? What is happening to me?"

"The trouble is, there seems to have been a slight problem with your personnel records."

119

I waited for him to continue, but he didn't, so I asked the obvious question. "What sort of problem?"

"It concerns the name of your maternal grandmother."

I had to think for a moment. "My maternal grandmother was called Sarah Rosen and she lived in Frankfurt, that's all I can tell you about her. What on earth does she have to do with anything?"

"The problem is Leibniz, that Jewish blood passes down the female line, from her to your mother, and then to you."

"But there is no Jewish blood, she was a Lutheran, I submitted her baptism certificate when I joined the party. You'll have all this on file. In fact I would remind you that I've been a party member for considerably longer than you."

He leaned forward, his face close to mine, and tapped his revolting wooden hand against my chest. "The problem, Leibniz, is her name. Her birth certificate shows clearly that she was not called Rosen, but Rosenberg. Her father's name is listed as Samuel. Now what does that tell us? Sarah Rosenberg, daughter of Samuel Rosenberg - what more do you want, a certificate from the Rabbi?"

"I have been a loyal party member for the last ten years, I have served the Reich without complaint, I have done invaluable work on radio location. This whole operation was personally entrusted to me by Reinhard Heydrich. How dare you question my loyalty, you deformed aristocratic throwback?"

Far from being perturbed by my defence, he simply looked thoughtful. "That's the trouble with you people, isn't it? You worm yourselves into every area of our national life, wherever we look, there you are - the eternal Jew. As for you being a party member since

120

whenever you claimed, that's no more than camouflage, you thought you could hide yourself amongst decent people. Looks pretty damned obvious to me. And immediately after Heydrich had spoken to you, he spoke to me, and he told me that once you'd fulfilled your function - I should clean up." He spoke the last words with perverted relish.

I was sweating, my heart was racing, this couldn't happen - not to me. "You can't expect Gebhart to do my work, he doesn't know the half of it." I wanted to say more, but didn't know what, I could no longer think straight. I was feeling faint, on the verge of passing out, and gasping for air.

"There's no need for you to concern yourself with any of that Leibniz, this is a simple matter of racial hygiene. People like you have dragged our country into the gutter once too often, now it's time we cleaned up."

Then he began to turn away. But Fuchs called to him from the window, where she had been looking down at the street from behind a curtain.

"There's a female Gendarme officer, and some old man, coming in downstairs, and they looked up in this direction before they did."

"In that case you'd better get rid of this thing," He waved his wooden hand in my direction, "Then we can get out of here."

I turned to look at Fuchs, for some reason she had wrapped her pistol in a towel, she slowly swung it to point at me, smiled and fired.

Sir Freddy Villiers
Paris, Tuesday midday, May 14th. 1940

The taxi took a wrong turning, and had to reverse out of a dead end, but at last we pulled up outside the apartment block. Martine threw a bank note at the driver and we ran into the building foyer, to check the flat numbers. Number six, Paul Schmitz, that's the one. We started up the stairs, passing a couple in one of the doorways engaged in what looked like vertical sex, their lunchtime baguette; what my boyhood friends and I used to call a knee trembler. As we passed, the woman looked embarrassed and tried to pull her skirt down and the man averted his face. No wonder the French are famous for it.

As I continued to clamber manfully upwards, my stick sounding like a third leg, it occurred to me to wonder if the French ever fitted lifts to their buildings. The door to number six was ajar, and we entered cautiously. Something about the complete stillness within said that there was no ambush waiting to be sprung, but it wasn't a feeling I wished to trust my life to. So we continued with a degree of circumspection.

There were two bodies lying on the floor, apparently dead, one of them was unknown to me but I recognised the other. He was a German scientist called Theo Leibniz, one of the many faces I had occasionally seen at international conferences. From what little I could recall he was a dedicated Nazi, and thus no loss to anyone. However, the bodies made it clear that not only were we too late, but that the perpetrators had gone.

Except . . . except for what? Except for the very strong smell, both of cordite and scorching, as if someone had burnt the ironing. Why? There was a towel on the floor, there were scorch marks on it, I bent down to touch the marks, and found them still warm.

"The couple on the stairs - it's them"

I abandoned all notion of limping and almost threw myself back down the stairs, holding my walking stick like a club. Adrenalin can make a mortally wounded deer bound another hundred yards across the moor, before it drops down dead, or a small woman lift the front of a car off her child. It propelled me down those stairs and out into the street as though all the hounds of hell were after me, but I was still too late. A dark green Citroen Avant was pulling away from the kerb, there were two men and one woman in it. I was so desperate to reach them that I even charged down the street in hot pursuit, as if a running man could catch a speeding car.

Then a delivery van pulled out from a side street, and the Citroen's brake lights came on, at exactly the same time as its horn sounded. Quite remarkably, it looked as if no one in the car was aware of my pursuit, there were no backward glances, all eyes were forwards, on the blockage. Perhaps it's as well they didn't know about me, or they might have wet themselves laughing at the prospect of an old age Pensioner with a walking stick, bearing down on them like Nemesis.

I was almost on top of them when the delivery van grudgingly pulled over far enough for them to get round, and they started to move forwards. But he hadn't left them a great deal of room, so they were only moving slowly. As I pushed my way alongside them, the woman on the back seat saw me, her mouth opening in astonishment at this bizarre sight.

It was a ridiculous situation, I had unthinkingly given chase, without any clear idea of what I would do if I actually caught them. Now here I was, alongside them for a brief moment, but armed with nothing more lethal than a walking stick. Not having any coherent plan of action, I behaved instinctively, impulsively. With a cry of rage I put all my weight into a two hand lunge forwards, smashing the point of the stick through the driver's window. There was no apparent resistance, the glass simply disintegrated in a shower of fragments.

It was the driver's misfortune that, alerted by the woman's shout, he had turned to look at me. The point of my walking stick hit him solidly in his left eye, his head shot backwards, his hands lifted spasmodically from the steering wheel and his right foot must have banged rigidly down onto the accelerator.

The engine screamed at maximum power and the car leapt forward, loudly scraping the side of the delivery van. I was vaguely aware that the man in the front passenger seat had grabbed the steering wheel, but even as I registered this, I found myself wedged forcibly into a doorway as the car accelerated and then I rolled helplessly to the ground. I had foolishly attempted to hold on to the walking stick, but it was stuck in the car, in fact I suspect it was stuck in the driver's head.

As I lay on the ground, my emotion receding, and the car disappearing, I wondered when was the last time that I had been so single-mindedly engaged in anything. I decided the simple answer was that I never had been. Martine knelt beside me, a look of concern across her face.

"I do hope that they were the right people." She said. "It's going to look very bad if you've just attacked some innocent passers by." Then she couldn't help smiling, and gave me a hand to get up.

I was shaking either from the emotion, or the exertion, perhaps both, and even putting one hand against the wall to steady myself, I found walking a struggle. She put my arm around her shoulder and helped me back along the street. The few parts of me that didn't actually hurt, ached, tomorrow I would be black and blue; but right now I welcomed the warm feel of her body and the smell of her, so close to me. This was clearly a day for inappropriate experiences.

At the apartment building she left me sitting on the bottom step, while she went up to use the phone to summon assistance and to secure the crime scene. I was content to catch my breath, and marvel at the stirring of so many dormant feelings. Then her voice rang down the stairwell, bringing me back to reality.

"Freddy, if you can manage, please try and make your way upstairs."

There was no further explanation, just the sound of the door closing behind her. The only obvious conclusion was that it was important but not life threatening. Holding firmly to the banister with both hands, I began to make my way unsteadily upwards. Taking it slowly, one step at a time, I climbed and kept on climbing. Who knows, the staircase today - the Matterhorn tomorrow.

I made my slow and uncertain way through the front door to hear the sound of Martine's voice, it was too low too distinguish the words. I followed the sound into the living room. She was crouched down by one of the bodies. It was Theo Leibniz.

"This one's alive and talking." She said, over her shoulder, having given a quick glance to confirm who it was. I went and crouched beside her, Leibniz had a large patch of blood in the region of his lower left rib. He was trying to answer whatever she'd said to him, but it wasn't making sense. Then he spoke quite clearly, in German, saying that he wasn't a Jew. Whoever he was addressing it wasn't us, his eyes were open but they weren't seeing his present surroundings, it sounded more like a rerun of an earlier conversation. Martine ignored him and used both her hands to rip his shirt open. There was an entry wound, and it looked messy, it also looked rather larger than I would have thought.

Martine used the end of a pencil to probe the wound, I winced and Leibniz groaned, loudly.

She looked up at me with a smile. "He'll live, that's the back end of the bullet I just prodded, it's hardly penetrated."

"How come?"

She pointed to his left hand, it was in a mess and covered in blood. "He seems to have had his hand clenched in front of him, the bullet went through the back of his hand and then through his clenched fingers, and only then through a heavy jacket and into his body. He was probably unconscious from hitting his head on the floor."

It made sense, that was why the entry wound looked more like an exit wound, the bullet was already deformed and tumbling by the time it hit his rib. He was a remarkably lucky man.

Within five minutes an ambulance had arrived and shortly after that, two more Gendarmes. While I had been engaging in my high speed car chase, Martine had taken the time to note the car's number plate, and had put it on a high priority watch list. It turned out that she needn't have bothered, the car was only two or three hundred yards down the road, embedded in the back of another vehicle.

It seems that the dead driver was fine with the accelerator, but not so good with the brakes. The two remaining occupants, the man and woman from the stairwell, had commandeered another vehicle and vanished. She arranged for two local *flics* to start asking

126

around for details of the second vehicle, somebody must have seen it.

Meanwhile, back at the apartment, Martine let the ambulance men put Leibniz onto the stretcher, and at her instruction they strapped him to it, then she told them to go and sit in the kitchen and have a cigarette. They looked surprised, but obeyed.

Leibniz turned his head to watch them go and then looked at Martine, his face, although screwed up with pain, still managed to register astonishment.

"What did you tell them? I need urgent help, I've been shot." He spoke poorly accented but perfectly grammatical French.

"You're a Nazi, you're a spy and you've been caught, why should we waste drugs on someone who's going to die anyway? Do you fully understand the procedure for being guillotined?"

"Guillotined?" He shrieked. It had never even occurred to him, and he was horrified.

"Well what did you think we were going to do with you, give you the Croix de Guerre? Of course you'll be guillotined, and under present circumstances it will probably be within the next two or three days."

"That's against the Geneva Convention, I'm a prisoner of war."

Martine laughed at him. "Wearing civilian clothes, and murdering French citizens in their own homes, I don't think so. You're for the chop my friend." Then having made a chopping motion against her neck with the side of her hand, she dismissed him and turned to me.

"The really clever thing is this idea of theirs for using Jews to do their dirty work. They must have reckoned that we'd never suspect a Jew, and he almost got away with it."

"I'm not Jewish." He was screaming by now, and thrashing about against the straps. "I tell you I'm not Jewish."

She turned to look at him, surprise and concern on her face. "Well you look Jewish to me, and your comrades certainly thought you were." I nodded in silent agreement.

"Look at my cock - that will tell you - look at my cock. I've never been circumcised, I'm not Jewish. And anyway I wasn't even sure, I guessed - I just guessed." He babbled on, completely beside himself.

She shrugged. "I have no intention of looking at your cock, that would be disgusting, you nasty little man. And so what if your not? The executioner can sort that out - he'll put your cock in first and make you a Jew - then turn you round and stick your head in next. The last thing you'll ever see will be your foreskin lying in the basket, you Nazi pig."

I was almost as surprised as Leibniz, this was a side of Capitaine Dumont that I hadn't even guessed at. It's an obvious truism that women are nowhere near as coarse as men, but when they are they can be surprisingly inventive.

Still, I suppose she hadn't been promoted solely on the grounds that I might one day find her fascinating. And that was another revelation, I had long thought that side of my life gone for good.

Martine said that Leibniz was too shocked and overwrought to get much sense out of him here, but thought that the clang of a steel cell door behind him, with the prospect of the guillotine in front of him should sober him up quite rapidly. Then at that stage we should start to get some useful answers.

She told the ambulance men to take him down to the van and drive him to the Montmartre police station, rather then the hospital he might be expecting. Then the two of us made our way downstairs, leaving the stretcher to follow at its own pace.

Chapter 9

Fraulein Heidi Fuchs
Paris, Tuesday afternoon, May 14th. 1940

I have to be honest, the astonishing sight of that mad old man suddenly there, running right alongside us, and shouting something at me through the car window - well it shook me a little. Not that I'd ever let a Prussian Arschloch like von Strenglen see that. But then when the crazy man took that wild swing with his stick, that was incredible. Had he been lucky or clever? It was difficult to be sure.

What are they going to tell Carl's wife: your husband died a soldier's death, struck down by a pensioner's walking stick? There was that case in Spain where some old woman kept a pig on her balcony, and one day the balcony collapsed - well it would with a pig on it - the pig fell three floors and killed someone in the street below. Imagine what they gave as the cause of death; killed by a flying pig? It doesn't look good, dying like that - it's unseemly.

Fortunately Gunther was able to lean over and grab the steering wheel, which served to get us out of the immediate area, and equally fortunately Carl was dead, otherwise we'd have had to help him on his way - you can't just leave injured people lying around to be interrogated.

Once we'd picked up another car and cleared the area Gunther had wanted to keep going, but we'd been seen and a dozen people had our description and the car's number. The Gendarme woman was only just down the street, she was going to have put the word out just as fast as she could reach a phone. Every patrolling *flic* and every police car in Paris was going to be looking for this car within minutes, what we needed was to be off the streets, and rapidly. I pulled in and stopped a boy, he was about seventeen.

"Can you drive a car?"

"Yeah, I can drive." You could see from his face that he was lying, just the sort I wanted. I gave him the keys and a twenty Franc note.

"Drive this to our friend, he's waiting for the car by the steps of the Opera House. He's a tall man and he'll be wearing a raincoat. He'll give you another twenty Francs, can you do that?"

"No problem, dead easy." He was still lying, he couldn't believe his luck, but I didn't care. Just as long as he got it out of here, and then when he hit a lamp post he'd run away to avoid the police. I took the box with Leibniz's electric thing in it, and he drove off with a crashing noise from the gearbox.

Von Strenglen was looking offended that I hadn't consulted him, I'd have to let him take the next decision, just as long as it was the right one. It's not that I don't like the man, he's an extremely efficient soldier and brave with it. It's simply that he isn't really suited to undercover work.

I can change my hair, change my clothes and, language permitting, I'll fit in anywhere I want. But with Gunther, no matter how he dresses, he is still very clearly a stiff necked Prussian. He might just as well carry a sign round with him saying: 'Achtung, Ich Bin Ein Kraut'.

Despite the military situation this whole area was still busy with visitors, most of them presumably various embassy staff or astonishingly self confident neutrals looking for a bargain. The same sort of people who would push to the front of the crowd to watch a building on fire, even with the risk that bits might fall on their heads.

We bought a suitcase, big enough to fit the thing into, and I bought a scarf, hat and sunglasses. Gunther went in the next shop for a hat and sunglasses, then he took his jacket off and slung it over his shoulder. We were so badly dressed that we fitted in as tourists, besides which, this was the last place they'd be looking. Just as long as nobody asked to shake Gunther's hand, we should be alright. We walked casually back in the direction we'd come from, carrying our suitcase, looking for a place to stay the night.

I was almost sorry that Leibniz had left us, he was such an innocent, from the first day we met in Switzerland he hadn't understood a single thing that was happening. He kept trying to give von Strenglen instructions, and von Strenglen kept pretending to take him seriously. I'll never understand how such an apparently intelligent man can be so dim in matters of everyday life. But at least we kept the show on the road long enough to verify that we'd collected the right piece of stuff, after that his time was up.

I still couldn't work out if that thing about his grandmother being Jewish was true, or had Gunther just made it up. On consideration, I didn't think the Sturmbannfuhrer would be very good at making things up, nimble mindedness isn't a Prussian trait, so it was probably true. It was just the sort of thing that a madman like Heydrich would be interested in, and have people researching. There had always been something about Heydrich's pale eyes and unblinking stare that made him look like so many of the murderers I've encountered, he wasn't a man that I'd be happy to leave alone with small children, or even animals. I do what I do because I think it's necessary, and I'm good at it. Men like Heydrich, and it is usually men, do it because it makes them feel bigger than they really are.

Despite the party's views on racial purity it wasn't Leibniz's Jewishness that bothered me, it was more a case of weeding out that level of stupidity from the gene pool. Besides which, when Leibniz had mentioned how low his party number was, I could see that had seriously annoyed Gunther, which can't have improved the man's chances. Anyway, once he knew about us leaving by plane from the Bois de Boulogne, he was a dead man, whoever his granny might have been.

It was half past five by now, time to be looking for a hotel. Gunther steered us into a flea pit called Le Petit Oisseau. I told him to look at some brochures and then leaned confidentially on the counter to explain to the woman that he and I were just *friends*, with a meaningful glance, who were having a night away from our other *responsibilities* - and did we really need to bother with the identity cards? Considering that every second building round here was a brothel it didn't take her long to make her mind up, and we went up to our room.

I suggested to Gunther that as we had a base now, it might be an idea to split up. If they were looking for us at all round here, they would be looking for a couple. He agreed.

"Since we lost the radio when we abandoned the Citroen, I'll have to use the emergency telephone number. I'll let them know we've got the magnetron and are ready to be picked up. I would imagine it could take up to twelve hours to organise the aircraft, so perhaps tomorrow afternoon, we shall see."

He always addresses me as if I'm a junior officer of his, I don't think that civilians have ever featured strongly in his background. When we were nearly caught leaving Roland's apartment, and I had to get him in a clinch on the stairs, most men would have grabbed a handful of whatever was on offer, but he didn't. Still I suppose that grabbing a handful, isn't quite as easy for him as it is for other men. Now there's an interesting strap on alternative you could make for a man with a wooden hand. I might sketch it out later. I decided to take a stroll and see if the excitement had died down yet.

Roland's apartment building was only three hundred metres along the road, and I sauntered past in my floppy hat and sunglasses, my coloured scarf draped round my waist to change the appearance of my skirt. I attached myself to a couple of earnest young Swedish women, what could be less threatening than three female tourists? Unless one of them was me. The ambulance was still standing in the street, its back doors open, waiting for trade.

At the top of the apartment building steps the woman Gendarme officer was standing next to the crazy old man who did tricks with walking sticks. I turned my face away, but swivelled my eyes to watch them through my sunglasses. The first thing that struck me was their respective stances, she was more aware of him than he was of her; I notice these things. She was standing just that little bit closer to him than was necessary, and her body was angled more towards him. She probably wasn't even aware of it, it's an instinctive sort of thing, you stand closer to someone you like, and you're more likely to be looking at them than anyone else. He hadn't noticed, or if he had he was repressing it.

I carried on casually strolling, my attention still surreptitiously on them. God alone knows what she saw in him, he must be every day of twenty years older than her, a tall, upper class English Gentleman type. Whereas she was a typically slim, short haired, hard faced French woman, who paid too much attention to her clothes. Just the sort that men seem to drool over. They probably think that the laced up prim exterior will be in contrast to a wild sex life, and come to think of it, that was certainly true of the last Frenchwoman that I slept with. It's funny what you can pick up, watching people who think they're unobserved.

A we passed there came a faint, but recognisable cry, or even scream, from above. One of the Swedish women half paused and lifted her head, as if to say; was that a scream? I carried on, unconcerned, and after a moment so did she. I knew the source at once, it can't have been the Frenchman that Gunther attacked, he'd had his head caved in. That left Leibniz, I'd only had time for that one snatched shot at him, I should have given him a second one to make sure. It's like mother used to say, on the rare occasions she was sober; more haste, less speed.

His left hand had been partly blocking me and, replaying the events in my mind's eye, I saw the hand shatter as the bullet passed through. Normally that wouldn't have been enough to save him, but the behaviour of bullets in the human body is an imprecise study. In my normal job as detective Sergeant with the Berlin Kriminalpolizei, the Kripo, I've seen a large variety of strange bullet paths, with deflections from bones sending projectiles on all sorts of wild tangents.

Maybe I should ask the Sturmbannfuhrer to give him the address of his wooden hand supplier, or maybe I should sit the two of them next to each other and they could make up one complete pianist. Or even better, maybe I should finish what I started, and kill the little bastard. If he hadn't already told them about the plane picking us up, he soon would – and even if he had, then he still deserved to die. There wasn't time to go and get Gunther, and he'd only get in the way if I did. The question was, what should I use? The gun would attract too much attention, and there were too many police around for that to be a good idea.

One of the tourist shops sold tents, for the traveller on a budget, I thought that was a good idea and went in for a better look. They had packs of slim steel tent pegs, little more than straight lengths of four mm. steel wire with a loop on one end, they came in bundles of twelve. I slid one out and held it pointing vertically up my arm as I wandered casually back into the sunshine.

By now there was another unmarked police car, next to the ambulance, reinforcements. There would be no chance upstairs, the obvious spot was going to be right here, on the pavement as they carried him out. They would be confident; the Gendarme and the old man, they'd been completely successful, capturing one of us and killing another. It was time that someone administered a corrective and back in my Hamburg days I'd run a nice little side line in administering correctives. It's true that in finding the magnetron thing, we had achieved the stated purpose of our mission, but I have always believed that it isn't enough just to win. For the real taste of victory the other party have to lose, visibly and obviously, and it should hurt.

There was a cake shop just across the road, I went in and spent ages choosing something, and then stood on the pavement with some other browsing tourist pigs, eating the cake slowly and messily. Then equally slowly I wiped and then licked my fingers. Eventually there was some action. A uniformed *flic*, in his cape and kepi, came to the apartment block doorway and stood, self importantly looking around. A clear indication that I should get ready.

Holding the camera that I had lifted from one of the Swedish women's bags, I snapped my way over to a group of six Japanese, three middle aged couples. I said hello in Japanese, some of my customers in Hamburg had come from the Land of the Rising Sun. And before you ask, yes, it's true what they say - they do have rather small pricks. In fact quite amazingly small in some cases, I think that's why they're so aggressive.

I gestured to one of their cameras, letting my own dangle from its strap round my arm. 'I'll take your picture' I mimed. The inarticulate response could be summed up as; 'Oh yes, oh yes, very good'. They all smiled at each other, then at me and then nodded. Very big on nodding these people, a sort of convulsive jerk of the head, as if they'd actually be happier bowing.

I steered them round so their backs were to the apartment entrance. The ambulance men came down the steps, there was no sheet over the casualty's face, it was Leibniz – staring vacantly upwards but still alive. The policeman had come down the steps and was stood by the back of the ambulance. Do it now!

I herded my group further backwards, with vague photographic gestures to the sun and the camera, they politely assumed I knew what I was doing, and they were right, it just wasn't what they thought. They were now in a row across the pavement with stretcher due to pass behind them.

As it passed, I pushed the middle two Japanese sharply backwards. They stumbled against the stretcher, both alarmed at my strange behaviour. As they did, I dropped their camera on the ground and leaned between them. The end of the wire tent peg nestled briefly in Leibniz's left ear and then I pushed it in, using the heel of my hand and my body weight to drive it home. After overcoming the initial resistance it moved quite freely. Just before the full length was embedded it encountered a solid obstruction, the far side of his skull. With a little more care and precision I could have had it emerge from his other ear, but it's one of those things you would have to practise. I had hoped he might have recognised me, one last time, but I think he had something else on his mind.

The ambulance men, the stretcher itself and the Japanese, were all now completely entangled. Turning to the man next to me I used the only other Japanese phrase I possess; Kiss My Arse. He shouted angrily back at me, so my pronunciation must have been good. In the group around us at least three of the others were screaming, but I'm confident that, this time, none of them was Leibniz.

I stepped away, anonymously disentangling myself from the melee, but as I turned, my eyes met those of the woman Gendarme. She was still at the top of the steps, with her boyfriend and, unlike the others, must have been able to see what I'd done. I smiled at her, and as her mouth opened to shout something at me, I turned and ran.

Hoity toity prim bitch in her expensively tailored uniform. Let's see how controlled you are when the Seventh Panzers roll into town.

Sir Freddy Villiers
Paris, Tuesday evening, May 14th. 1940

Martine grabbed my arm with one hand and pointed with the other. "That woman, over there, the one in the straw hat and the blue top, I think she just killed Leibniz."

The figure was visible through the crowds, fifty yards away and running fast. For a moment Martine scanned the street, looking for a usable Gendarme or police officer, but the only one in earshot was caught up in the free fight at the bottom of the steps. The people around the stretcher were shouting and pushing each other, and at least one woman had been pushed to the ground.

Logically I should have accepted that the woman in the straw hat was out of reach, but my success in chasing the car made me overconfident. I caught a last glimpse of her back vanishing round a corner, and started to rush after her. In view of recent events it's surprising that I made any progress at all, but gravity and boundless optimism took me down the three steps to the street, before my left knee buckled and I went over like a falling redwood. The Japanese man I hit on the way down seemed to be very annoyed and said something that I would probably have found objectionable, had I understood it. Mind you if I was five foot three, with glasses like Tojo and married to the woman he was stood next to, then I'd be unhappy too.

By the time Martine could have negotiated a passage over me and around the excited Orientals, it would have been pointless to chase such a determined and easily disguised assailant through the crowded streets, so she talked to me instead.

Having seem for ourselves that Leibniz was now finally and unmistakeably dead we sat together on the front steps, acknowledging my reluctance to face the three flights of steps back to the apartment. I was baffled, the parts I could see didn't fit together.

"Leibniz I can understand." I said, leaning my back against the doorway, the sun on my face. "He was the German version of me, the man they needed to verify that the item being acquired really was what Roland claimed. And the fact that they killed him must mean that he's already made that identification - so they've got the magnetron. From our point of view, anything else is just a waste of time."

"Not necessarily, you're forgetting what he was trying to tell us when we first found him." As Martine spoke, there were some people coming out of the doorway and she made more room for them by moving to one side, closer to me. I was aware that our hips and legs were now firmly and warmly pressed together, she seemed not to have noticed and carried on talking. It would be an awkward subject to raise, but I might need to speak to her about the unintentional effect she was having on me. I found it difficult to move beyond this sensory overload and concentrate on her words, but I tried.

"He didn't just go on about not being Jewish, he also said that he 'Wasn't Sure', that he had 'Just Guessed'. He didn't say what he'd guessed, but there are only a limited range of possibilities." She turned her face to me, waiting for me to fill in the rest, we were so close I could feel her breath. I didn't answer for a moment, there was a serious danger of me deluding myself about her undoubtedly innocent actions. This level of proximity with such a deeply attractive woman, who was young enough to be my daughter, could lead to misunderstandings. Our relationship was strictly professional and since Mary's death I have been emotionally damaged goods, and am now clearly in danger of ruining everything by imagining that a woman like her could be attracted to a man like me.

"No, go on, you finish the thought." I said, unwilling to share my own hot imaginings.

"Well as you didn't recognise the second body, it means that it wasn't Roland, and they must have known that, so they would feel the need to check even more closely that the item they were handling was worth whatever they were paying. That's what he meant when he said he wasn't sure. That woman and the other man must have shown him some sort of device and asked if it was a magnetron, and not wishing to appear unsure of himself he had just taken a guess and said yes."

"And then they shot him?"

"Why not? He'd fulfilled his purpose and would only slow them down while they made their escape. That business about him claiming he wasn't Jewish must have been because that was what they'd accused him of, before shooting him. Their problem was that we turned up half way through, meaning that they had to make a run for it before they'd made sure he was dead." She paused, but having finally managed to concentrate on the matter in hand, I found myself still unsure.

"Disposing of Leibniz as surplus baggage might account for shooting him the first time, but it doesn't cover the attack in the street. In broad daylight, in the middle of a crowd of people, with police officers all around, that smacks of desperation."

"Oh Freddy, you should have seen her face, she wasn't desperate, she was confident, in fact she was arrogant. That's why she laughed at me. That sign you make in England with the two fingers - she didn't need her fingers, she said it with her actions."

"That's still running an enormous risk, just to wave two fingers at you."

"It's not just me Freddy, it's you and me." She said putting her hand on my leg. "How do you think they felt when you killed their getaway driver using nothing but a walking stick? They must have been furious, whatever their original plans had been - you just cancelled them. Besides which you'd be astonished at the number of criminals I encounter who act irrationally, there's hardly ever any great master plan. You had just annoyed and seriously inconvenienced her and she wanted to hit back. If they already thought Leibniz was Jewish then they wouldn't have trusted him with any sensitive information. So I don't think she was silencing him - I think it was the two fingers." She took her hand back, to wave two fingers demonstratively in the air.

Now that the ambulance had removed the dead body, and the Japanese had gone complaining on their way, the street scene had regained some sense of normality, with only a handful of the incurably curious hanging around for possible developments. A uniformed police office approached us, from the direction of the crashed car. He solemnly presented Martine with a stick, my walking stick, which he must have retrieved from the wreck - or to be less squeamish about it - from the dead man's left eye socket.

She handed it back to me, the handle was scratched from being dragged against the wall and the last six inches of the tip were disgustingly covered in gore, the blood was still fresh enough to glint in the sunlight.

"If you're going to make a habit of this, perhaps I should cut a notch in it?" She suggested politely. Lacking, as they do, both wit and irony, Latin types sometimes have an excessive interest in mortality: Death in the Afternoon and all that. Although unhealthily obsessed with the woman, I managed to ignore the comment, observing only, "He could have wiped the bloody thing."

There was a silence between us, as we both considered where exactly our relationship and our hunt went from here. We had tried to stop them getting the magnetron, and we had failed, that seemed to remove any further reason for our partnership; a conclusion I found to be very depressing.

"How would you get it out of Paris, if you were them?" She asked.

"I would join the lines of refugees on every road out of town, until I reached some open stretch of countryside where the Germans could send a plane to pick me up. They must have some means of contact, probably a radio set."

"Or perhaps they won't even try to escape. Piecing together the likely truth from radio reports, it looks as if the Germans will break out of the Ardennes - Normandy area in the next few days, and if they do then I think they'll make it all the way to Paris. To be be honest I'm not confident of our ability to stop them. And if that happens they won't need to find the Germans, they can just hide in Paris and wait for the Germans to come to them." She sounded utterly depressed.

I remembered my conversations in London, and at the RAF base at Vraux. "Don't think too badly of us if Churchill decides to withdraw the British Expeditionary

Force, but we simply can't afford to lose that many men in a battle that has probably already been lost."

She put her hand on mine and squeezed it, in another of her innocent and companionable gestures. If only she were less tactile, less close. If nothing else my probable return to England in the next day or two should save me from blurting out some adolescent nonsense about how much I liked her. The feelings she had stirred in me had taught me that life goes on, perhaps I should join some local group, the Amateur Dramatic Society or some such, and find an accommodating widow of my own age. I might even work up some enthusiasm for the scheme - if I tried harder.

"Can you manage to make it upstairs again?" Asked Martine.

"Why, what have you got in mind?"

She screwed her face up slightly, as if to indicate the improbability of what was to come. "It might be nothing, and I know they've already got the magnetron, but if we interrupted them before they were finished, could there be something else they missed? Some technical drawing of the thing, or written notes about how it works - I don't know, anything. It has to be an improvement on sitting here looking like the last meeting of the suicide club. We could even get the end of your stick cleaned up."

Despite the fact that we were in Paris, the home of the *double entendre*, I resisted the urge to look at her questioningly.

The apartment wasn't a large one, and in the absence of its normal occupants, there was only a minimum of clothing in the wardrobes or food in the kitchen. We were thorough, we examined everything there was to examine, and yet we found nothing of any interest whatsoever. Feeling that I had exhausted my investigative skills, I went into the kitchen and made a pot of coffee . As I stood there I heard voices from the hall, Martine was talking to another woman. As the tone of the voices was casual and friendly I assumed that it wasn't the woman in the straw hat, come back for another go, and left them to it.

I walked through to the living room, carrying the coffee pot and two cups, and found Martine and an elderly lady sitting talking. Martine made the introductions; she was Madame Pradel from the apartment directly below this one, and I was Sir Freddy Villiers, a senior diplomat from the British Embassy.

The woman was nervous, sat forward on the edge of her seat, fidgeting with the hem of her ugly brown cardigan. She said that she had just come to find out what was going on, but you could tell that whatever the point of her visit was, it wasn't just that. Martine was being politely insistent in trying to tease out her connection with either Roland or the apartment's owners. The woman didn't want to be pinned down and was saying how impressed she had been by Monsieur Roland's work, which she understood to be not only Top Secret, but also of National Importance, and despite the pressures of his work what a very nice man he was. And after this trouble in his apartment was everything still alright with him? She had no intention of coming to the point.

Then as I sat there, listening to her wittering, I suddenly realised what was going on. It was as clear as day.

"Excuse me Madame Pradel, I don't wish to be rude, but it is important that you should understand that no matter what Monsieur Roland might have told you, he is actually a suspected fifth columnist, whom we believe to be in the pay of the Boche. Capitaine

146

Dumont and I are here today to collect the parcel he left with you." I didn't elaborate, I just shut my mouth and stared at her.

She flinched, as if I'd slapped her and turned to look at Martine, presumably for some female assistance. She didn't get any, just another demanding stare. At length Martine leaned forward.

"We knew all about the parcel, and I deliberately gave you every opportunity to bring this fact to my attention, yet you consistently refused to mention it. I gave you the rope and you hanged yourself Madame. You are already guilty of concealing evidence in a matter of state security, are you another one being paid by the Boche?" She was good, where someone else might have looked at me in puzzlement, she had picked up my lead without even blinking, and run with it.

Madame Pradel began to sob, holding a screwed up handkerchief to her nose and snivelling into it. With difficulty she managed to fit some words between the sobs.

"He made me promise that I wouldn't tell anyone, he said it was a state secret, and that people might come looking for it, but they would only look in here and not in my apartment."

Martine stood up, straightening her uniform jacket, she looked stern but magnificent. "Madame, the parcel."

Four minutes later I was examining a resonating cavity magnetron on the kitchen table. Apart from her tits, I had no idea what the woman in the straw hat had stuffed up her jumper, but this looked like the real McCoy to me - I'd put my shirt on this one.

Chapter 10

Fraulein Heidi Fuchs
Paris, Wednesday morning, May 15th. 1940

The Reich's Broadcasting Service news report this morning stated that Holland and Belgium have surrendered, and that two complete German armies have crossed the Meuse, meeting only light opposition, and are today moving deeper into northern France. The reporter said that the biggest problem our advancing armies have to deal with is not armed resistance, but the fact that the roads are choked with refugees, many of them deserting French soldiers. The war in the air seems never to have started, the Luftwaffe seized control on the first day and has held it ever since. Some British fighter reinforcements were reported to have arrived, but seem to have had little effect. Too little, too late.

I took care to change my appearance before venturing onto the streets, we were still only a few hundred metres from the scene of yesterday's action; but I was keen to read the French newspaper accounts, strictly for their entertainment value. Sure enough they were filled with stories about *our boys* standing ready to throw back the filthy Hun. Too late boys, the filthy Hun already drove straight past you, and is probably giving your wives a good seeing to, before heading for Paris.

Now that we have the electronic valve thing Gunther is more relaxed, not exactly singing and dancing, but a little less stiff and formal than before. To help him get over the fact that I had more or less taken charge yesterday afternoon, I gave him my warmest congratulations this morning on how brilliantly he'd handled the operation. He politely acknowledged my comments as no more than his due, probably wondering exactly which medal Himmler was going to pin on him when we got back to Berlin.

But my mind was a lot closer to reality. All this news about German forces storming through a collapsing French army didn't alter the fact that the two remaining members of our team were still two hundred miles behind enemy lines, surrounded by people who would shoot us on sight; if only they knew who we were.

Von Strenglen might be ready to lead a victory parade down the Champs-Élysées, but I was still in Detective Sergeant Fuchs' ultra cautious mode. It had been satisfying to spit in the snooty French woman's face yesterday, when I sent Leibniz on his way, but that wasn't the sort of behaviour I planned to make a habit of. Now that we had the magic box I was content to leave it to my Prussian friend to make the arrangements for our early departure, preferably later today, and in the meantime it seemed safer to keep our heads down. Don't rock the boat.

Having lost the two way radio in the crashed Citroen, our sole means of communicating with Berlin was by passing messages through the French phone number we'd been given for emergency use. Von Strenglen put on his black leather gloves, to disguise his hand, and a pair of sunglasses in the vain hope of making him look a little less like Kaiser Wilhelm. Then the two of us sauntered out, hand in wooden hand, to pass ourselves off as tourists. The device was with our very few possessions in a small cheap suitcase, it all helped the disguise.

I have often found, when interviewing witnesses at crime scenes, that the average citizen could walk past a gorilla raping a nun and completely fail to notice anything remarkable. Or, even less helpfully, later swear on oath that the gorilla was wearing a top hat and tails. As long as we moved at the same speed as the surrounding pedestrians and didn't keep shouting Heil Hitler at passers by, I reckoned we should be safe enough.

We went into a dive called the Sporting Bar, where four old men and the owner were gathered round a radio set listening to a description of a bicycle race. The German army is heading straight for you, all guns blazing, and you're listening to a bicycle race? I paid for a couple of Jetons at the counter and we went through to the back corridor by the toilet to use their phone. That's how the public phone system works in France, you go into a bar, buy these round tokens they call Jetons and then stand outside the lavatory, talking into a wall mounted instrument, while your eyes water from the smell.

Gunther dialled the number, which I watched and would later write down, he always wanted to be the one who made contact. That in itself was enough to ensure I got the number down. When he got through, he told them we had the device, and then started to ask about arrangements for the pick up. At that point even I could hear a sharp voice down the phone telling him to shut up. Then a different voice came on, I couldn't make out the words this time but the tone was angry and accusing. Gunther tried to break in with some comment about 'A most unfortunate accident', but the voice shouted him down.

Then a question was asked, and the voice stopped, waiting for an answer. Gunther looked puzzled, but replied, "In a box, in the bottom of the wardrobe." In response to which the single word 'Imbecile' came clearly down the line, followed by another torrent of abuse. It was some minutes before I was able to escort a shattered Prussian back onto the street.

The second voice on the telephone had been Monsieur Roland, the scientist from whom we should have purchased the device, and who we had tried to double cross. The man Gunther had clubbed to death had been no more than his messenger. I had no moral qualms about double crossing a traitor, or anyone else come to that, but the point is that you must do it properly, and we had botched it. Or as Berlin would discover, just as soon as I could safely tell them, their blue eyed boy Sturmbannfuhrer Gunther von Strenglen had botched it.

The fact that I had been right about the stupidity of killing an unidentified man was vastly compounded by the fact that we had the wrong magnetron. Apparently the thing we had found in the wardrobe had been a dummy, put there especially to fool idiots like von Strenglen and Leibniz, and it had worked. Now Roland was beside himself with rage at our perfidy, and that was the actual word he used: perfidy. He thought it was alright for him to cheat his own friends but all wrong when someone else tried to do the same to him. He now further claimed that the French woman and the old man had, unlike us, managed to find the genuine article, which had been hidden elsewhere in the building.

The message from Berlin had been clear, if we wanted to stay out of a labour camp for the rest of the war, we had better recover the item, and be quick about it. Another point that I didn't need Berlin to tell me about was the fact that if we failed to find the damn thing, then von Strenglen would have me in his sights. With me safely disposed of, any failure could be blamed on the policewoman with the interesting past, and I would be in no position to argue.

At least Gunther had kept his head sufficiently to tell the phone contact that we needed an identity on our two opponents, and the message had been to call back in one hour. We disposed of the embarrassing proof of our gullibility in a rubbish bin and went to sit on a marble bench outside the Sacré Coeur basilica, where we watched the passers by. There wasn't a lot of small talk. Fifty nine minutes later we went to find another bar and another telephone.

One convenient aspect of the German army's forthcoming arrival in Paris, was the willingness of increasing numbers of police officers and other public servants to take a pragmatic view about their future prospects. If it looks likely that you'll be working for the Third Reich by this time next month, then it doesn't seem too bad to pass them some information now, it's not really like treason, it's more like keeping in with your new boss. In similar circumstances even I might have given the matter serious consideration.

The Frenchwoman turned out to be a Capitaine Martine Dumont, based at the Chalons Gendarmerie, aged forty five, divorced, no children, with a home address in the same town. She had clearly found some way of tracking either us, or Roland from there to Paris, which was an impressive piece of work in itself. The old man was more of a problem, they knew he was an Englishman called Sir Freddy Villiers, which confirmed my own guess about his nationality, but beyond that - nothing.

So we have a senior Gendarme, with the hots for some mad old aristo, how does that work? It wasn't as if he was her boyfriend from earlier, who was hanging around on her account, otherwise he wouldn't have been missing all those signals on the steps of the apartment building. That means he was here for the mission, and from their point of view the mission would be to stop us from getting the device - which then meant that he was more than likely to be MI6, British Military Intelligence. They must have a great deal of faith in his abilities to trust a job like this to a man like that

So as things stand this morning they think they've won, they think that we're disorganised and running, well not just yet we're not. If she had the nerve, her best bet would be to destroy the device, but she won't do that, because Mad Sir Freddy will want to get it back to England. Even though they're already supposed to have one example of this thing, he'll still want this one, if only as a trophy. He'll probably want to hang it on his wall, to prove to his friends that even at his age, he's got what it takes.

This is good because it gives us one last chance at it. But if I was him I would have proved I still had what it takes by taking the Capitaine to bed. She looked to me like the sort of woman who might smell nice. But the English are so repressed that sort of thing would never cross his mind, God knows where they get their children from.

I suggested to Gunther that we should split up for an hour or two, to double our chances of finding them, then we could meet again at lunchtime and compare notes. I suggested that he should stake out the apartment building again, to see if there was still any continuing police activity there.

Privately, I thought that would be a complete waste of time, but it would at least get him out of my hair for two or three hours - which would then give me the time to do something more useful.

Sir Freddy Villiers
Paris, Wednesday morning, May 15th. 1940

Martine had wanted to deposit the magnetron at the Montmartre Gendarmerie, for safe keeping. It was difficult for me to explain my reservations about this, without seeming to imply disloyalty in her colleagues, which I had no intention of doing. In the end she understood my point about the likelihood of some opportunist officer wanting to curry favour with the invaders, especially as it was now almost certain that the woman who killed Leibniz would have identified Martine. My own preference was to entrust it to the British Embassy, who could presumably despatch it back to England with the benefit of diplomatic protection. However, as it was eight o'clock in the evening before the excitement finally died down, neither of us had the stamina for anything more than a drink and something to eat before going to our separate beds.

As I look at that last sentence I wonder what prompted me to insert the completely unnecessary word *separate*, it was perhaps one of these Freudian Slips, I shall need to be more careful.

I wondered what Mary would say, if she could see me, barely three months after the funeral, getting tied into emotional knots over my foolish infatuation with a young woman I met two days ago. Or even worse, what would my daughter Cassie say? You shouldn't be frightened of your children's opinions, but you can at least take them into account. It's no wonder that randy old men are universally regarded as figures of fun.

We stayed again at the same Pension as last night, with Martine's great aunt, or whatever, making a fuss of us both. My left leg was grateful for the lack of any fresh reasons to chase passing killers, having been shot down by the Luftwaffe and rammed by a getaway car it was probably time for a rest. This morning Martine had arranged for an official car to be supplied, which made our trip to the Faubourg Saint-Honoré a lot easier.

The British Embassy was under a state of high alert, it would have been astonishing had it not been. There were French police along the pavement outside, armed British soldiers inside, and crowds of people on the pavement milling around and looking worried. By a combination of Martine's uniform and my persistence we eventually managed to reach a harassed young man at a desk, with a sign which said he was a consular assistant. Although it took a great deal of browbeating and determination to do it, we were eventually taken upstairs to the office of the military attaché, a Brigadier-General Fraser.

Under all normal circumstances I dare say Fraser would have been a perfectly pleasant and reasonable sort of chap, but these were not such circumstances. His position at the embassy put him in the middle of a nightmare of conflicting pressures. The French government were using him as one of a variety of conduits for their increasingly strident demands for British reinforcements, and the British were telling him to prevaricate in any way he liked - because there weren't going to be any. On top of that there were the various liaison duties between our Expeditionary Force and the French military commanders like Gamelin, who were scarcely in contact with their own officers any longer, let alone their allies.

Then as the icing on the cake, some unknown female officer of the Gendarmerie and a retired civil servant descend on him with tales of a shot down military mission, and top secret electronic parts. Having listened to my story he said that he had never heard of a Major Lawrence Grand of Section D, and had no way of passing a message to him. He looked at me to see if I had any further suggestions, but I didn't. He reminded us that unless the French surrendered first, Paris would probably be bombed as severely as Rotterdam had been, only the previous day, with the wholesale destruction of the city centre and thousands of civilian casualties. He explained that he wasn't even sure if the Embassy staff would be safe, never mind stray packages from wandering strangers. In retrospect I find myself amazed that it took him as long as it did before he finally threw us out.

We stood outside on the pavement, apart from the crowds trying to get into the Embassy the rest of the Eighth Arrondissement looked fairly normal, the high end couture and luxury goods shops of this area were all open and looked busy. The situation was surreal, we were in a city at war, where everyone we could see was trying to ignore that fact.

The news of the Rotterdam bombing had genuinely shocked me, I was unprepared for that level of gratuitous brutality. Dutch resistance had all but ended even before the bombers had arrived, the attack had served no possible military purpose. Perhaps the stolid burghers of Rotterdam had the temperament to cope with aerial bombardment; but how would the more volatile French temperament cope?

An Air Ministry study last year, immediately classified as Top Secret because of its alarming content, had suggested that in the event of heavy German bombing of London the government expected there to be widespread panic, with a probable requirement for martial law and the shooting of looters; and that was in Britain. When it comes to steadiness under fire, the news from the French front line is not encouraging. Martine's official sources were reporting massive levels of desertion, with some whole units disappearing, even the officers were leaving. The panic was infectious, as men fled the German approach, they tried to justify their actions by telling any surrounding troops that they had been forced to run in face of overwhelming odds. Many of the deserters were fleeing the rumour, rather than the enemy.

At her suggestion, we went to the car to pick up a road map and then wandered round the corner to take a seat in an open air cafe, the package sat on the pavement between my feet. A folded newspaper had been left on the next table, Martine picked it up. The lead story was breezily optimistic, claiming that the Germans had still not encountered the main French forces, and that when they did they would get no further. The editorial comment once again reminded readers of the events of 1914, when the Germans had reached the outskirts of Paris before being thrown back. Martine and I looked at each other helplessly, this was wishful thinking on a massive scale, and she knew it every bit as well as me.

"You can't count on reaching the Channel coast, the speed of the German advance is increasing every day, you could find yourself trapped in open countryside with no escape. Why don't you just abandon the magnetron, or hide it somewhere, you said that Ponte had already delivered one of these to you in England?"

"I might have to do that in the end, but I'd rather not. We don't know for sure if the one that Ponte delivered actually works; whereas we know this one does because they were using it in field trials. If this thing gives us any sort of advantage in producing airborne radio location, it's worth making the effort. We were talking about the bombing of Rotterdam being repeated on Paris, well I'm more worried about it being repeated on London."

"What can I do to help?"

"If I can't get through to the British Expeditionary Forces near the Channel, then I'll have to head west, to Brittany or further south to Lorient, I should be able to pick up a boat, or even find an aircraft going to the UK. If you could organise a car and some kind of official travel document, to get me through any police check points."

She nodded. "That won't be a problem, I've enjoyed working with you, I'm just sorry that our time together has been so brief." She leaned across and squeezed my hand, she probably regarded it as a comradely sort of squeeze, one colleague to another. The French are so much more demonstrative than the British. The problem lay in my wilful misunderstanding of even the slightest physical contact between us.

"What will you do, when I've gone?"

"I have my work at Chalons, no matter what happens with the Germans, there will still be a need for a civil administration, people will continue to have lives to lead, families to care for and jobs to do. They will rely on people like me staying at our posts and doing our jobs. It's not glamorous, but if everyone like me were to run away there would be anarchy; looting, rape, murder - you name it."

"Will you cooperate with the Germans?"

She seemed close to tears and didn't reply for a while. Eventually she looked at me. "You make me sound like a traitor, but I'm not. I hate the Germans every bit as much as you, but the people have a right to expect order and continuity, and I can't abandon them. If I stay I might make a difference."

I was horrified, and this time I reached out and took her hand. "I didn't mean anything like that, I would never say that of you. I was simply worried about what would happen to you."

"Were you?" She sounded slightly surprised.

I felt myself blushing slightly, at the age of sixty six I was acting like a schoolboy on his first date. It is a fact of life that if an older man thinks a good looking younger woman is attracted to him but doesn't like to say so, he is a deluded fool. This was exactly the position I had hoped to avoid.

"I don't want to make you feel uncomfortable, we're from such different generations, I simply wanted to say how much I had enjoyed our professional relationship, and how impressed I was by your work."

"I see." This time her voice was somewhat terse.

At that moment the ascending pitch of the air raid sirens began to sound. I had grown used to these in London, and whilst I was in no mood to panic, thoughts of yesterday's Rotterdam bombing were still in my mind. Martine and I both glanced upwards, at a completely empty blue sky, looked at each other and ignored the piercing wail. Around us everyone else did the same. The thought occurred to me that we were all in the same fools' paradise.

There were Gendarmeries closer to where we were, but we had become a known item at Montmartre and so it seemed sensible to go there to make my travel arrangements. There was an expectation that the ports of Le Havre and Caen would soon come under aerial attack, as they were well within range of the current Luftwaffe operational area. There was a widespread assumption that whether or not the German advance included Paris, it would certainly include the entire length of the Channel coast. It was thus a less popular choice as an evacuation destination, unless of course, like me, you were trying to get to England.

Talking to the senior traffic officer, it seemed that my best hope of avoiding Germans was to head West, the two hundred kilometre run to Le Mans was suggested as a starting point. The road in that direction was still relatively clear, unlike a lot of the routes South. Once I reached Le Mans I could then decide either to head North to somewhere like St. Malo, or continue further West to Morlaix or Brest. According to the Embassy there were British commandeered merchant vessels running in and out of all these ports, picking up anyone who wanted to go.

A car was produced, with a full tank of petrol and an open letter, on official French military headed paper, stated that I was on official business and requested that all officials should render me whatever assistance they could. I was ready to make a run for it.

Chapter 11

Fraulein Heidi Fuchs
Paris, Wednesday midday, May 15th. 1940

The easiest method of approach, and one that I've used so many times, would be to seize one of Dumont's close family members: her husband or a child for preference. Then everything would fit neatly into place, and she would be falling over herself to cooperate. The fact that she had no close family was a definite complication, but that was only one way to approach the subject, there would be others.

Back in Berlin I would have put a discreet watch on her office, and then tailed whichever of the two we spotted, before picking them up somewhere nice and quiet, for a chat. The difficulty with that was not just a lack of manpower, but also the fact there was no time left for standard operational procedures. Now that they had what they wanted she would be returning to lonely provincial obscurity in Chalons, and he would disappear back to England, taking his prize with him. No matter what I did next it would have to happen very quickly, or it would be just a waste of time.

The British Embassy had to be my best option. An English Gentleman type like Sir Freddy would instinctively gravitate to authority, in the absence of any British military presence in Paris and not trusting the French military, he would make for the Embassy. I'd bet on it. The concern was - had he already spoken to them last night? His MI6 bosses must have given him some out of hours contact routine with the MI6 Station Chief in Paris, who would probably be listed as a Trade Attaché or something similar. The reality was that, if that had taken place last night, I was just too late and there was nothing I could do about it. But right now it was still worth playing the odds, and that meant staking out the Embassy.

I took a taxi to the British Embassy. The Paris Metro is supposed to be good but I'm not sufficiently familiar with it, and I prefer to stay on the surface, where I can see what's going on and feel more in control. This is still a largely medieval city in its layout and, apart from a few big well known avenues, the rest of it is a maze of twisting and narrow old streets. It might not be as bad as I've heard London is, but it's a lot less straightforward than Berlin.

The Faubourg Saint-Honoré is a fair example of what I mean. Long rows of four and five story nineteenth century buildings, jinking slightly this way and that, as they try but fail to follow a straight line through the middle of town. However, one thing's sure, it stinks of money, and lots of it. We passed the Hermès bag shop just before my destination. It looked like the sort of place where the staff would look down their noses at you and the stock wouldn't have price tickets, if you need to ask the price, you can't afford the bag. Had I been on foot I might have paused for a quick look, it would have reminded me of my place in life. Though if I'm still in town when the tanks arrive, I might just go and take what I want anyway.

I let the taxi take me past the front of the Embassy and drop me off a few blocks along the road. I had a cheap lightweight coat on today, with my hair tied back and a plain cloche hat. All that Dumont had really seen of me had been my mouth as I smiled, and my general build. She would need to be extremely smart to connect that woman yesterday with me today.

Because I'd started early it was still only quarter past nine, but already there was a press of people around the main entrance. The two French *flics* on the pavement were making no effort to impose order, and the Embassy staff were admitting people in occasional twos and threes. This could be a long day, Gunther was going to have to amuse himself for a while if I failed to keep our afternoon rendezvous. I had a worried thought about how long my bladder was going to hold out. That's sometimes a deciding factor on the streets, it must be so much easier being a man, but then they've got so many other disadvantages I've never fancied swapping.

On most observation jobs I would try to find somewhere nearby that overlooked the area in question, and then watch from there, but this presented a much better opportunity. I simply joined the throng waiting for admittance, and struck up conversation with the first woman on her own who looked interested. It turned out that she was a Frenchwoman married to an Englishman, who had been in Paris visiting her mother and was now trying to get passage back to her home in England. I said what an amazing coincidence, as I was a Dutch woman, also married to an Englishman, and so we chatted. Teaming up with innocent third parties can be the best cover there is. The off duty Swedish and Japanese diplomats in Montmartre had been a Godsend.

Far from it being a long day on the Embassy doorstep, it turned out to be no more than a brief stopover. After less than half an hour of friendly chat, I saw the Englishman's tall figure, followed by Dumont, emerge from behind the black Embassy gates. They didn't look happy, and he was carrying a bag of exactly the right size to be what I wanted. For some reason I couldn't guess, the Embassy hadn't taken the device off them, had they been directed somewhere else to hand it over? It didn't look like it, they were unsure of themselves and looking round, as if wondering where to go next. Then they decided something and walked straight past the group of people that I was in the middle of, they didn't so much as glance in my direction. I waited for a minute, detached myself from the Frenchwoman, and began to follow.

They went first to a car, which Dumont unlocked and reached inside for a road map, then she relocked it and they carried on along the pavement, He was still carrying the bag. That had to be it, he didn't trust it out of his sight. I felt for my pistol, I could shoot them both, snatch the bag and their car keys, and be on my way before anyone could stop me.

I would have to be fast, because although I wasn't sure about him, she would certainly have a gun and could be counted on to use it. Then I saw that there was another policeman coming in this direction. In fact with the various embassies around here there wouldn't just be uniformed cops, there would almost certainly be plain clothes ones. I cancelled my half formed plan for a street robbery.

I watched them settle themselves at a cafe table, but couldn't get close enough to hear anything. The expressions on their faces were almost as revealing, she was saying something personal, something that he wasn't picking up on. She was leaning slightly forwards and looking straight into his face, he was leaning slightly backwards and his eyes didn't want to settle on hers. She was being straight with him about something, and he was being utterly dim, but about what?

A waitress came out and took their order, neither of them seemed to focus on her, and I was wearing a black dress, the easiest things are often the best. I walked directly towards the cafe, they had no idea that I was anywhere near them, I carried on into the cafe interior, neither of them looked at me.

It was a fairly busy place, there were four waitresses on duty, I went straight to the one they'd spoken to. My French is good, but clearly accented, it's obvious that I'm foreign, with any luck she won't enquire beyond foreign.

"Hello, my name's Jane Smith and I'm an English enquiry agent," I said in my most precise French. "I'm collecting evidence that the tall Englishman outside is having an affair with that woman Gendarme officer. He has a wife, children and grandchildren in England, and it's my job to nail the bastard. Will you help me please?"

"My God she's young enough to be his daughter, the dirty swine. And you're right, there's definitely something going on between them. I'm not sure what - but there's something. What d'you want?"

I took off my coat and hat and gave her a hundred Francs. In return she lent me her apron, her head dress and the cloth she had over her arm; then she disappeared for a long cigarette break.

I took their coffees out and served them slowly, leaving the *addition* in a saucer. The woman muttered a distracted 'Merci' without lifting her eyes in my direction, then I turned away and started carefully wiping the next couple of tables. I was invisible, I didn't exist.

He was saying how much he'd appreciated their professional working relationship, with the stress on the word professional. She was taking that as brush off, and didn't like it, and he had no idea which day of the week it was.

I'd heard that the English were emotionally repressed, but surely not at this level. Despite his age, the man was probably a trained killer, organisations like MI6, and even some of our own security services, were known to use specialist assassins. Those sort are always a bit peculiar, and that would account for his inability to read normal human signals, and the bizarre but effective way in which he'd used his walking stick to deal with Carl. If this man had ever had a wife, she must have made all the running, he probably lived with his dog and did unpleasant things to schoolboys.

Then I heard him say that he thought his best bet would be to drive to the coast and find a ship to take him back to England. She said they should go back to the Gendarmerie where the traffic officers could help him plan the best route to avoid the Germans.

I was tempted to tell her it was a bit late for that, but didn't bother. I looked around, we were still in the Embassy area, and there were two men in grey suits across the road who positively shouted plain clothes copper. I would have been happy to give it a go but it just wasn't clear enough for a smash and grab, I went inside, changed back into Heidi Fuchs, took the time for a quick pee, before I got desperate, and left. I didn't reckon it was worth waiting for a tip from either of those two.

Instead I walked down the street until I found what I wanted, a scruffy looking black Renault that hadn't been washed for weeks, with an unlocked door. One of thousands of the same model and colour to be seen all over France. I like anonymous, I'm not a flashy sort of woman and hardly ever wear diamonds and furs - well not at the same time as any other clothes.

168

I drove round until I was parked fifty metres behind their car and waited. Now I had them in my sights I wanted to make sure they stayed there.

Sir Freddy Villiers
Paris, Wednesday afternoon, May 15th. 1940

Before I finally set off for the coast, Martine and I drove back to the Pension, her in the lead and me following in my newly acquired car. We had our overnight bags to collect, together with the washing that Martine's aged relative had been kind enough to do for us. Besides which, for reasons which weren't entirely clear I hadn't wished to say my final goodbye to her under the gaze of her colleagues at the Gendarmerie.

Tante Mimi, as Martine called the lady at the Pension, had been particularly welcoming when we first met, but in the last twenty four hours there had been a slight cooling in the atmosphere. I wasn't sure if she thought that I should accompany Martine back to Chalons, or what, but I felt there was some sense of disapproval in her view of me. Perhaps she had somehow discerned the way I felt about her great niece and thought that I should develop an interest in a woman of my own age. I could understand her disapproval.

Well I'm sorry Tante Mimi, I really am, but if you can just hold your horses for a little while, then I'll be gone for good. For some reason my imminent departure failed to thrill me as it ought.

We stood on the pavement, and I formally shook Capitaine Dumont's hand. I wished her the best of luck during the forthcoming months and thanked her for her invaluable assistance in recovering the magnetron. I almost crumbled and started blabbing about how much, how very much, I admired and . . . and what? Respected her? Liked her? If our ages had been closer, if I'd known her a little longer, then I might even have said - oh who the hell knows?

Fortunately I was able to control my emotions and managed to avoid an embarrassing scene. Foreigners make fun of the English stiff upper lip, but there are moments in life when I'm sure that it's the right thing to do. Emotional incontinence is always distasteful. From her distracted and strangely reserved manner I think she must have been equally worried about the possibility of me coming out with some foolish and impassioned declaration, and her own farewell was businesslike and almost brusque. She was visibly anxious to get this finished with.

I put the magnetron on the car floor, behind the driver's seat, and drove away, without any lingering glances through the mirror. My mind was resolutely set on finding my way to the Place de l'Étoile and then on to the Porte de St. Cloud. I drove automatically, half my attention on the road signs, and half of me wondering exactly what it was that I'd just done wrong. There was certainly something I hadn't handled properly, and that isn't like me. Mary used to tell me there were times when I was too much in control, when I should, as she used to put it, unbutton a little. Once again I missed the ability to talk things through with the woman who had been half my life for thirty eight years. Strangely, I had the idea that if the two women could ever have met they would have been friends, I'm not sure what it was but they certainly had something in common.

The traffic lights ahead of me changed to red and I drew to a halt behind two other cars. There was an immediate bang and I was thrown, first backwards against my seat as the car behind struck mine, and then forwards against the steering wheel as my own car struck the one in front. I felt the magnetron shoot forward and wedge itself beneath my seat. Parisian bad driving was the last thing I needed.

I switched off the engine and got out of my car, as did the drivers of the cars in front of and behind me. I just wanted to get moving, so my own approach was businesslike and to the point, the man from the car in front of me was less so. He was red in the face and shouting.

"What the hell d'you think you're playing at? This car's supposed to take me and my family down to Clermont tomorrow - now bloody look at it."

"There was nothing I could do about it, I was already stopped when the car behind hit me." I gestured to the car wedged against my buckled rear bumper, where a woman in her mid thirties was getting out. She clutched her handbag to her chest with one hand, while the other hand covered her horrified open mouth, as she surveyed the results of her carelessness. She was probably trying to work out what to tell her husband.

The red faced man stared at me in disgust, then simply said, "English pig." Before striding off towards the woman. So much for my French accent.

"You stupid bitch, if you can't drive a car you should get on the bleeding bus." Normally I would have told the man to mind his manners and his language, but all I wanted was to get out of this situation and out of Paris. My car was bashed at both ends, but still looked driveable. If I could just move one of the two cars that were sandwiching me in, I could get on my way - and who cares about bent mudguards?

The man was still shouting, and demanding answers from the woman, who didn't seem to have spoken yet. Some of the other traffic was already finding its way past our little drama, their occupants glancing casually at the tableau as they passed. I walked back towards the angry man and the shocked woman, one of them was going to have to move and I didn't care which.

The man was now standing nose to nose with the woman, jabbing his finger at her. "Well go on, answer me you stupid bitch, answer me."

As I approached, the woman dropped her hand from her mouth and, quite incredibly, she seemed to be amused by his behaviour. Then she turned her back to the passing traffic, to shield her actions, put the hand which had been over her mouth into the handbag, and grasped something inside it. Then without bothering to take her hand from the bag, she shot him. Just like that, without any warning, in broad daylight, in the middle of the street and right in front of me. There was no doubt what had happened, I saw the hole ripped in the end of the bag and the brief puff of smoke.

Now it's true that he'd been aggressive, coarse and annoying, and should certainly have had his mouth washed out with soap and water, but this was extreme. However, if nothing else, it did stop his shouting. He staggered half a pace backwards, into the side of her car, his mouth was still open but now silent and he stared at her in astonishment. Then he slowly clutched his belly, folded forwards and fell to the floor. It looked like Mabel and the offspring would be going to Clermont on their own, and probably by bus.

My immediate reaction was the realisation that she was a professional, she'd done this sort of thing before, she had fired only once, and was so confident of its effect that she didn't bother with a second shot. Nor did

172

she step back after she'd fired, she knew for an absolute fact that he was no further danger - that he was going down, and that she could simply stand there and watch him.

Then she stepped fastidiously over the fallen body, her right hand still in the handbag, and the bag itself pointing unwaveringly at me. This was the first time that I'd been threatened by a handbag; dismissing thoughts of Lady Bracknell I took the threat seriously, and kept my mouth shut. The Ministry of Information have a poster; 'Careless Talk Costs Lives', it had certainly cost him his, and I was in no hurry to make the same mistake.

"Good evening Sir Freddy." She said in German accented English. That stopped me in my tracks, but I soon recovered.

"You're the woman from the stairwell, the woman in the straw hat who killed Leibniz."

She smiled at me. "That's right, you may call me Heidi, and now I'm going to be the woman who takes the radio location device from you." She took another step forward to make good her promise.

My mind was working overtime: 'Heidi! - You can't be called Heidi, she's about ten and lives up a mountain in Switzerland, tending goats with her grandfather'. Fortunately, I was able to persuade my mouth to come out with the more useful assertion; "You're too late, I don't have it. They took it from me at the Gendarmerie, which is why I'm going back to England empty handed."

"Don't lie to me." She said in the weary tones of a primary school teacher dealing with a silly seven year old. "You will give me the device and then you and your garlic eating partner can go and do what you like to each other."

I was a picture of cooperative innocence. "You could have the damned thing for all I care, but I don't have it. I'll rip the car apart in front of you, I'll do whatever you want - but I still don't have it. The last time I saw it was in the Commandant's office at the Montmartre Gendarmerie. You must have been following me to be here, so you know that's where I've come from." I just hoped that she didn't look under the seat.

Her eyes narrowed, she didn't care if I was telling the truth, she only cared if I was going to give her what she wanted. "Then that is a pity, for you a great pity - If you had given me what I wanted I might have let you live." She gazed at me for a moment in contemplation, before she continued.

"At first I couldn't make my mind up whether you were dangerous or not, but since I've been watching you I have come to see that you are stupid, stupid but lucky. That business when you killed my driver with your walking stick, that was nothing but luck, and then in the pavement cafe when you told the woman that you enjoyed your *professional* relationship, that was just stupid - asking for trouble. You went out of your way to annoy someone who wanted to be your ally. You are, perhaps, one of these Englishmen who don't like women so much, only their old nannies heh? So you should understand that when I kill you it's not personal, it's for women everywhere, women who have to deal with stupid men like you."

How on earth could she know about that? I had no answer, only the knowledge that I had met my match. But one last thing puzzled me.

"How did you manage to find Roland's apartment, did he give you the address himself?"

"Hardly, I just followed the greedy little bastard's taxi receipts, nothing special, just basic police procedure. Your people should try it one day."

Feeling this had completed our conversation, she lifted the still deadly handbag towards me, and shamefully I flinched.

Before she could pull the trigger, somebody else, somewhere else, pulled a different trigger. I don't know who, but the incoming bullet ripped through the handbag, throwing her hand to one side. Shreds of material and broken contents flew about in the air, but there was no metallic clang of a bullet striking her gun and no painful cry of a bullet striking her hand. The shot had saved my life but, frankly speaking, it could have been better.

She identified the shooter's location faster than me, that's one of the signs of aging - my cunning might be intact but my reaction times are hopeless. She grabbed my left arm to swing herself behind me, for a moment I was useful to her. She might not know who the shooter was, but she wanted my body between her and them. The handbag having served its purpose she tore away what was left of it, to reveal her pistol. I'm not sufficiently well versed in these matters to have recognised its type, only its lethality.

With her still grasping one of my arms I turned my head to look down the road, in the same direction she had looked. There were several vehicles stopped behind us, and people could be seen looking back in our direction, probably wondering what the delay was. As I was screwing up my eyes to try and identify someone pointing a gun at us, two marked Gendarmerie vans squealed to a standstill on the far side of the road and men emerged - uniformed men with guns. I turned to see how these new arrivals would change an already confusing event, but as I did I was hit round the side of the head, by what I later realised was the butt of the German woman's gun.

I went down, not completely unconscious, but unable to prevent myself falling helplessly to the ground. As I looked, in vague surprise, at the pavement from a distance of half an inch, I could hear gun shots and more shouting. There was also the tinny sound of bullets hitting car bodywork, and of glass shattering, but it was all a long way away. Then I think I went to sleep.

Chapter 12

Fraulein Heidi Fuchs
Paris, Wednesday evening, May 15th. 1940

I had no idea what the hell I was supposed to do with the bloody woman. I object to being shot at, especially when I'm in the process of shooting someone myself. But even as I realised that I would have to deal with her, two van loads of trigger happy Gendarmes arrived on the scene, blasting lead in all directions. It was plainly time for me to vanish, and if I wasn't taking the gadget with me then taking the woman Gendarme was the next best bet.

I still wasn't sure if the the old man had been lying about not having it, though I had to admit his version of things made some sort of sense. He said the French authorities had taken it off him, which fitted in with the events of the last few days, as our invasion had put the Franco British alliance under enormous strain. The British were blaming the French for being generally useless and not stopping the Germans, and the French were blaming the British for not providing enough reinforcements, especially planes. The one thing that hadn't occurred to either of them was the very obvious fact that it would have taken an act of God to stop Guderian and his Panzers. And when it came to acts of God they should have paid more attention to the old Prussian motto: 'Gott Mit Uns'.

That left his story as being at least plausible, even if I thought the man was about as straight as a dog's back leg. His sort of upper class Englishman would lie as naturally as breathing, and even when I'd got what I wanted I was still going to kill him. People like him were no more than parasites.

Having hastily clubbed him to the ground, I grabbed my hat from the car, it was quite a nice one, and ran down the side turning. The Gendarmes were still shooting randomly in all directions to make themselves sound good. That's a very Latin sort of behaviour, never mind what works - just do something that sounds good. The result was that everybody was keeping their heads down, and some unknown woman running from the scene just looked like common sense. I took the next left, a service alley behind the shops, and put my hat on. Then I picked up a couple of empty boxes from beside one of the bins and turned left again onto the next street.

Her smart uniform was immediately visible, she was crouching behind one of the cars, gun in hand trying to see what was happening. I had come out onto the street behind her, and she wasn't bothering to look backwards, just forwards. Don't they teach them anything at their police training school? I go to the trouble of getting a decent disguise, and she never even looks at me; I sometimes feel my skills are utterly wasted on these people.

My approach had been direct, I quietly put down the boxes, pulled out my gun and crept slowly forwards. She was devoting half her attention to the body of her fallen friend, Sir Freddy, and the rest to keeping an eye on the Gendarmes from the vans who were now spreading across the street. Fortunately for him, he was lying on the pavement, behind the group of crashed cars, a reasonably safe position from the gunfire. I gave her the same treatment as him, a hard whack round the head with the butt of my pistol. I recognised the car she had been hiding behind as hers, and the key was still in the ignition, this would do nicely.

She was only light and so manoeuvring her limp body onto the back seat was no great problem. As I was doing so a woman came up and asked what was happening, I said that she had been hit by one of the stray bullets and I was taking her to hospital. The woman went into overdrive and started fussing: 'What can I do?' - 'Will she be alright?' I told her it was only a graze and everything was going to be fine, and then when she stood there watching me I told her to get off the pavement before the next bullet hit her. I didn't mention that the next bullet would be one of mine and luckily she left before we reached that point. I took off the Capitaine's stockings and tied her wrists and ankles, then gagged her and threw a coat over her. I hoped that she could breathe through her nose, she wasn't going to have much value as corpse.

Having missed our lunchtime meeting, my final rendezvous point of the day with von Strenglen was at the Place de Clichy, near our old hunting ground of Montmartre. It was a large busy square with lots of roads in and out and plenty of cafes for cover. I was ten minutes early, but drove to the cafe we had agreed on and sure enough, von Strenglen's uncomfortably Teutonic features were visible at an outside table.

It was fully dark by this time but the cafe's lights were almost at peace time levels of brightness. According to the newspapers they have a strictly enforced blackout in England, with patrolling wardens telling people to cover their windows, but in Paris they do things differently. Apparently, they think the Luftwaffe won't bother them, or perhaps, more accurately, they think that trying to hide from us is a waste of time.

Sitting alone at the cafe table he looked tired and nervous, and when he saw me approaching couldn't completely hide the wave of relief that came over him. He was a competent enough sort, but out of his depth when operating undercover in enemy territory. Give him an assault rifle, a couple of grenades and tell him to charge a machine gun nest and he'll be delighted to do it, single handed, but this sort of thing was a little too complex for his rigid military mind. There were too many variables, and the introduction of Capitaine Martine Dumont was one of them.

"What are we going to do with her?" Was his petulant first question, when he learned of my back seat passenger, and asked in such a way as to accuse me of an error in taking her.

"Would you rather I had come away from a major ambush empty handed? I believe in taking victory from the jaws of defeat, not the other way round. What about you?"

"My dear we mustn't argue, we need a united effort to pull this off. I didn't mean to criticise, simply to wonder where we go from here?"

"We inform the Commandant of the Montmartre Gendarmerie that if we don't get this bloody thing, and quickly, then first we kill Dumont and then we kill him. The Panzers will be here with the next week or two, and with them come the SS and the Gestapo. We tell him the same thing I told Gaston, that anybody who has interfered with our mission will be hunted down and exterminated, together with their wife, child and dog - it's as simple as that."

"How admirably direct Fraulein, and I agree with you completely."

As I say, although unoriginal, the man is basically decent, but you do need to lay things out quite simply for him. As I spoke to the waiter it struck me that in the last twenty four hours, in the dedicated service of the Third Reich, I had been conversing in German, French, English and Japanese, I should put in for a rise on linguistic grounds alone. We had *steak frites* and two beers each, keeping an eye on the car as we ate. You would have thought we were on holiday.

The option of staying in any sort of hotel wasn't open to us with our prisoner in tow, but that left two other choices. I would have liked to stay at Roland's apartment in the Rue Cortot, there would have been a magnificently brazen level of arrogance to it. We might have missed the genuine electronic thing, but that's a mistake that can be blamed on Leibniz. It was an address that could be almost guaranteed to be safe from official attention. They must have searched the place to the point of exhaustion, but now they'd left and it was a safe bet that they wouldn't be coming back again. The difficulty would be manhandling the bound female Gendarme up and down the stairs, with regret, I crossed that off the list.

That still left the CSF building out on the deserted industrial estate, the offices where we'd started our search for Roland, even better it was only about three kilometres from here. I told the waiter to fetch us some bread and cheese and a couple of apples, partly for Dumont and partly for our breakfast. Even if the diet was going to be a little restricted, there was a telephone, water, toilets and all the privacy we needed.

Dumont was conscious and trying to hide her fright when we returned to the car, she must be in pain from being left tied up for so long, and was probably beginning to panic from the thought that she'd been abandoned. That's generally the best condition for a prisoner, frightened and docile. I wondered if von Strenglen had any weird Prussian intentions for our defenceless female captive, it was a long time until breakfast and he must get a lot of refusals with that hand of his. Were there any frustrated desires, just waiting for an opportunity like this to float unpleasantly to the surface?

I took Dumont through the domestic requirements of lavatory, food and drink and then retied her. I didn't bother with the gag, there was nobody else to hear, and if she caused a problem I could silence her in seconds.

She had some strange idea that I either wanted or needed information from her, and went to some trouble to assure me that she wasn't going to talk - no matter what I did to her. In the end I told her to be quiet, because although her day tomorrow might be a very short one, my own was likely to be quite long. She was surprised by my lack of interest, but sensibly took the opportunity to bed down under some coats that we'd found in a cloakroom. I did likewise, in the same room as her, I wanted to make sure there was no escape or rescue attempt in the night and trusted my own vigilance more than that of my Prussian friend.

I didn't have particularly strong views on whether or not he was going to perform unmentionable acts on her in the night, but if so, then he was going to have to ask me politely to look the other way while he did so. In the end I suspect his embarrassment at having his nominal junior present while he displayed his animal lusts proved stronger than the lusts themselves, and he never turned up. It's always possible that I'd misjudged him, but I very much doubt it.

This morning, after some stale bread and dry cheese I settled myself down by the telephone, it was time to issue some instructions, and after an extremely uncomfortable night with nothing but a couple of old coats between me and the floor, I was in just the mood to do it. While von Strenglen sat with our captive in the next room, I dialled the Montmartre Gendarmerie.

Sir Freddy Villiers
Paris Wednesday/Thursday, May 15/16th. 1940

There was a raw feeling bruise on the side of my head and a trickle of blood running down behind my right ear. I was physically hurt but scarcely astonished by the fact that the woman, who I still had great difficulty thinking of as Heidi, had been able to overcome me quite so easily. I recognised that I was an amateur and she was some sort of professional, the fact that she had successfully hi-jacked me was no more than a reflection of these basic facts. But that wasn't the end of the matter, it was no more than a beginning.

The Sergeant Major with the mobile team of Gendarmes had told me that they had arrived in response to a call from Capitaine Dumont. It seems that as she and I had driven back to Tante Mimi's to collect our bags, travelling in our two separate cars, she had noticed that we were being followed. She had said nothing to me, as she assumed that the following car was more likely to be interested in her, but when I left she had watched what the other car did, and then followed us herself. The Gendarmes had been warned of our route and told to watch out for us.

The fact that Martine had been abducted by this one woman German hit squad was a lot more painful than my bruised head. I needed to take it as a warning signal, a warning that I should have to start operating in a more professional way. She had said to me that her tracing Roland had been achieved by tracking his claim for taxi expenses, and that hadn't needed any experience with a gun or cosh, just what she had described as basic police procedural work. As a retired civil servant I didn't see why my organisational skills should be any less effective than hers.

The authorities would undoubtedly take the abduction of a Gendarme officer seriously, but with the German army getting closer by the hour it had to be admitted they had other concerns, and I felt no compunction about elbowing my way into the investigation. I knew more than anyone about the circumstances and people involved. It was now crystal clear, even to someone as confused as me, that I should have voiced my feelings for Martine. I had been so desperate to avoid making a fool of myself, that in the end that was exactly what I'd managed to do. The road to hell is paved with good intentions, and with the purest of motives I had separated two people who should have stuck together. That was what Tante Mimi had been exasperated by.

But if I'm going to be practical, where to start? What about the scene of the crime? I spoke to the Sergeant Major and asked him to help me look for any of the items which might have fallen from Heidi's bag. Martine's bullet had ripped it open, scattering at least some of the contents on the ground. It was completely dark by now, but unlike London the street lights were all on, and one of the Gendarmes lent me his flashlight.

Working on my hands and knees, I managed to find a small hairbrush, a wallet containing a significant amount of French bank notes, a Yale type door key and a folded piece of paper with a Paris telephone number scribbled on it. Hoping that I wasn't interfering with the investigation too badly, I pocketed the wallet and door key, made a note of the phone number and then virtuously handed the original slip of paper and the hairbrush to one of the officers. The most surprising thing about this wildly untypical behaviour was the complete absence of any sense of guilt. I had a growing sense that I might find myself alone on this one, and that meant the only judges of morality would be success and survival.

Back at Montmartre, I spoke to Major Vernet, the investigating officer. He struck me as an uninspiring specimen, a man destined to follow the rule book and little else. From my meeting with Heidi I didn't imagine her to be a lady much troubled by rule books, and Vernet didn't look like the man to deal with her. The fact that he didn't bother to conceal his view that I was little more than a geriatric nuisance didn't improve my opinion of him. However, one of his junior officers established that the scribbled phone number was situated at the home of one of the Spanish Embassy consular officers. After a degree of arm twisting they agreed to arrange that all calls to or from that number should be, intercepted and recorded at the exchange, there didn't seem to be any Anglo Saxon nonsense about court orders being required. As if to compensate for this cooperation he then made it clear that, despite my previous involvement with Capitaine Dumont, he saw no further place for me in his investigations.

This came as no surprise and not much of a disappointment. Although the kidnapping of one of their own produced a ripple of activity throughout the ranks, I was unconvinced of the depth or likely duration of that activity. His attitude left me with sufficient time to make some arrangements of my own.

Driving my recovered, and only slightly dented car, I returned to the Pension, told Mimi what had happened and apologised for my earlier unwillingness to recognise what was going on under my nose. She reassured me that it wasn't entirely my fault, patting the back of my hand and telling me that, for an Englishman, I wasn't too bad. She even admitted that she had told Martine that as I was so obviously slow on the uptake that she, Martine, would have to give me more of push than most men needed; just to get me started. She asked me is I'd been to boarding school as a boy, and when I confirmed this she gave a 'Well there you are then' sort of look, as if that explained everything. I couldn't argue with her assessment of my emotional abilities, it matched my own conclusion, it had just taken me a lot longer to realise it.

Despite what I had earlier told the German woman, Heidi, the truth of the matter was that the Gendarmerie had in fact shown no interest at all in the magnetron, and seemed to wish only that it would somehow disappear. The general mood was that with the advancing German army, then whoever was holding the magnetron when the music stopped could well have questions to answer to the Gestapo, and they didn't intend that it should be them. This was an approach that I needed to change.

There was a radio shop near the Pension, and after a troubled few hours sleep I made my way there in time for their opening the next morning. I was confident that Heidi would have better things to do than follow my movements, as far as she was concerned she had Martine as the bargaining chip and the Gendarmes had the magnetron, grey haired old Freddy didn't feature. Nonetheless I had a heightened sense of my surroundings as I walked the half mile to the shop, but to my untutored eyes the streets looked innocent of prowling Boche.

One hour later, and back at the Montmartre Gendarmerie, I presented Major Vernet with 150 Francs worth of second hand AC/DC power inverter in a cardboard box, and asked him to take very good care of it. He looked at the box sitting on his desk, at first unwilling even to pick it up. "Is this it?" He gestured cautiously at the box. The expression on his face revealed the depth of his unhappiness at being passed this particular parcel, coupled with the realisation that he couldn't honourably refuse it.

"Yes, it must be safer in your care than mine, with all the trouble it's caused so far it needs to be kept under lock and key."

Fortunately for me, Major Vernet, like the overwhelming majority of the population couldn't tell the difference between an inverter and a magnetron, and didn't know of anyone else who could. This was my trump card, now that Heidi had killed Leibniz she had nobody left to authenticate the product. I was hoping that tent peg would come back to haunt her.

Vernet was polite enough to update me, strictly as a matter of inter governmental courtesy, on the overnight results of the phone tap. Late last night a man, referred to in the conversation as von Strenglen, had called the number to tell them that he hoped to have the device within the next twenty four hours, and could the person on the phone start to make arrangements for them being picked up? The other party had replied, that in view of their earlier bungling and incompetence there would be no arrangements made until they actually had the device in their hands, and that this had better be soon. The phone was then put down in the middle of von Strenglen's further comments. Clearly Heidi and her

187

chum were under a great deal of pressure to come up with the goods.

"Do you have any idea who this von Strenglen is?" I asked

"If it's Gunther von Strenglen, and we think it is, then we have a file on him. He's ex army, about thirty five years old and served on two of Heydrich's Einsatzgruppen action teams last year. He was a professional soldier until he had to retire on medical grounds two years ago."

"Medical grounds?"

Vernet, picked up the report on his desk and looked through it. "Yes, here we are, he lost his right hand when demonstrating a grenade, apparently the fuse mistimed."

"Well that should be easy enough, we just look for somebody with a surprised look and only one hand."

"No, it says that he wears a false hand, and gloves to disguise the fact."

"So, a Nazi madman with a mechanical hand, it sounds like something out of a nightmare."

"I don't know how mechanical it is, but he was obviously so highly regarded that they kept him on, even with a hand missing."

"It doesn't seem to have impressed his contact on the phone last night, from the transcript it sounds as if they've given him and Heidi an ultimatum - get the magnetron, or else."

"Which is why they have resorted to the unheard of and desperate measure of kidnapping one of our officers."

"I must make it clear Major, that I am leaving the magnetron in your hands, solely to safeguard it, my government's position is that it should not be traded with the Germans, no matter what the threat."

"You can safely leave all negotiations to me from now on, Sir Freddy. But I would remind you that the item in question is French state property, although we are obviously grateful to you for returning it to us."

The extent of the lies we were both telling each other was now so great, that it was in danger of becoming obvious. I had a worried moment, wondering if there had been a price ticket on the inverter that I had failed to remove, but on reflection I don't think there was. The Major stood up, extending his hand towards me to be shaken.

"If you will excuse me now, Sir Freddy, I must continue the search for my missing officer."

Back on the street I climbed into the car, already anticipating his next actions and the likely repercussions. With any luck, the two Germans might have taken their eyes off me, everyone was so sure that I was no longer involved. That was good, but I needed to move quickly, and above all carefully, if there was to be any hope of salvaging my earlier mistakes.

Chapter 13

Fraulein Heidi Fuchs
Paris, Thursday morning, May 16th. 1940

"Major Vernet, I am holding one of your officers, Capitaine Martine Dumont, and I imagine that you would like her back, preferably unharmed. Luckily I happen to know that you have the means to secure her release, a certain electronic device which you obtained from that elderly MI6 agent." I paused, to allow him to join in the conversation, it's so often important to let people think that they're making a contribution.

"I don't know what you're talking about, who exactly is this?"

I sighed. Why do some people insist on making such simple matters so pointlessly complicated? I had obviously underestimated his stupidity. Unable to deal with even this brief silence from my end, he prattled on.

"I'm just going to have this call transferred to another extension, please hold on for a moment."

I put the receiver down, lit a cigarette and stared out of the window, it looked as if it was going to be another nice day today. This morning's news bulletin on the Reich's Broadcasting Service had told of further extensive Panzer crossings of the Meuse in the area of Sedan. The British Expeditionary Force seems to be holding itself in reserve, although no one can work out what for, as we have now been advancing non stop through enemy territory for most of the last week.

Perhaps they'll wave their Union Jacks at us as we pass. Whatever they do, nothing now can save the French, or Paris, it's just a matter of time - two or three weeks at most.

That seemed to have been a sufficient delay, I stubbed my cigarette out and dialled the Gendarmerie again.

"I am an officer of German state security, and I have forgotten more about tracing telephone calls than you will ever know. Your stupidity has just caused my associate to hurt Dumont, quite badly, I know that many French women are such sluts they enjoy that sort of thing - but from the way she squealed I don't think she did. If you annoy me again we will hurt her again, more seriously this time. Do you understand me?"

I had kept my tone reasonable up to this point, but when he failed to reply promptly, I thought it was time to wake him up.

"DO YOU UNDERSTAND ME?" I shrieked, in full harridan mode, loudly enough to damage his hearing. Men, particularly bureaucratic little pen pushers like this one, are usually unnerved by irrational and unstable women. A little instability is often a useful tool in the armoury. I visualised his wife as being some dull little mouse who greeted his return home every night with a 'Have you had a good day at the office dear?' or 'Shall I fetch your pipe and slippers, Claude?' Or whatever his bloody name was.

"Yes, yes, I understand." He stammered.

"Is your first name Claude?" I asked. Again there was a pause, as he wondered what the hell I was on about, but he was learning and it wasn't as long as the last pause.

"No, I'm called Henri, but why?" We didn't need to take this any further, he was clearly broken.

"You will remain at your desk until I call you again. When I do so it will be to give you instructions on how and where you will hand over the device. Is that clear?"

"Yes."

"If you wish you may instruct your junior officers to search for us, but in the unlikely event that they find us, we shall kill Dumont first and then you second. Just remember that a Gestapo officer will be sitting in your chair, at your desk, within the next two or three weeks. It might very well be me. Imagine what you're going to say when that day comes."

"There will be no interference, you have my word."

I silently put the phone down on him for the second time this morning. Now I'd leave himsweating for an hour or two, it would ensure his complete cooperation when I did ring him back.

If this man had the sense he was born with, or even a small amount of backbone, he would hand everything over to that weird old man from MI6, but bureaucrats don't work that way. They cling desperately to their own little patch, even if it means their ultimate destruction. I would, bet a month's pay that Vernet had told the old Englishman that his assistance was no longer required, and would he please leave this to the Gendarmerie, the experts. And because the old Englishman had no local organisation and French officialdom was crumbling round his ears, he would have no option but to comply. Vernet would do half my job for me, and the growing antagonism between the French and British played directly into our hands. That was the one thing Leibniz had been right about, their whole structure was rotten, from top to bottom.

Gunther wandered in from the other room, he would have heard most of what I'd said.

"Will they cooperate?" He asked.

"Completely, they're too scared of what will happen after the army gets here. Even so we'll take all normal precautions, this is no time to get sloppy about things. Is she alright?" I flicked my eyes in the direction of the next room.

"She tried threatening me earlier, what her people would do to us when they caught us, that sort of thing - but she didn't even believe it herself. She's gone quiet now." I nodded, hostages often went through cycles of optimism and despair, even though most of them knew there wasn't any real hope. She wasn't stupid and must have worked out that we were only keeping her alive to act as proof that she was still in play as a bargaining counter. Once that usefulness had passed, probably later today, then she would die. Deep inside, she would know this, but would still try to cling to any small glimmers of hope. It's the human way, and it makes the captor's job so much easier if the victim retains some small vestige of hope.

I reached for the Paris street plan, we needed to make our arrangements. By this time Sturmbannfuhrer Gunter von Strenglen, the autocratic much decorated Prussian leader of our team, had finally worked out where brains were and where the real power lay. As long as I pretended to consult him and treated him with some surface display of respect, he would do what he was told.

The trouble would start when we got back to Berlin, he could never allow the possibility of me telling the truth about who actually ran this operation. That would mean he would either try to dispose of me once we had the device, or he would have some plan to discredit me on our return. Even more obviously it wouldn't have occurred to him that I might have worked this out. That's why the Prussians have always been keen to ride only the best horses money could buy, that way at least one of them has some brains.

What we needed was a two or three point route for them to follow at the handover, report here, and pick up a message, and then go there and deliver the device. That way we could dispose of any trailing hit team. It was the uneasy union of two competing requirements: I would have liked crowds in which to hide, and open spaces in which to look for followers, but I couldn't have both. I started by looking at the map.

As there were only two of us left on our team, that made it difficult both to guard and transport our prisoner, whilst simultaneously checking for anyone following the Gendarme's delivery man. The obvious way to deal with this would be to arrange their delivery man's route so that it went round in a circle, with one of us in the middle watching to see if he had a tail. One of us could be sat, for example outside a cafe on the Place de l'Opera, with messages left for them to pick up in two or three different shops, around the four sides of the opera house itself.

But I wasn't happy. That would be complicated and time consuming to set up, I wasn't keen. We didn't have time for complications, we needed a shortcut.

After I'd dropped off the woman and von Strenglen last night, I had ditched the car, stealing them is so easy that I never keep one for more than a day. I wanted the chance to speak to the woman, preferably alone, so asked Gunther if he could go and pick up another one. He looked awkward.

"To be honest it's not something I've ever had to do before." He hesitated, not liking to admit to an inability. "It would probably be faster if you did it."

I had no wish to embarrass him, not yet anyway, and so chose not to make an issue of it. But it did provide a perfect example of the difference between the military and a half way decent street cop. The military put in a requisition chit to central stores and then sit around waiting, while the street cop just goes out and does it.

"That's fine, if you wouldn't mind keeping an eye on her, for a bit longer. I'll be back in half an hour or so."

It actually took me about twenty minutes, and I came back with another anonymous looking car, but something a bit bigger this time. I might need to do some more shunting and grinding, and yesterday's model had buckled rather too much.

I sat down with the phone and dialled my old friend again.

"Listen carefully, I'm going to give you just the one chance to get this right, and if you get any part of it wrong Dumont will be dead, and you will wish that you'd never been born."

"There won't be any mist . . ."

"Shut up and listen. You are are going to be sent to pick up a trail of instructions, each one will tell you where to go to pick up the next. As you travel between each pick up we will be watching you to see if there's anyone following. If there is any suspicion that you are being trailed by anyone, or if you try to use the phone then you know what will happen. Make sure that you have some cash on you, because at least one of the instructions will involve you going on the Metro. Is that clear?"

"Yes, I understand I'll be going on the Metro."

"Take the device in a knapsack, so that it can handled easily, the person you hand it to will know exactly what to look for so it had better not be a brick in the bag. Then at one of the pick up points we will intercept you. Dumont will be tied up in a car nearby, if the device is genuine we will show you where she is. If not, all hell will break loose."

"I promise you that . . ."

"You will be at the south west corner entrance to Galeries Lafayette on the corner of the Rue de Mogador, you will be alone, you will be holding the knapsack in your right hand and you will be there in exactly thirty minutes. You will wait there until someone approaches you, they will say 'I have a message for Claude' and give you a piece of paper. You will then do exactly what it says on that paper."

I put the phone down and looked at Gunther. "The game's afoot Watson."

He looked as puzzled as I knew he would. "Watson?"

Sir Freddy Villiers
Paris, Thursday morning, May 16th. 1940

This morning's BBC news, which I eventually managed to listen to at ten o'clock, after leaving the Gendarmerie, was a revelation. Statements to the effect that French forces are offering *determined resistance*, and that the situation around the German crossings of the River Meuse is *confused*, can mean only one thing. The reality is desperate and the German army is effectively unopposed. Unlike Doctor Goebbels, the BBC rarely tell outright lies, but they can occasionally be very economical with the truth, and this morning's bulletin struck me as a case in point.

My first emotion was what a disaster for European civilisation that the forthcoming bloodbath should be visited on us all twice in a generation, swiftly followed by a feeling of failure. What was it that my own generation could have done to avert this. Someone at my level in the civil service has to be counted as part of the Establishment, which meant that some of the responsibility for this horror lay on my own shoulders. The young men who were already being called on, in increasing numbers, to die for King and Country, could legitimately point their stiff dead fingers at me and my colleagues, and ask; what had we done to prevent this. To which question there could only be one answer: not enough.

After yesterday's adventures and this morning's news I wasn't just looking my age, I was feeling it. But there is only so much wallowing in guilt that I can cope with, and I had already been up to my armpits in the stuff after Martine's abduction. I might not be able to do much about the German army, but perhaps I could have some small effect on the prospects of someone who had gone out of her way to help me.

Major Vernet was a well meaning nobody, he had risen to his level of incompetence and would sit there, blocking the path of better men, until his retirement. Had I been doing the same at the Air Ministry?

No I hadn't, that sort of accusation was both untrue and pointless. It was also a waste of time to spend my day reflecting on how the past might have been lived differently, I needed to concentrate on living today effectively. Mary would have told me to snap out of it, and she would have been right.

What had I got to go on? The Spanish Embassy phone number that had dropped from Heidi's bag had been useful, but only indirectly. The overheard conversation, along with my sighting of them in the car at Montmartre, told me that there were only two of them. A ruthless and thoroughly competent woman with the improbable name of Heidi and, even more

198

bizarrely, this one handed ex soldier called Gunther von Strenglen. A truly odd pair, but the fact remained that they had knocked spots of Martine and myself so far. The only other thing of interest from the phone conversation was the information that their masters, presumably in Berlin, were desperate for this magnetron, and were subjecting them to a great deal of pressure. Would that pressure cause any mistakes?

Then there had been that comment about how they had found Roland's apartment. Heidi had said that it had been because she followed the greedy little bastard's taxi receipts. Presumably those receipts would be for trips from his office to the borrowed apartment, and where would she have found his expenses claim? That could only be at his employer's offices. Heidi and her friend had searched the Paris offices of CSF, but I had never established where they were.

I rang the Montmartre Gendarmerie, I might no longer be welcome in the inner circles of this investigation, but the desk Sergeant, Cesar, still knew me as being British Military Intelligence, a misunderstanding that I had never bothered to correct. Sergeant Cesar knew exactly where they were, on an industrial estate in the north of the city, near the Porte de Clichy.

"But you'll be wasting your time going, there's nobody there, all the staff have been dispersed and they're spread all over the place. I would have put you through to Major Vernet, but he's just had to rush out, I think it's on this same case."

I thanked him, whilst privately thinking that an empty office made perfect sense, it's easier to ransack than an occupied one. And while we're on the subject, if it's empty, what's to stop them staying there? Since this operation had, from their point of view, been derailed by Martine and I, they were operating very much off piste. They were making this stuff up as they went along, just like me, which meant they probably hadn't considered the need for a safe house to be made available. If Vernet had just rushed out, then he was probably meeting Heidi, and whether they spotted the dud magnetron or not, that meant that Martine could soon be surplus to requirements. Well surplus to their requirements anyway.

Being the consummate master spy that I am, I had made a mess of Tante Mimi's bathroom this morning, using half a bottle of her black hair dye. I might have looked like something the cat had dragged in, but I didn't look like me. The eyebrows were particularly fearsome. I had then begged a pair of her dead husband's glasses, from which I had pushed out the lenses. That, together with one of his old trilbies made me look a good deal more French and even a few years younger. Mimi had stood back to give me the once over, before delivering her accolade: 'Not bad'. My final touch was to buy a packet of Gauloises and a box of matches, they tasted rough but at least I would smell right.

Armed with the CSF office address and my new look, but with absolutely no plan beyond that, I set off.

Following the Sergeant's directions took me easily and quickly to the Zone Industrielle, near the railway marshalling yards by the Porte de Clichy. As I drove into the estate, a black Citroen 8CV drove out, Heidi was at the wheel, and as we passed she gave me a hard stare. My heart stopped and I almost swallowed the unlit cigarette I had wedged in the corner of my mouth, but somehow I kept driving. Her stare had included no element of recognition, and I managed to avoid turning my head to stare back at her. There had been at least one other figure glimpsed in the back, but male or female I couldn't say. As I watched in the mirror, no face showed itself in their back window, which it probably would have done if she had made any sort of comment.

It required no deductive process at all to realise that they were going to meet Vernet, and if there were two of them in the car then Martine was probably either dead already, or in the car with them. Unless - unless they had taken a chance on leaving her tied up, while they went to collect the magnetron. I had to check.

I drove steadily on until they turned the corner, unsuspecting our encounter, then I put my foot down for the last two hundred yards to the CSF building. The Yale type key from Heidi's handbag fitted the door, and I ran in. As I ran I shouted, "Martine, Martine." There was no answer, no sound at all. It felt like a dead building. I raced from door to door looking in every office, without any thought that there might be someone lying in wait for me. There were unmistakeable signs that this was their hideaway; makeshift beds, food and drink, but nobody here, and more importantly no body here.

I was suddenly overcome by the idea that I should have followed them, and now I'd let them go, and if she wasn't here then they must have had Martine with them.

Then, just as rapidly, I changed my mind, no, I shouldn't have followed them. The idea that I could act as a tail, pushing my way unnoticed through crowded city streets, behind someone as wily and experienced as that woman was a ridiculous thought.

Then I realised that I was standing next to a desk with a telephone on it, they all had telephones on them, that was the other attraction of staying here, the phones. I picked one up and found there was dialling tone, I rang Sergeant Cesar. He had struck me as a solid old style copper, and I was betting that he had a very clear idea of Vernet's abilities.

"I know that you aren't supposed to tell me, but I promise you that Martine Dumont's life is in immediate danger. Vernet was going to meet the Germans with that device I left on his desk this morning - wasn't he?"

There was a long pause, during which I could hear nothing but deep breathing, he was weighing up the pros and cons. I couldn't wait.

"Is there anyone else stood near you who can hear what you're saying?"

"No, there's just me, I can talk."

"Listen, Vernet thinks he can outwit the German woman, but he can't, and when he fails they will kill Martine, if they haven't already done so. Would you trust your wife's life to Vernet's skill?"

"It's Martine is it?" He asked, but did he mean: 'So that's the way it is', or did he mean, 'So the hostage is Capitaine Dumont?'

I didn't care, it was the same answer. "Yes it's Martine. Please tell me, and I might be in time to do something about it."

"I never said this, but he's gone to meet someone at the south west entrance to Galeries Lafayette, at the junction of Boulevard Haussmann and the Rue de Mogador, and he's taken that thing you gave him in a box. He's supposed to be getting instructions to go somewhere else from there."

I think that I'd said 'Thank you' before I put the phone down, but it was close.

I knew Galeries Lafayette, everyone knows the place. It's the biggest department store in France, and a magnet for tourists, second only to the Eiffel Tower, and probably even busier. The crowds would make it easy for the Germans to lose themselves, but they would also make it easier for an unsuspected watcher to observe events. This was going to be fun. But before I took to the road again there was one minor point to sort out; how exactly does one get there from here. Somewhere round this office there had to be a street map of Paris.

Chapter 14

Fraulein Heidi Fuchs
Paris, Thursday midday, May 16th. 1940

Boulevard Haussmann was busy, there were cars queued up in both directions and the pavements thronged with people. The streets around Galeries Lafayette were even more crowded than the rest, with well dressed, comfortable looking people, bustling self assuredly about their very important business.

Who were they all? We were in the opening stages of what could turn out to be the biggest and most destructive war in history, and these people had decided to go shopping. Not just any shopping, Galeries Lafayette wasn't the sort of place you came to stock up on emergency supplies of corned beef and condensed milk. From what I knew of this place it was where you came to buy another chic evening dress for a visit to the opera, or some exotic lingerie with which to titillate your jaded middle aged husband.

By this time next month all the flags on the public buildings would have changed, and the military uniforms would be ours rather than theirs, but the sleek well fed people would still be here. The top layer of society didn't much care who's flag they saluted, they took pride in their ability to be as comfortable on Unter den Linden as on Boulevard Haussmann. It was always the little people, like me, who didn't fit in. One of the incidental pleasures of my work is the occasional chance to poke such people firmly in the eye, strictly in the course of duty, you understand.

"Lieber Gott, just look at them." Von Strenglen's voice came from the back seat, where he was sitting with the securely bound Capitaine Dumont." They seem to think the Panzers are coming to hand out flowers." For once the Prussian view of life coincided with my own. Dumont herself offered no comment, possibly because von Strenglen had said he would shoot her if she did.

What the crowds on the pavements hadn't realised was the scale of the changes that would follow our arrival. True, there would be the usual gang of well connected turncoats, all keen to kiss the Nazi arse, but there were going to be some surprised and unhappy people when they finally realised that National Socialism was more than just a slogan. The forthcoming racial purification would involve permanent changes, and a whole swathe of these fur clad freeloaders would need to run for their lives, or lose them. When the patient has cancer, the doctor reaches for his knife. That's the difference between the old France and the new Germany - belief - belief in core values and the willingness to do something about it.

I spotted the scared looking man who must be Major Vernet, standing on the street corner, outside one of the main entrances, clutching a black knapsack. The crowds swirled around him, but he remained rooted to the spot. He was scanning the passing faces, looking for his contact, I took care not to stare at him as I swung the car round the corner into the side street.

The street down the side of the department store, Rue de Mogador, had a row of garish stalls along the pavement, covered in hanging scarves and multi coloured wraps, all staffed by Africans. I couldn't work out why the store tolerated such competition, literally on their own doorstep, and especially from such obviously illegal immigrants. Yet at least it could be seen that these people worked for their living, unlike so many of their customers. As long as they knew their place and kept to it, they would have no problems from us. From what I'd heard on the radio, the French black colonial regiments were just about the only ones not to have deserted.

I pulled in to the pavement, near the back of the store, I was sure von Strenglen could sort out any parking problem.

"I'm not rushing this, so I could be fifteen minutes or more," I said. "I'll leave the keys in the ignition, then if you have to move - just keep driving round the block until you see me."

I entered the store through the side entrance, into the ground floor displays of perfumes and cosmetics. The effect of so many competing scents was, to me, the smell of money. There was a battalion of interchangeable assistants, all extremely thin, all dressed in black and white, and all of them wearing too much make up. If it weren't for the name badges, only their mothers could tell them apart.

I walked slowly to the middle of the ground floor, I had had no idea of the scale of this place, the whole centre of the building was open all the way up to the roof, except that it wasn't a roof at all, but a cathedral size massive glass dome. All around the sides of this open space were the balconies of the upper sales floors, like theatre balconies, one on top of another, up and up. Just for the briefest flicker of a moment I wished that I were the idle wife of a wealthy man, and able to spend my days and my husband's money moving easily between places like this. I shook my head to dismiss the thought, I was here to serve my country, not to be seduced by their superficial elegance.

As I moved from the perfumes to the expensive watches, Rolex and Longines all around me, I casually pretended to look at each of the counters, as if they could possibly be of interest to me. I was aware that I didn't fit in, my make up free face, my plainly brushed hair and my workday clothes, none of them fitted in; but that wasn't the important part. The important part was, that as long as I didn't do anything loudly obvious, then I could hope to spot trouble before trouble spotted me. The angle of my body and my face were directed to the extravagant displays of luxury items, piled high in every direction, but my eyes were looking at the customers.

If the Gendarmes had tried to put anyone into the area, they would stand out as intruders, being even less at home than me. I hadn't allowed Vernet sufficient time to arrange for suitably dressed female officers, if they were here they'd be easy to spot. I didn't spot them - so they weren't here, but I did another complete circuit of the ground floor, looking through the entrance doors as I passed. There was nothing, Vernet was clean I was sure of it, he had no back up. Time to hit the mark.

I walked out of the corner door, he was standing in front of me, his back towards me. By now he had been standing here for about twenty minutes and was almost uncontrollably nervous, hopping from one foot to the other, as though desperate for a pee. I was holding my gun in a new handbag, the last one having been abandoned yesterday.

He was going to be surprised that there was no set of instructions for him to follow, and no trip on the Metro, just me, taking what I wanted. As I moved through the crowd, to take control of Vernet and claim my prize, a heavy hand clamped itself onto my left shoulder, I froze.

"Excuse me Madame, could I enquire what you have in your bag please?" I slowly swung my head to look behind me. A tall almost square woman, who must have weighed ninety kilos, was standing very close behind, and staring down at me with a hard 'You can't fool me' sort of look. She was a comic book version of a store detective, and she had no intention of letting go of my shoulder, not until she knew what was in the bag. Of the many competing desires that flesh is heir to - she was going to find that a particularly unfortunate one.

I smiled at her. "Certainly officer, if I could just turn around, I'll be happy to show you." I used my little girl's voice, it makes me sound half witted. And calling them officer is usually another good move, private security staff are often failed police applicants, it makes them feel good to be mistaken for the law. Her eyes flicked briefly around the nearby crowd and then, confident that none of them looked liked my accomplices, she relaxed her grip slightly. She was a powerfully built dyke, and probably shaved more often than Gunther, she was also well aware that she could deal with me with one hand tied behind her back.

As I turned to face her, I did exactly the same thing that she'd just done, I scanned the crowd to see if she had a colleague. She didn't, which meant that it was time to say Goodnight Bertha, this wasn't the moment for a cosy chat and some girl talk. I pushed the muzzle end of the bag into her belly and fired, angling the shot steeply upwards, for maximum internal damage. She did nothing theatrical, like staggering around clutching herself and moaning, she just went down like a sack of potatoes being dropped on the floor. An extremely large and unevenly shaped sack of potatoes. Unfortunately, the shot rang out more sharply than I'd hoped, the metal and glass canopy over our heads seemed to have magnified it.

There were screams from the women nearest to us, and people stopped to stare. The previously mobile and flowing crowd had formed a circle round me, and congealed into an audience.

Not caring who saw the gun, I pushed through the crowd, towards the street corner. Vernet was next, where the hell was he? I reached the edge of the pavement, but there was no sign of him, I turned and looked back towards the shop doorway, just the same crowd - but this time with their mouths open. My plan was beyond salvage, it was in ruins.

Across the road two patrolling *flics* had spotted the crowd, and might even have heard the shot. They were crossing the road to investigate. Behind me, one of the idiot women in the crowd had finally worked out that the dyke on the pavement was dead, so not knowing what else to do, she began to scream, "She's dead, she's dead." I should have shot her as well.

Instead I ran round the corner, past the multi coloured African stalls, wondering what I would do if Gunther had moved the car. He hadn't, I flung myself into the drivers seat, groped for the ignition key and got us moving.

"Is there some sort of problem?" He asked, in exactly the wrong tone of voice.

"It was a set up - so you just shut your mouth and keep your eyes on that bitch." I was still breathing deeply and on an emotional hair trigger, it would only take a very small provocation to trigger a large explosion. The fact that it had been a massive cock up, rather than a deliberate set up, was not something I felt inclined to share with the Sturmbannfuhrer right now. As I looked for our fastest way out of here, he kept quiet, which was the smartest thing he'd done all day.

I followed the Rue de Mogador until it became the Rue de Clichy, then with a sigh of relief I knew where I was. I had no plans to stay at the CSF offices indefinitely, but right now I just wanted to get off the streets and think about what came next, and CSF was the easiest way to accomplish that.

"Can I speak?" It was the woman Gendarme.

"Go on."

"Vernet didn't organise a trap, he isn't capable. Whatever happened, he would have done whatever you told him."

"So what do you think happened?"

"I don't know, I didn't see it, but I'm sure that if something went wrong it can't have been Vernet. If you tell him to set up another meeting, I'm sure he'll do it."

"That's very helpful, but I preferred you with your mouth shut."

The really annoying thing about that sort of comment was that I agreed with it. Vernet hadn't organised this disaster, the question was - had anybody? I don't believe in accidents and coincidences, not if there's any possible alternative. Could it just have been a nosy store detective getting in over her head, and Vernet then running away when he heard the shot? Or was the old Englishman involved? They're cold and sly the English, they keep everything buttoned up, especially MI6, who seem to crop up everywhere they're not wanted.

Was he cold enough to abandon the Frenchwoman? Yes, I think he was. People say that we're arrogant, but it's the English who have that phrase: 'The wogs begin at Calais'. What a collection of arrogant bastards. That's why he'd ignored her advances, it wasn't that he didn't understand what was going on, it was simply that from his point of view she was just another wog. Someone like him probably wouldn't even put the end of his walking stick up a Frenchwoman, never mind anything else. Mind you she should be grateful - considering where his walking stick had been. I wondered if the English had a word for *untermenschen?*

It was going to be a sad end for our captive if neither MI6 nor her own people thought she was worth trading. She was smart, and had used the excuse of getting me to take her to the lavatory, so that she could say privately that she thought Gunther was running his own agenda. Of course he was, I already knew that. But it had been a worthwhile effort from someone with no other cards to play; to try and make me see her as human being, and put a wedge between the two remaining Krauts. She just hadn't realised that sort of thing was never going to work with me.

Still, I'd be sorry to kill her, she'd been close to catching up with me, I could almost imagine working with her. Her associates were even worse than mine, a deranged English assassin, who could benefit from a session with that Jewish charlatan Freud, and a shitty little bungler like Vernet. But there are certain rules I never break, and once her value reached zero, then she was gone - she had to be.

I left it to Gunther to manhandle her into the offices. The close contact should give one of them a thrill, while I left the car outside another empty unit, three along. When I got back Gunther had sensibly begun to make coffee, so I lit a cigarette and looked around for the street map, to see if there was another location as convenient as the last one should have been. I couldn't see it, so I called through to the next room.

"Gunther, where have you put the Paris map?"

"You had it in the car."

"No, there's one in the car, and it's still there. There's another one in the office, where have you put it?"

"I haven't touched it."

I looked around the office again, but this time I viewed it as a crime scene. I knew exactly where I'd left the map, and it wasn't there. I also knew where I'd left the telephone on that same desk, and it had been moved from the middle to the end.

"Gunther, come in here - quickly - we've had visitors."

Sir Freddy Villiers
Paris, Thursday afternoon, May 16th. 1940

I had no concern for the French traffic laws and neither, it seemed, did most of the other drivers. If Martine was about to be traded, like a piece of livestock, then I wanted to be there. I pushed my way through the afternoon traffic with abandon and frequent use of the horn.

If it was possible to make a mess of this transaction then Vernet was the man to do it, and that's assuming the Germans had any intention of honouring the deal, a ridiculous concept in itself. As far as Martine was concerned, Vernet and the Germans were completely at one, neither of them gave a damn whether she lived or died. It looked as though the only people to take an interest were myself and Tante Mimi, and she was even older than me, the poor old dear.

The huge bulk of Galeries Lafayette loomed ahead of me. Mary had bought a dress here on our last visit to the city, it was probably still in the wardrobe at home, I haven't been able to face clearing her things out just yet. If my memory of the map was correct, this should be the Rue de Mogador, I craned my neck to look for street signs, yes, that's it, I'm on the right street. So the meeting point must be up there on the corner, behind the clutter of pavement stalls. There were pedestrians everywhere, even in the road, I nosed my way through enough of them to reach the kerb, and set off on foot. Two things were readily apparent; first, I was at the right spot and second, I was too late.

A crowd of shoppers, mostly well dressed women, were gathered round to look at something or someone lying on the ground. Not really wanting to look, but knowing that I had to, I elbowed my way through. The fallen figure of a large woman in a severe blue suit, was lying on the pavement, she had fallen on her back and there was a large spread of blood across the front of her jacket, she looked to be unmistakeably dead. I could feel the involuntary release of breath, as I saw that it wasn't Martine lying there, I hadn't realised I'd been so tense.

The crowd had formed a circle around the woman, at a distance of about ten feet, but standing by her head were two men in suits, chatting casually and managing to ignore her. They were some form of authority, and were demonstrating their professionalism by taking no notice of the dead woman at their feet. A little way apart was Major Vernet, clutching a black knapsack to his chest and talking to two uniformed Gendarmes.

"No, I saw her, she was right there." He pointed back to the body. "A madwoman with a gun. She just shot that lady, point blank. I've never seen anything like it. Naturally I tried to intervene, but I wasn't close enough. As soon as she'd shot the woman she ran away, before I could get to her."

I recognised this self justifying tosh as being no more than a distant relative of the truth. My bet was that if Heidi, for whatever reason, had shot this woman, her next move would have been to shoot Vernet and take the knapsack, Vernet hadn't tried to intervene, because if he had he would have been lying there dead, next to the big woman. Something had spooked Heidi and she'd shot her way clear, but had been obliged to leave empty handed. As soon as Vernet heard that shot he must have taken to his toes, that's why he was still alive, and it's also why he was still completely useless.

Confidently concealed behind my black hair, glasses, hat and drooping Gauloise, I sauntered easily round the crowd; just another passer by seeing what all the fuss was about. I paused by two middle aged women. "What's happened?"

They turned to me, acknowledging a shared interest in watching someone else's misfortune. "She was just doing her job, she'd obviously spotted there was something funny going on. Then the woman she was following pulled out a gun and shot her."

"So the dead woman was a store detective?"

"That's right. She'd followed this hard looking piece out onto the pavement, and then asked her what she'd got in her bag. And now look what's happened, just for doing her job."

I sucked my teeth; I imagined that people who habitually had cigarettes drooping from their mouths probably sucked their teeth quite a lot. "There are some real bastards about."

The other woman leaned forward, to share a confidence. "Gypsies, take my word for it. It's the east Europeans, they're all gypsies, and they've all got guns."

The three of us nodded our agreement. I gently eased myself away and headed back to the car. There was a police officer standing next to it, he had his notebook in one hand and was feeling for a pencil with the other.

"I'm sorry about the car officer, but I saw the woman escaping from the shooting, while I was driving past, so I stopped. Then that Major Vernet wanted me to give a statement." I pointed back towards the store entrance. "He said the car would be safe here for a while." The officer silently replaced the notebook in his pocket, touched the tip of his cap and left.

Those Nazis have got a lot to answer for, if I ever get out of this in one piece my moral standards are going to be in a shocking state. I now find myself myself lying quite fluently, without a second thought, and to policemen of all people.

Driving back up the Boulevard de Clichy, heading once again to the CSF offices, I was aware that it was a waste of time, but it was waste of time that had to be gone through. I had to see if she had gone back there. But as the Boulevard came to the entrance to the Place de Clichy, the traffic was at a standstill, one car had run into the side of another at the traffic lights. This time it wasn't an ambush, the two drivers had emerged and were stood in the middle of the road, squaring up to each other, with a great deal of noise and Gallic huff and puff. Beyond them, the traffic in the square itself was flowing freely. I sounded my horn, but was ignored by everyone. I waited for an impatient two minutes, for the combatants to either do something or just go away, but they didn't.

This was intolerable, even if Martine was still alive at the moment, she might not be for long. I shunted my car backwards and forwards two or three times to get out of the queue, and then drove down the wrong side of the road - clearing the oncoming traffic with my lights and horn. One advancing driver seemed unwilling to move over and put his arm out to shake a fist at me, thinking this might deter me. I accelerated directly towards him, ready to change his attitude with the front of my car, at the very last moment he swerved out of my path, his eyes wide in astonishment. Later I would be appalled by this performance, but at the time I was breathless and exhilarated.

Entering the Zone Industrielle I slowed down, hoping to pass as an innocent third party, but it made no difference for as I rounded the last corner the building looked unchanged, and there were no cars parked in front of it. I let myself in once again, using the key from the pavement, and then paused just inside the door, suddenly aware of the folly of my behaviour. What did I think was going to happen if the German woman was here, never mind her single handed henchman? I stood with my back to the inside of the closed front door, acknowledging that this level of audacity was little better than madness. I should have called the police rather than charging in as a solitary knight errant, but it was too late to run away now.

I tried to calm myself, and looked around for a weapon, before remembering that I was already holding my cleaned up walking stick - that should sort the Gestapo out. Take a deep breath and go for it.

Finding the place once more deserted came as a slight let down, although when I felt it, the coffee pot was still warm - very Marie Celeste. I must have missed them by minutes. I couldn't decide whether to be annoyed or grateful for that delay at the Place de Clichy, it had caused me to miss Martine, but almost certainly saved my life. So probably a good thing.

Thinking about it, I knew why they'd gone. Heidi was smart, she would have spotted at once that someone had been blundering round the office, leaving items in different places - oh, and don't forget, I'd stolen their street map. In the same way that shouting abuse at oncoming traffic was newly acquired skill, I was also going to need some improvement in my breaking and entering technique. I went back to the coffee pot, it wasn't just warm it was actually quite hot, so I poured myself a cup and thought about my position.

The sensible course would be to recognise that I'd chased this particular fox about as far as I could, but now it had gone to earth and I was stumped. Martine had never been my responsibility and certainly wasn't now. She and I had had certain interests in common for a while, but that moment had passed, and any foolish notions I had ever entertained of there being an attraction between us were just that: foolish. She was a serving officer of the French Gendarmerie and had the full professional resources of that organisation available to assist her, not some damn fool old man with a walking stick.

I took another sip of coffee and stared out of the dusty window at the car I had just been using as a battering ram, and I knew that all this careful rationalisation was just evasive nonsense. If the fox had gone to earth then it was time to reach for a shovel and start digging.

That phrase: 'The full professional resources of the Gendarmerie', was just another way of saying, Major Vernet, and he was a waste of space. He was already trying distance himself from the fiasco at Galeries Lafayette, and he wasn't about to get any better. As the Wehrmacht moved unstoppably towards the capital, French administrative life was moving into a state of suspended animation. No matter what local newspaper and radio bulletins were saying about throwing back the invader, the mood amongst a lot of public officials was not to do anything which might upset your new employers, and chasing Heidi would most certainly do that.

I had no idea where to look next, all they had to do was break into another empty office or house, and with the number of people leaving town there were plenty of those around. Once they'd done that I would have no way of tracking them. They had used a different car each time I'd seen them, so that wasn't much help. Even I knew that cars were supposed to be easy to steal, well perhaps not for me, but certainly for someone like her.

Their next move would probably involve contacting Vernet again, as they believed that he had the magnetron, but that wouldn't help me as he would deny everything if I asked him. That is assuming that he even bothered to try and arrange another swap, it meant nothing to him if Martine took a bullet, just as long as he didn't. There had to be some other way; if Mohammed won't go to the mountain, then the mountain will come to Mohammed. If I can't go to them, what can I do to encourage them to come to me? What can I do that will annoy Heidi sufficiently to make her come looking for me?

Short of taking out an advertisement in the local newspaper, or putting a long distance call through to Berlin, there was still one possible method of communication. The Spanish Embassy man's home phone number. I poured myself another cup of what was, by now, slightly tepid coffee, and thought of how best to use it.

219

Chapter 15

Fraulein Heidi Fuchs
Paris, Thursday evening, May 16th. 1940

Von Strenglen came through to my office to see what the problem was, and I explained the signs of there having been someone else in the building.

He was dismissive. "It could have been anybody," he said, "Just some petty thief going through the empty buildings around here, looking to see what he could steal."

I looked at him in astonishment, this wasn't even worth having an argument about. The only possible reason for saying such a stupid thing could be that he was unable to bring himself to accept my superior observation and judgment. He had seen everything that I had seen, and reached absolutely no conclusion whatsoever. Yet when I politely point out the obvious, he prefers to bury his head in the sand and wait for someone to kick him up the arse. Perhaps Prussians enjoy being kicked up the arse, well I don't. This whole relationship was approaching a tipping point much faster that I'd intended; I needed to keep the show on the road for another 24 hours, after which Gunther's value would have sunk to absolute zero - with the inevitable consequence for his continued wellbeing.

I swallowed my sarcastic retort and concentrated instead on taking him seriously, for as long as I possibly could. "I don't think so, when I walked back from parking the car, none of the other buildings showed any sign of a break in. We have to assume that this is the result of someone either following us, or following exactly the same clues as us. Whoever it is, they now know that we're staying here."

"Who do you think it could be?"

"Well I'd bet my Saturday night knickers it's not the Gendarmes, and that pretty much leaves us with the mad old MI6 man."

"The sooner he gets taken care of, the better."

I was grateful to him for this razor sharp tactical assessment, and nodded my considered agreement.

"One last thing, before we leave here. You can use this phone to speak to your Spanish Embassy contact and tell them that we'll have the device tomorrow, so they'll need to get the pick up aircraft organised, because we'll probably be in a hurry."

"They refused to discuss it last time."

"You just tell them that if they want this bloody thing, whatever it is, then that's the deal. I get the device, they produce the transport and we bugger off back to Berlin - I'll do the Eiffel Tower next time I'm here."

"How can you be so sure you'll get it tomorrow?"

"I can't be sure the sun will come up tomorrow, but sooner or later one of us needs to take control of this continuing cock up, and tomorrow's as good a day as any. Besides, the army's only 130 kilometres away, so things might be about to turn very ugly indeed around here. I've got a doctor's note excusing me from artillery fire and aerial bombardment, so I say we go with tomorrow. Alright?"

He didn't look happy, his last conversation with this man had been a humiliating experience for him, but we all have our problems to deal with and this was one of his. Then I had another thought.

"Just remember he's Spanish, and Franco would never have got into power without the Condor Legion and Luftwaffe pilots. We bombed the shit out of Guernica on his account; perhaps he'd like us to do the same to Madrid on our own account. You don't need to take any crap from a fat little tosser like that."

I left him to it and went to bring the car round; I didn't want Dumont visible to any watchers for a moment longer than was necessary. When I got back in the office he was bursting with pride, he'd clearly put the man in his place, it's amazing what some people can do - if you only tell them how. The next thing he'd be telling me it was all his idea.

"They say that a Fieseler Storch will be on standby at a forward air base from noon tomorrow, and will be available to take off at one hour's notice and will then need another hour to reach Paris. From what I've seen of them previously, as long as it has something like seventy or eighty metres of ground run it should get off with both of us, and the pilot."

I wasn't sure if either of us really believed it would need that much lifting capacity, we were both privately imagining a solo departure, with the subsequent ability to write the mission report just the way we wanted it.

He pulled out his pistol. "I'll just go and deal with Dumont." He said, operating the slide to chamber a round.

"Deal with her?" I said in surprise.

"Well we can hardly take her into a hotel with us, and she was no use last time, so we need to get rid of her."

"Like hell we do. We're still a long way from friendly forces, and she's a senior Gendarme officer, which makes her a valuable hostage. As long as we can produce her with a gun to her head we can talk our way out of trouble. Her life might not mean much to the MI6 man, but most French police would hesitate to pull the trigger if they thought that she was going to die with us. Until we're ready to climb in the plane, we keep her in one piece."

He shrugged and uncocked the pistol, but then smiled unpleasantly. "Does that mean you're keen on her?"

"You know what I'm like, show me a Frenchwoman who hasn't had a bath for three days, and I'm panting." He made a disgusted face, but I was thinking - that might not be such a bad idea. You can miss out on a lot in life by being too picky.

"So where do we stay tonight, if we're dragging her around with us?"

I sighed. "God knows, but I'll find somewhere."

I couldn't be bothered to replace the car, if the police had known the number they would have picked us up this afternoon, but nobody had so much as looked at us. There had to be an upmarket housing area, somewhere the houses had individual drives, but this wasn't it. I'd seen some suitable areas between here and the middle of town, so I headed that way. In fifteen minutes I had us on a quiet tree lined avenue, with large individual houses set back from the road.

Two slow trips up and down the road, identified the likely prospects. I parked on the street and walked up the first drive, there no lights showing and it was seven thirty in the evening, if it was occupied then somebody should be home. I rang the front door bell and waited, then I rang it again. A light came on in the hall, I straightened my skirt and smoothed down my hair. An elderly gentleman opened the door. "Can I help you?"

"I'm awfully sorry to disturb you, but I'm looking for a Madame van de Meeren, she's a Dutch lady, my aunt.

I'm afraid that all I know is that she lives at fifty something along this road." I let my eyes wander to his own house number of fifty two.

He didn't know her and apologised for this omission, explaining that in this sort of area people often didn't know much about their neighbours. He then expressed his regret for what the Boche were doing to my homeland. We parted friends.

I walked along for another five houses, to the next prospect. This time nobody came, even after repeated ringing, so I looked through the windows. It was just what I wanted, there were dust sheets over the furniture. The drive continued round to the back of the property, there was still just enough daylight not to need a torch, but not for long. I took out the long screwdriver I had with me and forced open a window. There was a board in the back hall, with carefully labelled keys hanging in a neat row, I took the back door key and let myself out to fetch the car.

The larder was well stocked with tinned goods and the immersion heater soon produced enough water for baths, it was like staying at the Ritz. As I found a secure bathroom in which to let Dumont wash herself and her clothes, she used the opportunity of us being alone together to speak to me.

"I heard what happened earlier between you and the man, and I just wanted to thank you. I can imagine how difficult it must be for you, always having to guard what you say for fear of bringing the situation to a head. You do realise, don't you, that no matter what happens to me, and even if you get the magnetron, he will never let you get back to Germany alive?"

"You're a smart woman Dumont, but don't get too smart for your own good. You'll never succeed in playing mind games with me, because I don't give a damn about a lot of the things that other people care about. If it's necessary for my mission, I'll kill you as soon as look at you."

She said nothing, but looked at me for a moment, with an expression on her face that said; 'Will you, will you really?'

She had come very close to going too far, and might even have done so, because, as she suspected, the truth of the matter was that I didn't actually know if I was going to kill her. Despite the surface gloss she had originally presented, there was something of me about her, and not just a willingness to drag into the open things that others would prefer hidden, but also a depth of perception that most people couldn't approach. It had been dangerous for her to be that open, I hadn't realised the strength of the similarity.

So on reflection this wasn't going to help her, I was never going to allow another one of me onto the streets. Nothing had changed, she was expendable, just like von Strenglen - if not more so.

Sir Freddy Villiers
Paris, Thursday night, May 16th. 1940

The Spanish Embassy contact had to be worth some attention. Perhaps I could simply call them and make an offer for it, somebody in this chain of events must be susceptible to bribery. The trouble was that all the world and his wife knew, for an absolute fact, that the Germans were going to win this war. The Germans, the French, the Russians and most of all the Americans, they all thought so. The American Ambassador in London, Joe Kennedy, was an unashamed and enthusiastic admirer of Hitler's new Germany. You would need to be blind or British not to see which way the wind was blowing. So this was always going to be about much more than a financial transaction, it was about being on the winning side. There wasn't enough money in the world to cover that point.

Similarly, with an approach to Vernet. True, he was an incompetent nobody, but more than that, he was a French incompetent nobody. This meant that his view of my countrymen was coloured by the forthcoming French defeat at German hands. He might not be sure exactly *how* this was the fault of the British, but he knew that somehow or other that is what it would turn out to be. He would give me nothing that he didn't have to. I was hedged in, with no resources to rely on, but my own, and no reinforcements to summon. Even the British Embassy had turned me down, and I couldn't blame them.

The unpalatable fact about the German woman was that she was good at what she did. Maybe if the original team that I'd flown in with had not been shot down and killed, then they might have dealt with her. But they had been, and in the event she'd only had to deal with me, which had caused her no trouble at all. Compounding my inadequacy with Heidi, had been my inability to respond to the simplest of human feelings when it came to Martine. If she and I had been together, she would never have been in a position to be captured.

I recognised that I was talking myself into a depression, I should stop being so gloomy and try to look for the positive aspects. So I tried, but there weren't any, it was not a helpful exercise. However, the one luxury of being at the bottom of a hole is that every direction is up. I had nothing to lose, whatever I did couldn't make things any worse. I reached for the phone.

After two rings the receiver was lifted and a Hispanic voice said simply: "Ola."

"Good evening Senor, my name is Grand, Major Lawrence Grand of British Military Intelligence. I understand that you are acting as a clearing house for offers on the Ponte magnetron."

As I don't speak Spanish, I was using French, it would be inconceivable that the other party didn't speak it. Grand's name had seemed a better bet than my own, they would probably have it on file somewhere, and no one likes to sound like a one man band.

"Good evening Major Grand, I regret that I cannot help you, in fact I don't know what you are talking about." He pronounced Major in the Spanish fashion as Mayor, which always seems to take me by surprise. His voice had been too slow, he was trying to do something else at the same time as he was talking to me. If my guess was right, he should be scribbling a note to someone, telling them to do something - urgently.

"The Ponte magnetron, that is the cavity magnetron developed by Professor Maurice Ponte. Certain agents, with whom you are in touch, collected this today at Galeries Lafayette, from an officer of the French Gendarmerie. We have been informed that your team now wish to sell this item to the highest bidder, we simply wish to register our interest, and enquire if there is any particular figure that you have in mind?"

"Where did you obtain this telephone number? There are very few people to whom I would give this, so you will understand my curiosity."

"I understand completely Senor, but you in turn must understand my own reluctance to enter more fully into such operational details. I think we should both simply be happy that we can speak to one another. Should we come to a financial agreement, on behalf of our respective principals, then perhaps such matters could be discussed more fully."

"One moment, if you please."

There was the sound of a hand being placed across the receiver, and the vague sibilant murmurings of an inaudible conversation. Although the words themselves could not be distinguished, at least part of the conversation sounded angry. The delay was extended, but I hung on the line and eventually the hand was removed and he returned.

"Mayor, I know nothing of these matters personally, although I did hear a report on the radio of some disturbance at that location, I understand that the two parties involved did not actually meet each other."

"On the contrary, the hand over most certainly took place, one of my own agents witnessed it personally. If we weren't sure of this we would scarcely be offering to pay you a large sum of money for something you don't have. The female agent collecting the item, which was contained in a black knapsack, was observed leaving the scene carrying it. There was then a diversionary performance carried out by two Gendarmerie agents, in which a female employee of the store pretended to be shot."

"Why would such people produce this performance? I do not understand their purpose."

"I must confess that puzzled us at first, but now I see why. They don't wish it generally known that they have the item, I would imagine they seek to conceal this fact from their original employers, the Germans, in order to be free to offer it discretely to certain interested parties. However, this is of no interest to us, we merely wish to acquire the magnetron. We understand that the Russians have already made an offer, and we are willing to increase that by twenty five per cent. Would that be acceptable?"

"Mayor, I am afraid there are certain matters here requiring my urgent attention, is there perhaps a telephone number on which I may reach you?"

"I think it would be better if I called you again tomorrow morning, but please be aware that my government will only be interested in making this offer for another twenty four hours. We would be unwilling for the product to be inspected by every other potential buyer before acquiring it ourselves."

"I quite understand. Good night Mayor."

I replaced the receiver and wondered if I had done enough, not merely to inconvenience Heidi, but to enrage her. An enraged opponent just might be a careless opponent. There is a precept that if you're going to lie at all, then the closer you keep your lies to the truth, the safer you will be. I felt my recent efforts had maintained a semblance of plausibility, but how believable that would be was unsure.

It hadn't been diplomatic for me to mention the fact, but it was obvious from the earlier intercept I'd heard on this line, that the Spaniard was a German agent, and also in touch with Ponte's missing assistant, Roland. His masters might discount my call as nothing more than attempted trouble making, which of course it was, but in my experience there is always some of the mud that sticks.

If, despite any holes in my story, Heidi's bosses in Berlin came anywhere near to believing that she was lying, and secretly trying to run some sort of fraud, their response would be devastating. The possible effect this could have on Martine worried me, but not as much as leaving her fate exclusively in Heidi's clinically ruthless hands. Whatever I did could result in disaster, but doing nothing was probably even more dangerous, they would just kill her when they left. I shook my head to clear unwelcome thoughts, and concentrated on the here and now.

One last job, before I abandoned the convenience of a freely available telephone, was to ring Chalons Gendarmerie. The desk Sergeant at Montmartre had been grudgingly cooperative, but there were limits to the assistance he would give to an Englishman, even if he did think I was with MI6. If there was to be any hope for Martine, beyond me randomly annoying people, then I was going to need help, and Martine's Sergeant at Chalons, Jacques Barnier, was the most likely candidate.

Luckily he was on the premises to take my call, and sounded pleased though curious to hear from me. I told him the whole story, everything that had happened since he left us at Tante Mimi's. His immediate reaction was to advise me to talk to the local Gendarmerie, but when I explained that this was being handled by Major Vernet, who showed no signs of serious interest, he wearily agreed that this sort of attitude was spreading throughout French officialdom. The oncoming German army was a fact of life, and he was well aware of the consequences on morale.

"What about you, how do you feel about working on this?" I asked, needing to get to the point without too much delay.

"I'll tell you when I see you. I can leave here within the next fifteen minutes, where can we meet?"

We agreed to meet in the bar of hotel I'd passed, not far away, and he reckoned he should be there in two and a half hours. He had sounded keen and determined, two attributes that I was running short of

231

I switched off the lights and locked the front door behind me. If the hotel looked half way decent I would suggest staying the night there. I didn't want to draw any more attention to Tante Mimi's, if they thought there was a connection between us, even of friendship it could be dangerous for her.

As I drove away into the darkening night, I realised that I had just played every card in my hand, and wasn't at all sure if I'd played them well. Until Sergeant Barnier arrived I was still just a foolish amateur dabbling in a professional's world, how was I going to feel if my actions were responsible for Martine's death? I was sickened and horrified at the prospect.

Chapter 16

The luxury of waking up in clean sheets and on a soft mattress meant that, even when fully awake, I just lay there for a minute enjoying the sensation. I could hear Dumont's breathing, but the rhythm of her breath wasn't natural, she was controlling it. I've woken up next to lots of different people over the years and can tell the difference. Which meant that she was already awake, and listening to me.

There was no particular reason why it should, but the fact that she was awake before me made me feel unusually vulnerable, not a feeling I'm used to, or happy with. Last night I'd dragged a single mattress from another bedroom to go on the floor of the room I was using. Gunther had asked me earlier if I planned to share the double bed with her, I had just looked at him with contempt until he had to look away, the sneer frozen on his lips. The truth is that I had actually considered that possibility, and rejected it. Not on moral grounds, I don't have any, nor for the danger that she might overpower me in the night, I'm not only stronger than her, but infinitely dirtier.

The problem was more a question of misunderstanding. Having her in my bed and then killing her might alert the Sturmbannfuhrer to my readiness to kill colleagues whom I consider to be either an obstacle or a danger. It remained a fact that von Strenglen had the cross hairs of my gun sight resting right between his eyes and, unlike Martine, there was absolutely no chance of me going to bed with him before I pulled the trigger. The charade I'd staged with him in the stairwell two days ago, while Martine and the MI6 man had rushed blindly past, was about as far as I felt like going in that direction. A Prussian's idea of foreplay is to blow a whistle to let you know he's starting, they approach the whole thing like a military campaign. Well if von Strenglen felt like invading Poland all over again, he wasn't going to use my body as his battlefield. Even if I did still harbour occasional, and slightly unconventional thoughts about that hand of his.

Unless I'd tied her tightly enough to cut off the blood supply, she was too smart to be left alone overnight, and that had meant sharing a room with one of us. Sleeping under a pile of coats on an office floor, with Gunther snoring nearby, is not remotely intimate. Whereas sharing a luxuriously fitted bedroom, behind a closed door, most certainly is - whether I wished to acknowledge the fact or not. And while I've had more sex with more people than I can remember, there has been remarkably little intimacy, at least until this strange episode. My only security in the night had been to handcuff one of her wrists to the leg of an extremely large and heavy armoire. Let's see her bite through that. The cuffs themselves came from a bedside table drawer in the master bedroom, where they had been neatly lined up with a variety of other interesting items, things that I hadn't seen since Hamburg. I was quite impressed by their cosmopolitan tastes.

Then she broke the silence. "Thank you for letting me use the mattress, I'm well aware that the man would have left me tied up in the garage - or worse."

She spoke quietly and confidentially, as if she didn't want Gunther to hear - her comments were just between the two of us. She can't work out what level of personal safety she'll get from being close, or even intimate with me. Like most people she includes too many emotions in her calculations and is unable to understand the distance I see between sex and friendship. The fact that we were naked and had slept next to each other meant nothing to me, this wasn't a schoolgirl's dormitory, where we all got crushes on each other. It was time she remembered that, it was time to restore the status quo. I retrieved the pistol from under the pillow and slid out of bed to unlock her cuffs.

"Go and use the bathroom, with the door wide open, then when you've finished I'll tie you up again."

She paused, directly facing me, looking down at my chest. Having spent a considerable part of my working life in this condition, I was untroubled by my own undress and unexcited by hers, even though she looked as good out of uniform as in, which in her case was saying quite a lot. Still, it's not what you've got beneath your clothes that matters, it's what you do with it - and who you do it with.

We were of a similar height and could have been eye to eye, but as I looked at her face, she continued to look down at my body. She reached a hand out, but paused with it half way towards me and looked up. "May I?" She asked in a low voice. Unsure what she had in mind, I still said, "Yes", unthinkingly. When she completed the movement, however, it wasn't my breast that she touched, but the eagle and swastika pendant hanging there. I smiled to myself, the whole move had been a subtle display of game playing, I liked that. As she examined the pendant, tilting it from side to side in her

235

fingers, I put my own hand up to hold hers, and she looked me in the eye.

"Go to the bathroom."

She carefully placed the pendant back against my chest and meekly turned to obey, and in doing so made sure that her bare arm brushed slowly against my nipple. The firmness of my nipple was caused by me standing around with no clothes on, rather than arousal, but I didn't want her to get the wrong idea, so as she turned I gave her a stinging slap across the backside. The devious bitch.

"Ow."

I knew she was just doing her best, under difficult circumstances, but she still needed keeping in place. When it's a matter of life and death you do what you have to do. It was my job to determine how far that went and I still wasn't sure of the answer.

As I was in no mood for managing other people's affairs this morning, I was quite perfunctory in dumping her onto von Strenglen, it was time for the professional to take control of things, sole control. I warned him to keep a low profile, no venturing out of doors, and no noise, and then I left them to it. She could always try charming her way round the Sturmbannfuhrer, that should be a laugh.

I knew that I was wildly overcompensating in the way that I was distancing myself from her, but as I was firmly in control, what would it matter if I did take a brief diversion down that route? It wouldn't affect my subsequent behaviour in any way. I'd been in firm control of my emotions ever since, just after my thirteenth birthday, I had pushed that dirty bastard 'Uncle' Emil down a flight of stone steps. They say you always remember your first, and I can certainly remember killing him. He hadn't been quite dead at the bottom, though from the way he flopped about I'd say his back was broken, and I'd had to put a hand over his mouth and pinch his nose until he obliged me by dying. And all the time I crouched over him his eyes were staring at me and saying; 'But I thought you liked it'.

With the two of them safely in the kitchen, I spent half an hour going through bedroom drawers and wardrobes, until I found what I wanted: a blonde wig, a change of clothes, and the right sort of make up. Then I shut myself in the bathroom and set to work.

When I was happy with my appearance, and it was past nine o'clock, I went down to the hall and rang the Montmartre Gendarmerie, introduced myself as a Le Figaro reporter and asked if Major Vernet would be available this morning. "Yes, he'll be here till lunchtime." Excellent, I picked up my bag and went out to the car. It was show time.

The Montmartre Gendarmerie lies just off the Rue Damrémont, about half a mile from the apartment on Rue Cortot, where all the excitement had been. I had a basic familiarity with the area, so I wasn't going to get lost. Leaving the car close, but out of sight of the entrance, I swivelled the mirror round for a final check of my make up, and then set off to limp my way slowly in through the front door.

The only part of the building accessible to the public was the front desk, to get past there you needed to produce official identity or be a local officer with a key. I had decided to go with plan B. I made my way painfully to the front desk, with tear streaked make up and dark glasses, which tried but didn't quite manage to cover a large black eye.

"I want to report an assault." I said haltingly.

"What sort of assault?"

"Sexual assault."

He looked at me more closely, now noting the state of my face and the disordered appearance of my clothes."Sexual assault, including rape?"

I nodded, my embarrassment making me unable to meet his eye.

"Just wait a moment, while I get someone to talk to you."

"I can't talk here." I said, looking around the reception area.

"No, of course not, we'll bring you through, just give me a moment."

"Wait." I said, as he turned to fetch someone. "I can only talk to a woman, it was . . . well it will have to be a woman." I was twisting a handkerchief in my hands and looking only at that.

He came back to the desk, and spoke softly. "It's alright, I'm going to fetch a colleague, she's called Mirielle, you'll be able to talk to her. She's seen it all."

I would have preferred someone who hadn't seen it all, if she was as experienced as he said then she would probably spot me as a phony in the first minute. I'd just have to move faster.

She was near enough to fifty, and about my height with greying hair, she took me through to an interview room on the first floor. Still standing in the open doorway, she gestured me to a chair and asked if I'd like a coffee.

I sniffed into my twisted hanky. "No thanks, but please, just shut the door." I said, clearly on the verge of tears. She did so and came over to put a hand on my arm. I stepped back and pointed my pistol straight at her.

"If you attempt to get help I will kill you, and anyone else who comes in the room, do you understand me." Her expression was more disappointment than anything else, she had been trying to do some good in the world, and then she met me. She nodded her understanding.

"The fact that I am wearing a wig and dark glasses is the best indication you could possibly have that I don't intend to kill you, unless I have to - remember that and you should stay alive." I paused and looked at her, she appreciated the point and had relaxed, very slightly. "You are going to take me to Major Vernet's office right now, if there is anyone else there, or he has a secretary who wishes to interfere, you will simply say that I have vital information that he must hear about immediately, and in private. Is that clear?"

"What will happen to Major Vernet?"

"Exactly the same as you, unless he tries to be a hero. I intend to be out of here in less than two minutes, taking with me just what I came for. Remember - don't even dream of being brave, that will get people killed."

Vernet's office was on the same floor, and sure enough there was an outer office with a secretary. Mirielle took care of her, as instructed.

"Is he in?" She asked, with me standing to one side of her, my handbag clutched to my chest in both hands, as if defending me from a cruel world. The secretary looked enquiringly at me, and then at Mirielle, her eyebrows raised to invite some further explanation.

"She came in reporting an assault," Mirielle nodded her head in my direction. "But it turns out to be directly connected to what he's currently working on. He'll want to see her without delay, it's urgent."

"Go straight in."

Vernet took longer to get over his shock than Mirielle, but then yesterday had been almost as bad for him as it had been for me. I pulled the pistol out of my bag, to remove any possible doubt in his mind about the reality of the threat.

"Good morning Major, I am the German woman you were supposed to meet at Galeries Lafayette yesterday. Since you didn't bother waiting to meet me I thought I'd come here to see you." After a brief moment spent with his mouth hanging open in astonishment, he resorted to incredulity.

"You can't do this, we're in a police station, in the middle of Paris. You're surrounded by police officers, this is utter madness." Eventually he ran out of steam, and just stood there looking aggrieved.

"I couldn't argue with you, but I'm still going to do it. Now don't bother telling me that you don't have the damn thing, just get it, before I blow your balls off."

He started trying to mouth some sort of protest, but I cut him short. "Get it now." I accompanied the words by putting the gun to the woman's head. That way he could feel better about cooperating with me - it had all been to save her, rather than himself. These little details help the job to go much more smoothly.

He picked up the same black knapsack I'd seen yesterday, it had been on the floor beside his desk.

"Take it out and show me."

It was a black metal thing about twenty centimetres by ten, with electric wires attached to both ends. It didn't look like the last one, but then that hadn't been the real thing, so it would have been wrong if it had looked the same. How on earth would anyone know? I should have brought Leibniz with me. Dear old Theo, where is he when you need him?

I told Mirielle to take her stockings off and then sit down, Vernet obligingly tied her hands and feet. I then had him call in the secretary and do the same for her. I shoved a hanky in each of there mouths and we were ready for off.

Vernet carried the knapsack and we walked down the corridor side by side, with me to his right, my handbag encased pistol pointing straight at him. He was nervous but cooperative, whilst I was on an operational high, as if I'd just taken Benzedrine. I can sometimes get a little fretful in the build up to a job, but once the die is cast and the characters are in motion I'm at my best, confident and controlled.

We went down the stone steps, my every sense on high alert for the first sound of the alarm being raised. As we walked past the front desk to reach the street, the desk Sergeant, who had been so sympathetic with me, stopped what he was doing to look at us. He looked vaguely disturbed, and took a step forward.

"Is everything alright sir?"

"Yes, of course it is, why shouldn't it be?"

Vernet was a little too snappy with the man, but then I'd criticised every other aspect of his behaviour, so why not this? The desk Sergeant clearly thought that something was wrong, but wasn't sure what and given his chief's unequivocal answer there wasn't a lot he could do, so he simply watched us as we walked out of the front door.

Going down the front steps, I quietly told him to turn right, and we disappeared round the corner. This was going remarkably smoothly, even for one of my operations, any chance he ever had of causing me a problem had evaporated as soon as we left the police station, now it would just be him and me. I reached the car, still not having given his future prospects any serious thought. In my view, Vernet himself didn't rank as serious in any department of life, even in the question of whether or not he should leave it.

I unlocked the driver's door, and swung the knapsack across to the passenger seat, keeping the gun pointing squarely at him, then a thought occurred to me.

"You haven't asked me once about Capitaine Dumont - have you? The fact is that as long as you keep your greasy little skin intact you couldn't give a shit about her - could you?" Now that I'd thought of it, I was quite annoyed by this blatant lack of concern for a colleague, and had shoved my face quite aggressively into his.

He took half a step backwards, surprised by the accusation, "But I've given you what you wanted, I've given you what you asked for. If Dumont's as smart as she thinks she is - she can look after herself."

"That really was the wrong answer." I said, and shot him. I gave him two in the chest at close range, I didn't want a repeat of Leibniz, besides which I was fresh out of tent pegs.

As I drove away, I heard a siren start in the background, and looking through my mirror I saw Gendarmes come running round the corner, to where I'd been parked. Their fallen Major conveniently marking the scene of the crime. They could take turns in drawing chalk outlines round him, coppers always enjoy doing what they've seen in the movies.

Sir Freddy Villiers
Paris, Friday morning, May 17th. 1940

The inclination last night to wait in the bar for Sergeant Barnier's arrival, with a comforting succession of drinks had been strong, almost too strong, but I resisted. Even though I did wonder what exactly I was saving myself for. I was clueless and hopeless. The

German pair had disappeared, and taken Martine with them, unless they showed themselves in some unexpected way, there was nowhere even to start looking for them.

Instead, I had somewhat hopelessly played out my last hand, parking the car out of sight and loitering on foot on the industrial estate. If my prodding the German contact at the Spanish Embassy was to yield any results at all, it would probably be sooner rather than later, which meant tonight. It was dark, I was cold and hungry and had lost all confidence in what I was doing. As I peered round the corners of empty industrial units, my hands in my pockets to keep warm, I was sure this was a ludicrous waste of time.

So it came as a surprise, when after an hour of increasingly chilly boredom and with an aching left knee from all the standing, I heard a car engine approaching. I told myself it was probably a courting couple looking for somewhere quiet. But the engine came closer, and then the head lights swung onto the front of the CSF building. I shouldn't have been surprised, after all I'd been careful to give them enough time to trace the call, so I should have expected them to turn up. But it still came as a bit of an eye opener when they actually arrived.

There was no soft shoe subtlety in their approach, they drove straight to the main entrance, four men got out of the car, kicked the front door open and went in. They were all carrying guns, and I instinctively shrank further back into the shadows. I had obviously prodded the right hornet's nest. All the office lights came on, upstairs and downstairs. Figures could be seen moving around, searching for whatever there was to be found. As far as they were concerned this was the location from which Major Lawrence Grand of MI6 had telephoned their contact, so there had to be something for them to find.

Invisible in the darkness, to the people inside, I walked across the car park, to make a note of their registration number. Having come close enough to read the unlit plate, I thought why not go the rest of the way and look inside the car? Checking that all four of them could still be seen rummaging through the offices I opened the front passenger door, and was immediately startled by the interior light coming on. What a professional, I hadn't even thought of that, it might just be seen from inside. A very hurried look round the car interior revealed nothing of apparent interest, nothing marked 'Secret Code Book', in fact no documents of any sort. I quietly closed the door, and prepared to make myself scarce. The four figures were still visible in the offices, I was torn between a rapid and sensible retreat to safety, and a childish gesture. The gesture won.

I crouched down by the rear offside tyre and pressed the centre of the valve. In less than a minute the tyre was flat. What did you do in the war Granddad? Well sonny, I let down one of the Gestapo's tyres - I heard later that Hitler was absolutely furious. Creeping away into the darkness, I wasn't sure whether to be pleased or ashamed at the extent of my offensive action. Although to be fair, when they did emerge three of four minutes later, there was a certain amount of Teutonic effing and blinding as they changed the wheel.

Having waited for them to clear the area, I drove round to the hotel and went in the bar for an overdue large Scotch. Sergeant Barnier arrived just as I was ready to order a refill. He said he was starving and so we had something to eat while I explained what had been happening. His first reaction was one of disgust that the Montmartre Gendarmerie hadn't even notified the office at Chalons of Martine's abduction. But by now it was too late for any useful action, he had just finished a full day's work followed by a two hour drive, and I was exhausted, emotionally and physically and my leg hurt. Using his official status, to ensure anonymity we booked a room each and went to bed.

I woke up this morning glad that his arrival had stopped what could well have turned into a heavy session with the whisky bottle, whatever was going to happen today would be better without a hangover. After breakfast Barnier spent some time on the phone to Chalons, informing Martine's boss of her disappearance. However, beyond deploring the lack of information and cooperation from Montmartre, there was very little they could do. It was agreed that Barnier would pay Vernet a visit this morning, to get a full and official update on how the investigation was proceeding.

Before he went anywhere, we round to the CSF offices, to satisfy Barnier's curiosity. But there was nothing of interest to be found, after last night's visitors the place was wrecked, even the front door was hanging off its hinges. We left the place to be stripped by vandals.

Barnier dropped me back at the hotel, before making his way to Montmartre, we both agreed that he would make better progress without me, than with me. I bought myself a selection of morning papers and settled down in the now deserted bar to see what they had to say for themselves. In recent days, the censorship of French newspapers has struck me as self defeating, no one takes their contents at face value, at best they can be used to infer the opposite of whatever the printed word actually says. For example, this morning all the papers report the statement by their Prime Minister, Reynaud, to the effect that the government has no intention of leaving Paris; everyone reading that will know straight away that the government is probably already half way to Bordeaux.

To my great surprise it was also reported that Churchill had arrived in Paris yesterday, although beyond saying, somewhat obviously, that he was having talks with Monsieur Reynaud, no further information was given. One can only hope that they decide to be a little more candid with him than they're being with their own people.

The breakfast waitress this morning said that, yesterday, from the top of the hill near the Sacré Coeur you could see columns of smoke rising from several points in central Paris, she had heard this was caused by government ministries burning their files and sensitive documents. That sort of third hand hearsay is about as reliable as news gets at the moment, and I have to say that it sounded entirely credible to me. Despite listening to the radio bulletins and reading the newspapers, I still don't have any clear idea of where the advancing Germans are, only that they must be within a day or two of Paris.

Will they declare it an open city, or will they have to be bombed into surrender? I suspect the former. Come what may with the search for Martine, I would soon have no option but to run for it. That phrase about rats deserting the sinking ship came to mind. I was sure to feel wretched and blame myself no matter what happened. I kept looking anxiously at my watch, longing for Barnier to return, with whatever news he could gather.

It was almost noon when he finally reappeared, and I was nervously wondering if he'd abandoned me. He looked to be in shock, and when he told me about Vernet's murder I felt the same myself. The cool way that the woman I knew as Heidi had walked into one of the biggest police stations in Paris, and then calmly walked out with what everyone but me thought was valuable piece of state property was astonishing all on its own. The fact that she had then shot one of their senior officers dead on the pavement outside the station, was almost too much to take in. Heidi didn't need tanks, she was a one woman blitzkrieg all on her own. God help anyone standing nearby when she discovered that she'd got the wrong thing.

The two women in Vernet's office who had seen what took place, said there had been no mention of Martine, by anyone, it seems that she had just been forgotten by all parties. The situation was now clear; I had encouraged a country Gendarme, albeit a very smart one, to join me, a retired civil service meddler, in thumbing our noses at the German security services. We hadn't won, we'd just annoyed them - so who could honestly be surprised at the results? My previously peaceful life in Putney seemed a million miles away.

Barnier had arrived at the scene only minutes after the event, with Vernet's body still lying on the pavement. While he had still been gathering what information he could, from anyone who would talk to him, two big shots from the Cinquième Bureau, the French counter espionage organisation, had arrived. They had immediately taken full control of events, which included ejecting a non resident staff member like Barnier. His assumption was that, considering the wider pattern of events and the German connection, both Martine's disappearance and Vernet's murder were now firmly in secret service hands, and that the role of the Gendarmerie would be strictly limited to doing the leg work on someone else's behalf.

Beyond discovering what he had about Heidi's activities this morning, Barnier's main achievement was to have obtained a name and address to go with the registration number I had written down last night. Information of any kind was an advance, but I recognised that the four men I'd watched searching the offices were unlikely to have any idea where Heidi and von Strenglen were, and thus no idea where Martine was. If they'd known that, they wouldn't have been wasting their time kicking down doors at CSF.

Chapter 17

Fraulein Heidi Fuchs
Paris, Friday midday, May 17th. 1940

I drove unhurriedly back to our temporary accommodation, partly to avoid drawing attention to myself, and partly to enjoy the exhilaration of a perfectly executed operation. Whether the equipment I had just picked up from Vernet turned out to be genuine or not, he himself had clearly thought that it was. Even so, I still needed to recognise the possibility that the MI6 man was deceiving Vernet, his idea of a full and frank cooperation with his closest neighbours and allies was very similar to my own.

Von Strenglen and Dumont were in the kitchen when I got back to the house, he was sitting on a chair at the table, his sleeves rolled up, cleaning a stripped down pistol; she was sitting on the floor with her hands tied behind her back. Oddly, the sight of his false hand openly exposed, with its stainless steel supporting rods, emerging from the leather straps around his forearm, looked less peculiar than the rigidly black gloved object one normally saw.

Unfortunately, even this failed to make him any more agreeable, he was still a walking cliché - his constant desire to assert his military capabilities coming a close second only to his desire to assert his masculine superiority. Yet when the chips were down, it had been me, not him, who had just run rings around the massed ranks of the Gendarmerie. Perhaps he was going to continue with this masculine display by pulling his dick out next, and cleaning that, it would probably make him smell better. I reflected, not for the first time, that Martine and I would probably make a much better team.

I looked at her briefly, but she hadn't been touched. Her face showed no signs of the shame, defeat or outrage which are the usual markers of recent rape. I sat down opposite him at the kitchen table and slid the device out of the knapsack, putting it down between us. We both stared at it.

"Is this the magnetron?" He asked.

"I can't tell you, that's what Leibniz was for. All I can tell you is that Major Vernet thought that it was, he wasn't smart enough to fool me."

We both stared at it for a little longer, as if it would burst into speech and give us its own opinion.

"This has to be it, Vernet wasn't going to risk his life at yesterday's meeting with a dud, and he wouldn't have known that you were coming for him this morning, so he wouldn't have had a replacement waiting for you." From the smug expression on his face he clearly regarded his logic as unassailable, and with him being the senior officer present, I wasn't going to get into an argument on the subject. Perhaps he was right, but just in case everything turned to dust in our hands later, it was always going to have been his decision.

He seemed to have no intention of asking me exactly how I had managed to retrieve the item from an upstairs office in a heavily guarded police station, and in less time than it would take most people to go for a shit. He didn't want to listen to any tales of me outwitting the enemy, while he risked life and limb looking after a tied up woman. The deeper we got into this, the more certain I was that he was not going to want my version of events to surface - ever. This was turning, with increasing speed, into a single ticket event.

"In that case we'd better contact the Spaniards." I said. "The sooner we're on the plane and out of here, the happier I'll be."

He nodded and went through to the front hall, where the telephone was. I went to Dumont and helped her to her feet, before guiding her to a chair. I didn't say anything to her, there were more pressing things for me to deal with, instead I half filled a tumbler with tap water and held it to her mouth. She was still a hostage, and hostages need to be in a tradable condition. She drank the water but didn't thank me, it wasn't that sort of occasion.

I took a chance on leaving her for a few moments and walked through to the hall. He was already talking to someone, I stood next to him, my ear close to the phone. A German man's voice was speaking and saying that 'They' would come and collect us from where we were now, and could von Strenglen give him the address. I grabbed his arm, and his attention, and shook my head vigorously, quietly hissing: "Not a chance - we meet them at the plane."

Von Strenglen looked panicked, he didn't want to say this to the man on the phone, so I repeated myself, even more dogmatically and with a threatening look to go with it.

He got the message. "No I'm sorry that won't be possible, we'll meet you at the plane, at the Bois de Boulogne as planned."

I heard the faint German voice persisting. "It will be much more convenient if we come to you, just give me your address."

But he was too late, von Strenglen might have been listening to the voice, but he was looking at me, and I had my headmistress face on and was shaking my head. I was closest, and I won.

"No, as I said, we'll meet you at the Bois de Boulogne, what time will you be there, and how will we recognise you?" Feeling that it was safe to leave the housekeeping details to him, I went back in the kitchen.

Dumont had managed to get to her feet, and had already hopped half way to the back door. Hearing me come in from the hall she stopped where she was, and looked guilty. I yanked her round to where she'd come from, and shoved her back down to the floor.

Having finished the phone call von Strenglen came in from the hall, he looked slightly puzzled. "I don't know what's happened to the Spaniard, but that was a German who answered the phone then. Why didn't you want them to come here?"

Beyond gut feeling, I didn't really have an answer to that

"I'm not sure, but it felt wrong in some way, he wanted us somewhere quiet and unseen. I've stayed alive by listening to feelings like that, and that's the way I like it."

The arrangement was for us to meet at three o'clock at the planned pick up point in the Bois de Boulogne, once a Royal hunting reserve but now just a small forest and equestrian area, directly to the west of Paris. Although most of it was quite thickly wooded, there were some football pitches at the northern end, and an area of open ground, suitable for operating a short take off aircraft. I was uneasy about the whole idea of meeting these people, even though my plans weren't fully formed, the appearance of this previously unknown group was a serious disruption.

Somewhere between leaving here and boarding the aircraft, it had been my intention that von Strenglen should meet with an accident, leaving me as the brave sole survivor of this desperate mission. That was the sort of performance that was going to work best without an audience. Whether von Strenglen's friends on the phone wanted to steal the device and bury our bodies, or simply wave us *bon voyage* I didn't know, but I did know they were an intrusion. This was a fork in the road, and I needed to start taking decisions, before someone else started taking them for me.

I turned to von Strenglen. "I want us to be in position well before the time, we need to see what we're dealing with. She still needs to come with us, I want her available to trade, in case the French are somehow involved in this. We don't know who these people are, but just remember - you don't need to come from Berlin to speak convincing German."

He pursed his lips and raised his eyebrows, in surprised acceptance of a thought that hadn't occurred to him. That was the first seed of doubt sown.

Then I looked down at Dumont. "I'm going to unfasten your feet, and then we'll go upstairs to use the lavatory and get changed; if you try anything I don't like - your dead." I followed her upstairs, my pistol in my hand.

Upstairs, I swung the bedroom door shut behind me, and then wordlessly herded her ahead of me into the en suite bathroom. I knew that I was taking a chance, in fact more like a stupid gamble, but I've always lived my life on a tightrope, one false step and I'm a goner. Yet somehow I'm still here.

I pushed her backwards to sit on the lavatory seat, whilst I sat on the edge of the bath. "You will have worked out by now that your chances of surviving the next few hours are practically zero, the Sturmbannfuhrer thinks you've outlived you usefulness, he thinks that you are a piece of excess baggage that we should dispose of."

She looked grim, but nodded her understanding. "I can tell by the way he looks at me, he can't decide whether to rape me first and then murder me, or do it the other way round."

I smiled, she'd certainly summed him up. "I'm going to increase your chances of survival from one per cent to fifty percent."

"Should I be grateful, what's in it for you?"

It's partly to annoy von Strenglen, and partly because I like you."

There was a long pause, as she looked at me, unable to work out what was going on. "Am I supposed to have sex with you?"

"If you feel like it, then why not? It could be fun"

But she was still looking puzzled, thinking there was some extra bit that she hadn't worked out. Finally she smiled. "No, of course not, if you'd wanted sex we would have shared the bed last night. You think there's going to be a shoot out, and you don't trust von Strenglen, so you plan to release me and let me make a run for it. You want me as a running target, to draw their attention from you."

"You really are good, you should have been doing Vernet's job, you would have been a lot more of a challenge."

"What happened to him?"

"I asked him if he wanted to include you in the deal, he said he wasn't interested and that you would have to take care of yourself."

We looked at each other silently for a couple of heartbeats. "And then?"

"And then I shot him, it was altogether the wrong answer."

"Do you understand that I'm a patriotic French officer, I deplore your murder of Major Vernet and will do anything in my power to disrupt your plans?"

"Of course you will, my dear, I understand perfectly." I was relaxed about her statement, I knew she had to say these things. The earnest declaration had been a diplomatic necessity, rather than any sort of meaningful communication to me personally. Having finished our cosy chat I found her a coat with sleeves long enough to disguise the handcuffs and took her downstairs. It was time for us to take our stroll in the country.

By my reckoning, all three of us were now actively planning to kill the other two, no matter what happened this afternoon, it was unlikely to be boring.

Sir Freddy Villiers
Paris, Friday afternoon, May 17th. 1940

As I had with Martine, I managed to persuade Barnier to drop the 'Sir', although his Gallic sense of propriety was vaguely offended by this revolutionary removal of the officer class. Our working relationship was a good deal easier simply as Jacques and Freddy, and talking as equals enabled me to see that, despite being happily married, Jacques also had a regard for Martine which went far beyond the strictly professional. We were like flies round a honey pot.

The address attached to the registration number of the car which had responded to my telephoned provocation, turned out to be an outfit called Axel Buro, a supposedly Swiss office equipment company. Identifying yourself as Swiss or Austrian helped to explain your German accent, together with the fact that you ate a lot of sausage and wore lederhosen at weekends. The British have been criticised for being a little too ready to intern suspected enemy aliens, but I would rather have that than squads of Gestapo roaming the streets. It's not even as if I've got the time to let down all their tyres.

Axel Buro's office was on the Avenue Mozart in the 16th. Arrondissement, to the west of the city centre. It's a busy commercial street, lined with trees and with parking down one side. The buildings have the usual suburban mix of shops, bars and restaurants on the ground floor, with apartments above. When we arrived it was busy with both pedestrians and cars.

Driving down here from the hotel at Clichy had given us an overview of the city centre off to our left, and standing out incongruously, as the waitress had said yesterday, were several narrow columns of black smoke. The ministries and government offices were still at work, burning their records. In several of the parks there were cars parked haphazardly on the grass, with makeshift tents and tarpaulin shelters, where refugees had bedded down for the night. Branches had been torn from trees to make campfires, around which people were squatting to make breakfast. There would of course, be no arrangements for lavatories in such a set up. It was all so very squalid, so very un-Parisian.

Despite there being an almost schizophrenic divide between the desperate refugees and the residents, many of whom were still trying to carry on as normal, there was overall an almost tangible awareness that time was running out, and nobody was quite sure what would happen when it did - when the Nazi tanks actually rolled down the Champs-Élysées. Clearly life would continue in some form, but what form, and would that continuation apply to everyone? The French have an inbuilt race memory of the marauding Hun.

Where Martine had been appalled but practical, Jacques was appalled and ashamed. There were men in military uniforms on every street corner and in every cheap bar, but they weren't serving soldiers, they were deserters. The uniforms were dirty and dishevelled, the buttons undone, the wearers unshaven. They looked surly and mutinous, and I thanked God they'd thrown their rifles away when they ran; it was just unfortunate that they seemed to be reserving their hostility for their fellow citizens, rather than the enemy. I wondered how I would feel to witness such a public collapse of an entire army had they been British, and how would I feel if these were the streets of London?

There was nothing I could say to Jacques that would gloss over the situation, so we talked of practical matters and I told him what I knew about Heidi. His first reaction had been similar to mine, what a wildly improbable name for a ruthless killer. The name evoked peaceful Swiss meadows and cow bells, not stabbing someone through the ear with a metal spike, and then smiling about it.

"How old is she and what does she look like?" He asked.

"I'm not very good with women's ages, but perhaps thirty five years old and about so high." I held out my hand to indicate a height. "But it's difficult to be sure as she uses disguises. On the two occasions I've seen her she had black hair one time, and blonde the other." I realised my answer had been less than helpful, but it was all I had.

"Would she actually kill Martine, just because she wasn't needed as a hostage any longer?"

I didn't need to consider my response to that one. "Without hesitation." And that shut us both up.

Having found a suitable parking spot on the Avenue Mozart, we took it in turns to walk slowly past the premises, a small but stylish glass fronted showroom with typewriters and mimeographs and suchlike, professionally displayed on spot lit plinths. An attractive young woman sat at a desk, they were clearly open for business. If this was a cover operation, they apparently ran a genuine commercial set up to hide behind.

There was a vehicle entry to a yard at the side, and lurking at the far end was a black saloon car, its back end towards us and, just discernible in the shadows, it's registration plate could be seen. It was the same number as last night. No matter how fancy the front of house, there was darkness visible at the back. Somewhere round here were the four men with guns, who had gone out to find and no doubt kill me last night.

We agreed that in the absence of any other leads, and our limited manpower, we had little option but to wait for their vehicle to move off, and then follow it. Since Vernet's killing even Jacques was denied access to the investigation and its results, and that included any information from the phone tap on the Spanish Embassy number. We were following our one and only clue, the amateur status of my position remained sharply highlighted.

My street skills for discretely trailing another vehicle were unlikely to fool the German security services, who were presumably trained in that sort of thing, which made Jacques all the more useful. He had spent six years in Paris, before moving to Chalons, and his expertise should help cover my own shortcomings. After learning what little we could from walking past the premises, Jacques and I settled ourselves in the car and prepared for a long wait. I was familiar with the supposed tedium of 'stake outs', I've read enough Erle Stanley Gardner and Raymond Chandler novels to have an idea of the basics. It was just that doing it for first time in real life seemed a lot slower than it does in a novel. That's the trouble with real life - you can't skip the boring bits.

We had a parking spot about seventy five yard from the front of the showroom and, traffic permitting, had a good view of their vehicle entrance. It wasn't that we couldn't see, it was simply that there wasn't anything to look at. The typewriter trade seemed to have died a death, the only sign of activity being when the young woman came out, locking the door behind her, returning five minutes later with what looked like her lunchtime sandwich in a bag. I was beginning to worry that our one and only clue might be a complete waste of time.

Having exhausted the immediately obvious topics of conversation, Jacques was looking at the Paris street map I'd brought with me. Something about it had caught his eye, and he was examining it at close quarters to try and make something out.

"What is it?" I asked.

"Probably nothing, I'm just trying to see what you've written on this bit." He tapped a finger on a green area of the map.

"I haven't written anything, let me take a look."

He was right there was a word scribbled in. "It looks like *Shorck*." I said, passing it back to him. "It's the map I took from the CSF offices, I assume it's the one Heidi and von Strenglen were using." Even as I said the words we both suddenly realised that this might be significant.

He held the map up to the car window to get more light. "No, the second letter isn't an *h*, it's a *t*. What it says is *Storch*, but what does that mean?"

As soon as he said the word I was sure I knew, but there was one more question.

"What's this green area here?"

"The Bois de Boulogne, it's a wooded area, for horse riding and that sort of thing." He waved his hand vaguely, to indicate that sort of thing.

My Air Ministry background had already given me the answer, an answer I should have spotted earlier, but the truth was I hadn't even noticed the scribbled word. "Storch will be short for Fieseler Storch, it's a type of small German aircraft, and it's what will be used to pick them up."

"Well they can't land there, that particular bit's a football pitch, and it's surrounded by trees. You can't land and aircraft in the middle of Paris."

I corrected him. "The Fieseler Storch can land in thirty metres, and take off in sixty. Even with three people onboard it can take off in the length of a football pitch."

We looked at each other, and most unusually I allowed myself to say: "Oh bugger." at the thought of what I'd missed. Then our minds working in unison, and anxious not to miss anything else, we both looked back at the Axel Buro showroom, there was still nothing happening, at this rate they'd go bust.

"Wait here." He instructed, and fairly leapt from the car. He ran into the nearest ground floor doorway, an accountant's office. For the next ten minutes it was like being at a tennis match as my eyes flicked from side to side; from Axel Buro to the accountants and back.

What would I do if the car we were waiting for came out and drove off? I was still debating the point when he emerged, looking seriously unhappy. The car springs rocked as he dumped himself angrily back behind the wheel.

"A complete waste of time that was."

"What was?"

"I rang Army Command at Vincennes to inform them that a German aircraft was due to land there in the next hour or so, to collect two of their agents and a top secret radio part. I suggested they should either send a fighter to intercept it in the air, or troops to seize it on the ground."

"And they said?"

"That I should submit my report in writing, through the proper channels, and it would be evaluated." He then hit the steering wheel several times. I could imagine how he felt.

There was a faint sense of guilt at the back of my mind, about the number of people I was allowing to believe that the device I gave Vernet was the genuine article, but as I say, it was only a faint sense.

Then, finally, at long last, we saw the black car reversing out from the Axel Buro yard. It was too far away to be sure, but there looked to be four people inside. Jacques pulled out, about ten cars behind them.

At the junction at the top of the road they turned left. "Chaussée de la Muette." Jacques muttered, half to himself, as he followed them round the corner. "Then if they're going to the spot marked on the map, they'll turn right up ahead, onto Avenue Prudhon."

They did, and we followed, but now hanging back a little further. Now that we all knew where we were going we could be a little more relaxed.

It was a sunny afternoon, springtime in Paris, what could be nicer? The Wehrmacht were coming, the British Embassy didn't want to know me, French officialdom wouldn't touch Jacques with a bargepole, and the two of us were planning to jump out of the bushes and surprise the Gestapo. There simply had to be a downside to this somewhere.

Chapter 18

Fraulein Heidi Fuchs
Paris, Friday afternoon, May 17th. 1940

Despite heavy traffic, the drive to the meeting point took less than half an hour. Gunther was driving, it pleased him to demonstrate his ability to change gear with that wooden hand of his. All around us were the early signs of chaos, not in the open yet, but waiting - just a millimetre below the surface. The people on the pavements were looking rushed and nervous, and even by Parisian standards, the driving was more dangerous than usual, with more frequent recourse to angry gestures and the horn. The whole city was unstable, I could imagine there being outbreaks of public disorder, but couldn't foresee it becoming sufficiently organised to represent any serious resistance to our troops. Most of these people would be grateful for any sort of competent government, then they could simply get on with living their lives. I didn't feel any sort of sympathy, for the last twenty years they had consistently voted for either clowns or communists. They shouldn't blame us if they didn't like the results.

I was sat in the back of the car with the Frenchwoman. We had decided that I would stay in the background with Dumont, while Gunther met the supposed welcoming party, carrying the device with him. I couldn't work out any particular reason why we should distrust these people who had insisted on meeting us at the pick up point, but that didn't remove my awareness that their behaviour was unexpected and inexplicable - two things that I didn't like.

Berlin should be delighted with our performance, we had fought our way through every obstacle put in our path, and my own performance in capturing the device from Vernet was outstanding. Even in the worst possible case, if the device turned out not to be genuine, we were doing no worse than the expert Leibniz, who had also picked a dud; and at least we had obtained the item that the French authorities themselves had believed to be the right one. Despite all that, von Strenglen's belief that any other members of the German military structure must, by definition, be on our side, struck me as dangerously naive. The pair of us spent all day, every day, together - and even I wasn't on his side. I would just have to wait for events to play themselves out.

The meeting place was a sports area at the northern end of the Bois de Boulogne, we were due to meet them by the changing huts at three o'clock. I wanted to be an hour early, to look at the surroundings, to check on lines of approach and even more importantly, lines of departure. The theory was that we would leave here by plane, but I grow steadily older by always having an option up my sleeve.

Dumont turned to me. "Do you know these people you're supposed to be meeting?"

I looked at her, the model of innocence. "Don't build your hopes Martine, they're German, they won't be coming to help you." I enjoyed calling her Martine, it seemed to disconcert her slightly, she knew the undercurrents, but couldn't work out if they would save her life. And to be honest, neither could I.

"No, they won't be there to help me, but will they be there to help you? The man doesn't think there's any danger, but there's something going on that you're not happy about, isn't there?" The eye contact was direct and her voice soft and warm.

I was sat on the right hand side of the back seat, so that the pistol in my right hand was out of grabbing distance, I put my left hand out to take one of hers, and squeezed it slightly. "Part of the reason that I like you is that you're clever, and you know it. But remember that I warned you before not to be too clever, it could be unhealthy."

She pursed her lips and looked away. If there were going to be any mind games played around here, it was going to be me who played them, that's how life works. I do enjoy hostage taking, the dynamics are fascinating, someone should write a book about it: one person totally dependent on the other for everything in life, including life.

"We're here." Said von Strenglen over his shoulder, as he pulled off the road onto a dirt track, leading to a couple of football pitches and a sad looking wooden hut. The place was deserted, which was a good start, the rest of the population must have better things to do at the moment.

"Keep your eye on her." I said, and got out to take a look around. There was only one door into the hut and that was securely padlocked on the outside, nobody was going to jump out of there at us. I walked slowly round the hut, scanning the area, The two football pitches were side by side, with at least a twenty metre clear strip around the edges, before the trees began. It was a long time since I'd taken geometry, and I hadn't been very interested in it then, but even so I reckoned that going diagonally, from one corner to the other, this should give a runway distance of something like 250 to 300 metres. Even with the plane being overloaded and the trees all around, that would be plenty for a short take off aircraft like the Storch.

I walked over to the thin belt of trees between us and the public road, I wanted to see where the ditches were, where there was any cover and where the nearest parked cars were. There had been many times I'd checked out sites in this way, and then never needed the information, but twice that I could think of it had been the only difference between me and a variety of people who were now underground.

Satisfied there was nothing else to learn, I looked at my watch and walked back to the car, von Strenglen had wound his window down and was watching me. I went to the car boot and took out the steel jack handle, and then levered the padlock off the shed door. There was nothing of interest inside and it smelt of old socks. I shut the door, leaving the broken padlock lying on the ground. We had forty minutes to go. I bent down and ripped out some blades of grass and then threw them as I high as I could in the air, they fluttered off to one side as they fell.

"The plane will land over there." I said, pointing to one corner.

"How do you work that out?" He asked.

"It will land into wind, it will then want to turn round and taxi back to the same spot for its take off run. So that's where you need to watch, to see it coming in." He looked anxiously in the direction I'd indicated. Oh for God's sake, not yet von Strenglen, not yet.

I opened the back door, and took Dumont's arm to help her out. "It's a fact of life that you can't run as fast with your hands in cuffs as you can without. Furthermore, although that tight uniform skirt of yours makes your arse look good, it would be a swine to run in."

"You think the skirt makes me look good? I never liked it personally."

"Yes it fits you perfectly, you look ten years younger from the back."

"Was that a compliment to my bum or an insult to my face?"

"It doesn't matter, just remember that I'll shoot you if I have to."

"I believe you."

I told von Strenglen that I would wait around the far side of the hut and then, in the event of there being any sort of problem, I would give him back up from there. A gun fight might be convenient, just as long as there weren't more than one or two people coming to meet us.

"What sort of problem?"

I shrugged. "No idea, but there's something strange going on, so better safe than sorry."

At quarter to three a black car came slowly down the track from the road, to my horror there were four men in it. I hadn't got any sort of plan for dealing with that many, and why did they need four men if there wasn't going to be trouble. I kept myself out of sight and warned Dumont to keep her mouth shut.

The car drew up behind our own, and they all got out. Four large, serious looking men, three of whom were carrying handguns. Von Strenglen climbed out, carrying the knapsack in his left hand, or to put it another way, his only hand. This meant that for as long as he was holding the knapsack he couldn't use a gun even if he wanted to. The one who wasn't carrying a gun, presumably the leader walked up to von Strenglen, while the other three spread out in a loose line, their eyes slowly covering the surroundings.

Poor old Gunther, even he must have realised by now that things weren't right, but he tried to pretend that everything was normal by saying hello, it made him sound nervous, he would have been better not to have said anything.

"Get it out and show me." Said the man.

Von Strenglen looped the knapsack strap over his right forearm and then used his left hand to take out the device. He handed it to the man. The man took it, turning it over in his hands to get a proper look at it. Then he looked up at von Strenglen for a long silent moment, before carefully holding the device out at arm's length and dropping it on the ground.

He took a step closer to von Strenglen. "How much did you get for the magnetron?"

"What do you mean? That is the magnetron." He made a futile gesture to the dropped item.

"That," said the man, quite calmly, "Is an AC/DC power inverter, it's a standard radio component. I'll give you one last chance, how much did you get for the magnetron?"

"I don't know what you're talking about, we stole that from the private office of the senior French police officer on this case, it has to be right." He was trying to sound confident, but he was pissing upwind.

"We know for a fact that the Russians have made you an offer, and that you have been in personal contact with an MI6 agent for exactly the same purpose, so don't waste my time."

"What personal contact? I know nothing about selling the magnetron, Fuchs told me that was it, the thing I just gave you. She must be trying some sort of trick of her own. She's completely degenerate, she's got the hots for some female Gendarme we took as a hostage, I wouldn't put anything past her. Go and get her, she's listening to everything we're saying." He gestured back to the corner of the hut, to indicate that I was behind it. Unfortunately, his gesture also encompassed the door to the hut, with the broken padlock lying brazenly on the ground in front of it.

The leader pulled out his own pistol and then waved two of his men forward to search for me. They moved past von Strenglen, who was rooted to the spot facing his accuser. Then instead of looking behind the hut, they followed the obvious clue and went to look inside.

I put my face right up to Dumont's face and whispered urgently. "Go straight to the edge of the wood, where we were before, if you can run fast enough and quietly enough you might get away." Then on an impulse gave her a kiss, straight on the lips. She was astonished, but at the kiss or the offer of freedom I couldn't tell. "Go now." I whispered and gave her a slight push to get her started.

As I looked round the corner of the hut, I was fifteen metres away from von Strenglen's back, and considered rewarding his version of my character with a bullet, but that would be a waste. Instead I braced myself against the planking and carefully lined up on the leader. Neither of the two men were looking in my direction, but that could change. It was important not to rush this first shot, but I needed to move quickly. Using a two handed grip I settled the notches of the open sights, first on the leader's face, and then slowly dropped down to mid chest, and then as I exhaled, I slowly but firmly squeezed the trigger.

Even before I saw him drop I was running round the back of the hut, Martine had almost reached the edge of the trees but had fallen and was struggling to get up. From the far end of the hut I fired a shot in her direction, it hit a tree just in front of her, and she obliged me by squealing. Not a lot, but enough. The fourth man came round to see what was happening, his gun held out ready for action, Martine was directly ahead of him about thirty metres away, and he stopped to aim at her back. As he did so he suddenly realised that I was stood to one side of him, just five metres away, he tried desperately to swing in my direction. That's the trouble with rushing into these things, you miss the obvious. Happily though, I didn't miss him. In fact from the look of the ugly bugger I suspect that not many people would miss him.

That left von Strenglen and the two inside the hut. I pivoted against the rough timber of the last corner to swing my pistol round to where they should be. They had both come out of the hut to see what was going on, and were stood pointing their pistols at von Strenglen, the only visible suspect. Taking the same care as before, I shot them both in the back. If you do this well in the shooting gallery at the Tiergarten, they give you a teddy bear.

My next shot would have been the Sturmbannfuhrer, but as luck would have it the first one of the two I'd just shot, had stumbled against von Strenglen, pushing him to the ground, where he lay beneath the man's body. Von Strenglen, with a quick wittedness that surprised me, had snatched the fallen man's gun from the ground beside him and started shooting back at me. Shooting while lying flat on your back, with a dead body on top of you isn't likely to improve one's aim, and it didn't his.

As I swung back into cover, two things happened all at once. Another car came bouncing down the track from the main road, the speed indicating that this was no casual visitor, and simultaneously a small aircraft started to drop itself carefully onto the football pitch. This place had become too interesting for me to linger any longer. It's important to remember not only that I'm good, though I am, but also that I'm not invincible, I turned and ran for the trees. Me and my best friend Martine would have to find somewhere to lie low for a while, until I could work out what the hell was going on.

Sir Freddy Villiers
Paris, Friday afternoon, May 17th. 1940

Jacques, suggested that as we knew where they were going, it would eliminate any possibility of being spotted if we took a slightly different route. I wasn't entirely happy to lose sight of them, but remembering how Martine had spotted a car tailing me, I agreed.

"Unless they know the area as well as a local, they'll go up to Tassigny and swing left onto Sablon." He said. "Because that's what looks best on a street map." From looking at Heidi's map, I agreed with him.

"We'll be able to tell at the next junction. And then I can take a different route and beat them to it."

They went in the direction he'd predicted, still driving at the same steady and perfectly legal speed. I suppose that's the way with hit men, they don't mind killing people, but tend to shy away from breaking the speed limit. Jacques swung us off to the left, across some park land, following a blue sign to the Lac Inférieur. "This way's slightly shorter and will have a lot less traffic on it."

The route took us past the end of the boating lake and through a forested area, and there really was much less traffic, exactly as he had predicted. That is until we came to the junction with the Allée de Longchamp, also known as the N185, a main road which cuts right across the Bois de Boulogne. Today it was carrying a military convoy, a long line of trucks with unhappy looking troops sat in rows in the back of them. Then every so often a low loader with an anti aircraft gun on it. The whole lot were travelling extremely slowly, and the junction was blocked by military police. We had no option but to sit there, fuming. There was no way either of us could have predicted this, but he clearly felt that it was his fault.

Eventually the last of the convoy ground laboriously past and the road was open again. Jacques' foot went all the way down as he angrily pushed the car to whatever it was capable of, hoping to recoup what he saw as his own misjudgement. Unfortunately, he wasn't the most competent motorist I've ever been driven by, and the result was more frightening than exhilarating.

After three or four hair raising minutes, he announced that we were nearly there, and swung us down a track between some trees, marked by a sign showing a matchstick man kicking a football. As we jolted our way along the track, we saw through the trees ahead of us the incredible sight of a green and brown camouflaged aircraft slowly, almost impossibly slowly, coming in to land on the football pitches. There was no doubt that we had found the spot.

Even with the car windows open there was no sound audible from the aircraft, but there was the sound of gun fire. Jacques brought the car to a halt at the back of a long wooden hut, presumably the footballers changing rooms.

"Get your gun out." He said.

"I don't carry a gun, I'm just a private citizen."

He made an exasperated noise and rolled his eyes at this fresh example of Anglo Saxon trickery. As every Frenchman has learnt at his mother's knee, you can never trust the English. Just because you can't see how they're tricking you doesn't mean they're not doing it. He hurriedly rummaged around in the glove compartment, until he came upon a small pistol, which he thrust at me. I found this rather surprising, all you'll find in my glove compartment will be an old AA book, a torch that doesn't work and a packet of Mint Imperials. Nonetheless I levered myself out of the car, pistol in one hand and walking stick in the other, and started towards the corner of the building, Jacques at my side. As we approached we passed an unknown male body lying untidily on the ground.

Even this blatant warning failed to persuade either of us to exercise the least degree of caution, we simply marched round the corner, oblivious to any possible danger, which, if nothing else, saved us some time. There were three further grey suited male bodies, lying around the front of the shed, all apparently dead, and one man struggling to his feet. He was wild eyed and covered in blood, and as soon as he was aware of our presence he aimed his pistol right at me and pulled the trigger. There was a click, but nothing happened, until Jacques fired his own gun. Demonstrating his superb marksmanship, the German's apparently empty pistol flew away to one side. I never even got my gun up to the firing position.

While Jacques and I had been preoccupied by this performance, over to our left at the far corner of the football field, the Fieseler Storch, which I recognised from pictures, revved its engine and turned round to taxi back for its take off run. It was difficult to know to which activity we should pay more attention. Jacques was faster on the uptake than me.

"Where are Dumont and Heidi?" He shouted at the wild man, presumably the surviving member of the

Gestapo team, but I couldn't work out who their astonishingly lethal opponents had been.

"Licking and pawing each other, for all I know, the dirty perverts. They went that way." He gestured round the far end of the shed.

I presumed this talk of licking was supposed to be an accusation of lesbianism, but from my limited knowledge of that subject I had never thought licking to be a central part of their activities. I'm a reasonably well rounded sort of fellow and I've read Radclyffe Hall, it's important to try and keep up with these things, but I'm fairly sure that she never mentioned licking - perhaps I missed something.

Meanwhile, Jacques had advanced on the man. "Where were they going?" He was aggressive and direct, which was what we needed if we were ever going to catch them.

"You'll never find out, she's too smart for you, even I couldn't control the bitch."

"Are you Gunther von Strenglen?" I asked, finally realising that this must be her fellow assassin from the original team. As I asked this, Jacques turned his head to look at me, perhaps acknowledging that we should have realised this sooner. This momentary diversion was all the man needed, and in one sudden movement he used his left hand to rip off his false right hand, then with a devastating backhand swing he hit Jacques across the side of the head. The makeshift club was a powerful weapon, a solid wooden hand on the end of two steel rods, and Jacques fell directly to the floor. Von Strenglen turned to swing at me, but I was just out of range of his prosthetic weapon. I pointed the pistol at his belly and fired, except the trigger wouldn't move - I should have checked the safety catch.

There was no time for examining the weapon, so I did what I was good at in the days when I played rugby. Instead of running away, I lunged towards him, feinting round his right side as I did. The old skills were still reasonably intact, certainly enough to fool him, and the next thing I was standing behind him and he was still turning to follow. Not wanting any more truck with the pistol I brought the silver knob on the end of my walking stick down on his head. That did the trick and he joined Jacques. The old ways are often the best.

I looked around me, there were enough bodies to start a small mortuary. A voice called out something indistinguishable from across the field. I looked up and saw that the aircraft pilot had got out and was walking across towards me, his engine was still running and ready for a fast departure.

I waved a confident greeting to him, and then held up one finger, shouting: "Einen moment bitte." Then I waved him back to the aircraft. He looked a little puzzled but went. I crouched down beside Jacques, I could do with some assistance. Fortunately he was emerging from the effects of Gunther's hand. Leaving him to recover I turned to von Strenglen, and found that he was still breathing. Being somewhat feeble, I lacked the iron resolve to finish the job by clubbing him to death as he slept, instead I removed his braces and tied his elbows as tightly as I could behind his back. A civil service desk job was obviously about my limit.

Having stood up and shaken himself, like a dog emerging from water, Jacques gave von Strenglen a sharp experimental kick in the ribs. Satisfied that he was still unconscious, he strode off towards the plane. I tailed along in his wake, having discretely made sure the pistol safety catch was off, I couldn't face looking stupid from the same cause twice in five minutes.

The pilot obligingly turned off the engine, and climbed out again, faced with two pistols at close range it was his only sensible course. I thought he must have been enormously self confident, or simply a bit dim, not to have taken fright at what he could see was a fight to the death over by the changing hut. If I'd been him I would have opened the throttle and gone, you wouldn't have seen me for dust. But on consideration, the fact that he was now Jacques' prisoner was never going to be anything more than a temporary inconvenience. When the French surrendered, which had to be in the near future, then all German prisoners would be released and free to return to their units. From the pilot's point of view this entire episode would be no more than an interesting tale to tell in the mess. By this time next month they would all be having a good laugh about it. I sighed to myself, what an utter cock up this was, and it was going to be Britain's turn next. God help us.

"Lock it up will you." Jacques called, as he marched his captive back to the car. "We can hand the key in later, then someone from the air force can come and move it." I obliged, locking the aircraft's single flimsy access door, and then followed them.

Jacques found enough belts and braces to bind the pilot securely, and left him in the back of one of the other cars we had found parked there. Then we returned to von Strenglen, and Jacques gave me an object lesson in how to elicit answers. He propped him against the wall of the changing hut and slapped him viciously about the face two or three times, just to attract his attention. He soon had it.

"Even if I were to pretend that you were an enemy soldier in uniform, like the pilot we just arrested, and not a common spy, what do you think is going to happen? If you don't help me to find Heidi, you will be a prisoner in Paris while she makes it back to Berlin on her own, and then she will give her version of events without any input from you. Think about it man, whatever it was that caused the Gestapo to want you dead, will still apply." He waved his hand at the surrounding bodies, "If she gets back first she can throw all the blame for whatever your problem was onto you. At that point I won't need to kill you, your own people will do the job for me as soon as they get to Paris."

The two of them had their eyes locked, each feverishly calculating the best way to get themselves out of their respective problems. Jacques wanted Martine back in one piece, and von Strenglen wanted Heidi dead so that he could tell his own story. Unlike Jacques I knew exactly why the Gestapo had turned out in force. Even better, the story of the magnetron being offered to the highest bidder, had been amply confirmed when von Strenglen had produced a fake. Whichever of them got home first could tell the winning story. I thought it best not to confuse matters by mentioning my own role in these events.

Jacques had stopped talking, and von Strenglen was slowly nodding to himself, it seemed that he agreed with our version of events.

"If I help you to find Heidi, then you will kill her, and hold me until our troops arrive?"

"I have no interest in your death, with only one hand I would hardly describe you as able bodied, so you're not really much of a threat. And after a fiasco like this I can't imagine Heydrich giving you another job." As Jacques spoke I could see von Strenglen's facial muscles go rigid with the strain of not responding to this put down, the fact that he managed it proved how important it was to him.

"In principal I am willing to help you, because she is a traitor and I want her dead. The difficulty I have is that I don't know where she can have gone. After we lost our two way radio in the car crash at Montmartre, the only connection we had to a possible safe house was by using a Paris contact number. I can ring them for you and try to find her." He looked at us hopefully.

"Are you talking about your contact at the Spanish Embassy?" I asked.

"You know about this?"

"Of course we do, it was them who sent this bunch out to kill you."

"You are the old man from MI6, yes?"

"No, I am the old man from Putney."

"I don't think I know them."

"Just concentrate on thinking of something that might save you from your own people."

But he was at a loss, you could almost see his brain cells working overtime, trying to think of another possible destination that Heidi might have run to. He shook his head. "She could go anywhere, she can steal cars and open doors, she is very dangerous. I will do anything you want me to, but I just don't know where to start. You could try looking at any contacts the French slut had in this area, they will want to get off the streets."

Jacques hit him hard, across the face. The word slut had been a mistake.

"I am sorry, I should have said the Gendarme officer."

I might be gullible, but I believed him, if he knew something he would have told us. Jacques looked baffled, which meant that he believed him as well. It was an impasse, the three of us were silent, we didn't have a single idea between us.

"Then I'm afraid you are no longer of any use to us." Said Jacques, his manner indicating that the talking had ended. He moved his pistol to point directly at von Strenglen's heart.

"Wait, please wait, there is just one possibility. I cannot say it is a good possibility, but it is an idea so outrageous that only that woman would consider it." He was staring at us wide eyed, desperate to be listened to, if not believed.

We listened to him, but it was a ridiculous story - and we didn't believe a word of it.

Chapter 19

Fraulein Heidi Fuchs
Paris, Friday evening, May 17th. 1940

Clearing the immediate area was not quite as problematic as I had allowed for, and that's as it ought to be. Plan well, train hard, fight easy. As I caught up with the slow moving Martine, still stumbling through the trees in her slim line skirt, there was at least one more gunshot and then car door slamming noises, to indicate that the new arrivals were joining the fight. Whoever they were, they weren't likely to be friends of mine, so I kept going. I knew just where I wanted to be: out of here.

The first car I started had an almost empty tank, so I switched off and moved on. The next car was more than half full. As we drove off I turned to Martine. "Don't even try and tell me that wasn't more exciting than arresting flashers in Chalons. Even losing your virginity wasn't that good."

She tried to stop herself, but it was a waste of time, so she relaxed into a smile. "Actually I didn't much enjoy losing my virginity."

"Neither did I, but give it a while and it grows on you."

"Did you kill all those men?"

"All except Gunther, and he was the one I really wanted, the rest of them were just getting in the way. I know you and your friend found the proper device at

Montmartre, but I don't think he had it with him when I stopped him on the road, so where did it go?"

"You must realise that even if I did know, I would have to lie to you."

"Alright, so lie to me."

"Major Vernet took it off him, and then tried to fool you with some dummy."

"So Sir Freddy was really going home empty handed, and leaving you like a lemon?"

She seemed a bit choked up and wasn't sure if she could manage to say anything to that, so she just nodded her agreement.

"What is he - homosexual, stupid, or does he just not like foreigners?"

"I don't know, I tried to work it out, but I still don't know."

"I was listening to you in that cafe, after you'd left the British Embassy, when he said how much he'd enjoyed your *professional* relationship. I thought you'd been making things pretty clear up till then, you should have hit him for that."

She sniffled a bit, but then realised what I'd said. "You can't have been listening to us, nobody knew where we were going, and there was nobody anywhere near us."

"Did he say what I just said, or didn't he?"

"Well, yes he did, but how can you possibly . . ?"

"I was the waitress who served your coffee, and then I cleaned the next two tables. Nobody looks at waitresses, you certainly didn't."

She turned her head to look straight at me.

"Close your mouth, you'll catch flies." I said.

Then just to confirm things I asked. "So having come all this way, and succeeded in finding the device, he just gave up and left it with Vernet?"

"He felt that he had no choice, all the proper professionals on his team had been killed in the plane crash, he was just a bureaucrat, he was only on the team to identify the proper magnetron if ever they found it. Then when the British Embassy refused to help he wasn't left with much option, he knew he couldn't take on professionals like you and von Strenglen."

"And that's the lie you promised me is it?"

"Yes, I promise you, that's the lie."

Then we both laughed, because we both knew that I believed almost everything that she'd told me. She needed watching, but she was still relaxing company. Though I still couldn't decide if she'd been running as fast as she could, when she was supposed to be escaping from me at the football ground.

I was driving back towards town, without any more coherent plan than clearing the immediate area. The car had only just been stolen, it was safe until at least tomorrow morning, the Paris police had their hands full dealing with refugees. There was no pressure on me from that direction, but there was still no forward planning. I pulled over in front of a bar, I needed time to think.

I put my hand on her leg. "No matter how I feel, you know what I'll do if you try to run, don't you?"

She nodded, and so I reloaded my gun, took off the handcuffs and then we went in for a drink and something to eat. The last time I'd eaten in a pavement cafe Martine had been left in the car, tied up under a coat. She should regard this as promotion.

The only question of real significance was whether or not I was going to abandon the device, and save myself, relying on my native wit to get back to Berlin faster than von Strenglen; thus making sure that my version of events was the one that stuck? Or, should I sacrifice myself in a vain and pointless search for a device that I wouldn't even recognise if I saw it?

When you put it like that it doesn't take a lot of thinking about, and I couldn't think of any other way of putting it. There was no chance of him having jumped on that plane for a quick way out, because for him, as mission leader, to arrive in Berlin empty handed would be just as bad as him arriving with the wrong thing. That wasn't the sort of mistake he'd recover from. No, if von Strenglen was still alive, he was still in Paris, and desperate. Whoever had sent the four men I'd shot, would no doubt have plenty more to replace them.

My best hope was to stick with the story that I'd been obeying his direct orders throughout, even when I was shooting the Gestapo, it was only because he had told me they were foreign agents. What they'd said to him about suspecting that he was trying to sell the device to the highest bidder was exactly the sort of acorn that I could turn into an oak tree.

Unlike von Strenglen, my danger didn't lie in Berlin, it lay right here in the next twelve or twenty four hours. My own people were looking for me, the French were looking for me, and the English toff from MI6 would like to get his hands on me. The part of Martine's story that I found hardest to swallow was that he was going home empty handed. She might believe his lies, but I didn't. No one else had ever tracked me as successfully as him, and I don't believe in coincidences, he was no more a bureaucratic amateur than I was. I needed to be somewhere untouchable for a while, until I could work out a decent exit plan.

And then it came to me, why hadn't I thought of it earlier? The meeting I'd attended two months ago, on the direct instructions of Rudolf Hess's personal office, where detailed plans had been laid for an earlier

Einsatzgruppen raid on Paris, plans that had, in the end, been cancelled. But before they were I had learnt some rather surprising information, and it was information that could be useful in exactly this situation. Written notes had been forbidden at the meeting, but I hadn't needed them, the information itself was sufficiently astonishing to be memorable. Of particular significance to me now, was the fact I could remember the address; twenty four Boulevard Suchet. This would get us off the streets - was it even possible that the original plan might work. Now if I could pull that one off, I would be untouchable - by anyone.

I unfolded the map, and began to look for the Boulevard Suchet. As best I could recall it was somewhere in the west of the city, I moved my finger, methodically, block by block. Yes, there it was, only a couple of kilometres from here. I put the map down, lit a cigarette leaned back and smiled at Martine.

"You're going to enjoy this." She looked doubtful, but who cares? I hurried her back to the car, the sooner we got this started the better.

"What I'm going to want you to do in the next few hours might not make the British very happy, but it won't damage French national interests in any way. You have my word on that." As she hadn't stopped looking doubtful, I emphasised the point.

"You're a clever woman, just follow my lead, and if at any time you think I'm cheating you, come straight out and tell them that I'm a German agent. How's that?"

"What would you do about it, if I did?"

"I'd kill everyone in sight, starting with you, but at least you'd die pure. Perhaps you should change into something white, like for your first communion."

She sighed heavily, to indicate that I was being more tiresome than amusing. But I knew that she knew, that I

285

meant every word of it. My dear Martine and I, with her sexy little tight skirt, understood each other very clearly indeed. It had always been von Strenglen who was the excess baggage.

In films and magazines people have to tell each other that they're in love, but not in real life. For me it has always been a growing awareness, rather than a direct statement; and the confirmation, the certainty, has usually come from some otherwise unobtrusive touch. When you're sat next to each other, the unselfconscious placing of a hand on a thigh. That sort of thing is far more reliable than talk. Martine just did it to me, as I turned the car towards the entrance. She put her hand on my arm, it was half touch, half stroke, and the clincher was that she did it without even realising she was doing it. I might be too hard bitten to feel quite the thrill I once did, but a bulb lit up on my circuit board, and I noted the fact, with interest.

The premises were immediately recognisable from what I could remember of the briefing photographs. A large white three story corner property, with striped awnings at the principal windows. A bored looking Gendarme was standing on the pavement near the front door, and twenty five yards along, at the end of the building another one was guarding the striped traffic barrier leading to the back of the premises, which was where I was heading.

I took out Martine's official identity card, which I'd been carrying since I kidnapped her, and left it ready in my lap. From this moment on it was all about confidence.

"Whoever you meet, and whatever is said - you don't blink, you don't look evasive and you do not allow anyone to intimidate you. Is that clear?" I was aware of sounding like a sergeant major, which was exactly the effect I was aiming for.

Although I was looking at the road, I was aware of her stiffening in slight surprise at my tone. "I will be every bit as confident as you."

"Good girl."

I swung across the pavement, brought the car to halt with our bonnet next to the striped barrier and wound down the window. The Gendarme put his head down to look at me.

"Capitaine Martine Dumont, Royal Protection Division, lift the barrier."

He scrutinised the identity card picture. "This doesn't look like you."

"Congratulations, but it does look like her." I prodded a finger in Martine's direction. "Now open the barrier."

He crouched lower to peer across to my front seat passenger, then handed me back the card and turned to lift the barrier. All without a single further comment. I passed the ID back to Martine, drove through and parked next to two large black British limousines, with diplomatic plates. As I was doing this, Martine breathed in an astonished whisper. "I know who lives here."

"Then it's congratulations to you too." With the Capitaine in my wake, like a destroyer following a battleship, I swept through the open door leading in from the car park.

There was a portly middle aged man, with a red face and a well cut suit, even before he opened his mouth, he was English. He stepped forward. "Can I help you?"

"And you are?"

"Metcalfe, just helping out with security. Friend of the family normally, you know, but it's all hands to the pump just now."

We had spoken in English, and although it was not my favourite language it seemed sensible to stick with it for the moment. Especially as I have been told that when speaking English I sound unmistakeably German. "Gendarme Capitaine Martine Dumont, acting for the Foreign Office, has accompanied me here. I need to speak to His Royal Highness without delay."

He looked surprised by this, and turned to Martine, who was by now holding out her official identity card for his inspection. He turned back to me. "I'm afraid I must ask who you are, and exactly what this is about. You see I've heard no mention of you being expected."

"My identity need not concern you, please simply inform His Royal Highness that I am the courier he is expecting concerning Operation Unity, as discussed with the Duke of Hamilton."

Metcalfe stepped back, as if I had struck him. I recognised his name as a close confidante of the former King, and his reaction proved that he was well aware of Operation Unity, and what it involved.

Looking about him to confirm our privacy, he leaned closer and asked in an astonished whisper. "Do you mean that you're from *Germany*? I mean actually from *Germany*?"

I like to give people their money's worth, if I can, so I gave him the correct response. I straightened up, clicked my heels, briefly bowed my head and said "Ja, naturlich."

His eyes goggled. "Shh, we don't want to alarm anyone. Please just wait here, for a moment." Then he looked about, presumably for someone to wait with us, in case we set fire to the place. "Ah, Johnson, yes - could you come here for a moment, and keep these ladies company for a minute, while I go and speak to HRH?"

Then turning back to us. "I shall be back in a moment, if you wouldn't mind . . er . . yes . ." He left without quite managing to finish his sentence, but I think we'd got the essence of it. Johnson kept us out of mischief for the five minutes it took for Metcalfe to confer with his master, and then we were ushered through a green baize door into a large tiled hall and up the wide curving staircase. Throughout this time Martine and I had avoided looking at each other for fear of laughing.

On the first floor Metcalfe led us in to an ornate and typically French salon, decorated in gold and silver. It was the sort of room you would expect someone with a great deal of money and very little taste to occupy. The desks and sideboards were over decorated, and the chairs were that spindly sort the French are so attached to, the sort that no matter which way you sit on them you are always uncomfortable. There was a brothel I'd worked at once in Hamburg that had tried for this look, and I hadn't liked it then.

Metcalfe stopped, and made the formal, if somewhat vague, introduction. "Your Royal Highnesses, the two persons of whom I spoke."

Until I saw which way he'd been facing I hadn't noticed the rooms occupants, the exaggerated height of the room had reduced its human occupants to insignificance. The legendry Duke of Windsor and 'That Woman' were sat facing each other on a pair of sofas, he had a small dog on his knee. We had been warned at the briefing that, despite being specifically barred from using it, Mrs. Simpson, or as she now was, the Duchess of Windsor always insisted on being addressed by the title Royal Highness. But then you simply couldn't list the various things that different people are turned on by, and I've seen a few of them myself.

I started in my strongly accented English. "Your Royal Highnesses, I wish to extend the Fuhrer's personal delight at your agreement to accept our protection. Both the Fuhrer and Reichsministers Hess and von Ribbentrop hold themselves at permanent readiness to be of any assistance that might be necessary. The Fuhrer also wishes me to say how very much he enjoyed meeting you both at Berchtesgaden, and looks forward to seeing you there again in the very near future. With immediate effect, this area of the city has been declared a prohibited area of activity for all Wehrmacht forces, no matter what happens in the rest of Paris, this area will remain untouched." Not wishing it to sound like a public lecture, I paused to let them catch up.

The Duke had stared, first at me and then at the Duchess, unsure what his correct reaction ought to be. He was clearly astonished by my unexpected appearance, the Duchess, however, rose to her feet, astonished or not she was doing the driving.

"Why didn't Joachim let us know that Operation Unity was back on track? We're almost ready to leave for Biarritz, the cars are loaded and we plan to be on the road first thing tomorrow morning. Don't we David?" She turned back to the Duke for confirmation.

I'd forgotten about that, although he had been known as King Edward, she always called him David, the upper classes could be very confusing. He spoke. "That's right dear." Where she had a strong almost masculine American voice, his was weak and petulant. The difference between them was every bit as strange as the gossip columnists had suggested. Then I remembered something else, it was said that she had

290

worked in a brothel herself, in Shanghai. That could account for her taste in furniture.

"Reichsminister von Ribbentrop, wishes to apologise for this, but an earlier messenger had been sent, two days before the Blitzkrieg began, unfortunately it now seems that he was intercepted by French Intelligence. As soon as this was discovered, I myself was sent."

The thing to keep in mind about these two was that they were desperate to see 'David' back on the British throne, but this time with her as Queen Wallis, and with a German occupied Britain that was exactly what was going to happen. In the meantime they would turn any trick it took to get themselves there. Desperate people believe what they want to believe, they're the easiest people in the world to fool, they'll do half the work for you.

"To allow for the possibility of my capture I was not permitted to travel with any written identification, I was, therefore, instructed Sir to give you the password Siegfried."

"By Jove, that's it, that's what we arranged with Joachim." He said to Wallis, but she still wanted more information about me.

"What's your name, my dear?"

"Heidi Fuchs, Madame."

She gave a brief smile. "Sure honey, I just bet you do, but it was your name I wanted - not your hobby."

Since my days on the game I had forgotten what simple delight the Anglo Saxons took in misspelling Fuchs. For a while I had even used it as my professional name, though frankly the repetition and lack of subtlety soon became boring, and I went back to being Hot Heidi. Perhaps an outsider wouldn't have spotted it, though I knew straightaway, the main difference between the Duchess and me was how we were paid.

But with my mouth I said sweetly, "Then please just call me Heidi."

"Isn't that cute David? Heidi, just like the little Swiss girl." She said, over her shoulder, unconcerned with any reply.

Photographs had not prepared me for her appearance. Despite the clothes, the jewellery, the big hair, the makeup, despite all that, there was something distinctly unfeminine about her, a squareness, an angularity; and remember - there had been no children from her three marriages. Of course I've seen, and even worked with, the lady boys in the bars down the Reeperbahn, and they go big on the hair and the make up. She couldn't possibly be, could she? Surely someone would have noticed by now? I brought my wandering attention back to earth.

"The Fuhrer suggests that you should remain here, until advance units of our forces arrive. With your permission, I have been instructed to remain and act as your communications link, to ensure that all future messages are delivered efficiently."

The Duchess walked over to a writing desk, where she pressed a button twice. Within seconds another middle aged Englishman came in. He ignored the Duke and looked directly at the Duchess.

"Ah, Gray, you had better tell Hale to start unloading the cars, it looks as if we shan't be going anywhere for a while." The two of them had smiled at each other, and she spoke more warmly to him than she had to her husband. If I hadn't known it would be immoral, I would have bet she was sleeping with the staff. Though in her case, who knows if such a union would be homosexual or heterosexual?

292

The man she called Gray flicked a casually enquiring glance at Martine and I, and asked. "Operation Unity?"

She nodded. "I knew Joachim would come good - and the way those stuffed shirts patronised him in London - well we shall see about that. Won't we David?"

His response was so inevitable, I almost said it with him. "Yes dear."

Sir Freddy Villiers
Paris, Friday evening, May 17th. 1940

It proved a challenge to handcuff a man with one hand, and in the end we left von Strenglen and the pilot tied up together, against the front wall of the hut. The four bodies we left where they lay, someone else was going to have to tidy up. Then Jacques drove us to the nearest bar, to call in a report and get us both a drink and a sandwich.

The fact that Heidi had left the site with Martine, only minutes before our arrival, was no help at all. Once she'd cleared the scene, she could be anywhere. I was obliged to acknowledge that it had been my lack of engagement with Martine, when she had so clearly extended the hand of friendship, that had led to us operating separately, which in turn had allowed her abduction. If we had been together that day, instead of me pompously going off on my own, then this whole disaster could have been avoided. My concern about not making a fool of myself had ended up ruining everything.

As I had the magnetron, the German's sole ace was the fact that they were holding Martine hostage. From a

British Military Intelligence viewpoint the answer was simple, abandon her and head for home. But if I ran for cover, then Heidi would almost certainly kill Martine, and that would be something that I wasn't sure I could live with - such a grubby and cowardly end to an otherwise honourable career. No, this game was going to be played right up to the final whistle, no matter what the cost. And if Major Lawrence Grand of Section D in London didn't approve, then Major Grand could do the other thing. I was aware that a few days on the front line had noticeably coarsened my reactions, I had once been willing to look at the other chap's point of view.

We left the bar, no wiser than when we'd arrived, my renewed determination providing no practical assistance. For a lack of any serious alternative, Jacques drove us back to the Avenue Mozart, to take another look at the offices of Axel Buro. Needless to say, they were deserted and shut for the night, what else had we expected?

"I'm not ready to call it a day just yet, do you want to take a look at the Duke of Windsor's place?" He asked.

"That story of von Strenglen's about a Nazi plot to install Edward and Mrs. Simpson on the throne, as Nazi puppets, surely that's the stuff of fantasy. The British people would never stand for it."

"Are you suggesting that we support what's happening in our country right now? Or the Dutch, the Belgians, the Czechs, the Danes, the Poles . ."

"Alright, that's enough, I take your point, it's a growing list and we could be next. But Edward abdicated two years ago, he can't just walk back in and say he's changed his mind."

"He wouldn't need to, Goebbels would orchestrate such a public demand for his return that he would simply be bowing to popular pressure. Don't forget that most Americans couldn't care less about the Nazis and they'd be delighted to have an American Queen. She would be on the front cover of every glossy magazine ever published; Queen Wallis."

He was right, Ambassador Kennedy had been predicting a Nazi walkover for years, he would see nothing wrong with Stormtroopers marching down the Mall, and Churchill being publicly hanged. Why we tolerated that man in London was a mystery. I was gripped by a deep feeling of frustration, there were so many things going so very wrong, and so little I could do about any of them.

"You could be right, at least we should take a look. But how do we approach it? We can hardly just walk up to his front door and ask if he's seen any crazed Nazi killers recently."

"Not crazed, whatever else Heidi is she isn't crazed. According to von Strenglen, she'd been involved in the planning for some kind of German kidnap of the Duke and Duchess of Windsor, so that they could be produced after a successful invasion of Britain. She will probably have some routine for contacting them, or identifying herself."

"I hadn't really thought about it before, but what von Strenglen had said might just have some element of truth in it. And I was wrong to say that she was crazy, she's anything but, in fact I suppose she's remarkably efficient in some gruesomely Teutonic fashion. That's the trouble."

Jacques had been driving as we talked, presumably towards the the Windsor's house. "Do you know their address?" I asked.

"Twenty four Boulevard Suchet, everybody knows where they live, they're in the papers every week.

Anyway, it was a fairly well known address even before they moved in."

I looked at him, my eyebrows raised, waiting for more.

He glanced back at me, looking slightly unsure. "Have you ever heard of Anaïs Nin?"

"Never."

"She was a writer, an erotic writer, who lived here nine or ten years ago. The house became something of a literary salon for people like D.H. Lawrence and a group of people associated with a publishing company called the Obelisk Press."

"The Obelisk Press?" I knew the name, but couldn't place it for a moment, then it came to me. "Were they the people who published James Joyce and Henry Miller?"

"You know these authors?" He sounded surprised, as if we didn't have sex in England.

"I've got a copy of Miller's Tropic of Capricorn, it was Christmas present from my brother."

"And did you enjoy it?"

"To be honest I thought it was impenetrable tosh, he was too concerned with shocking the reader to take enough trouble over his plotting and prose. Mary, that was my wife, said that it had taught her a couple of things she hadn't known previously. But in the end it was more of a novelty than a novel."

"Good Lord." Was his only comment. I didn't enquire if he'd read it himself, he didn't seem much of a literary type, but you never can tell with dirty books they attract all sorts, especially if they're illustrated.

The house was a large imposing place on a corner, opposite a small park, there must have been some money in pornography to have afforded somewhere like this. Though I suspect that I'm a bit old to start a new career, and the research would be exhausting for a man of my years. He pulled up just short of the building while we reviewed the situation.

"How are we going to get in?" I asked

"I was hoping that you could think of something, I'm not a sufficiently senior Gendarme to simply request admittance, without some very good reason."

Well his old private secretary Tommy Lascelles is the younger brother of a chum of mine, Sandy Lascelles, we were at Marlborough and Trinity together, and I've met Tommy and some of his crowd a few times. I could try getting in on personal acquaintance. We were silent for a while as I pondered the chances, the main uncertainty being the level of security to expect in the home of an exiled former king. It was hardly an everyday situation. In the end we decide to wing it, we lacked the time and the resources for anything more complicated.

Jacques drove the last hundred yards to park by the pavement, near the front door. The duty Gendarme came to attention as we approached, Jacques produced his official ID. "Sir Freddy Villiers, an official messenger from London, for the Duke."

"Wait a moment, please." He went through the black railings to the front door, and pressed his finger to the button on an intercom box mounted on the wall. After an exchange of squawking he beckoned us forward, and the door was opened from the inside. A tall middle aged man stepped forward to meet us, he stared for a moment, trying to place me.

"Sir Freddy, haven't we met before?"

It was easier for me; although I hadn't known he would be here, I had known him to be one of the Duke's inner circle, so his presence made sense.

"Fruity Metcalf - good to see you again, I should have expected to find you here. Always rely on Metcalf when the chips are down." For that first instinctive moment he had been genuinely pleased to see me, but his natural smile of welcome, at meeting a known face in foreign parts, soon faded. Our presence here was some sort of problem.

"The Gendarme said you had a message from London, but the fact of the matter is old chap that I think you might be a bit late, what with the Hun beating down the door and all that."

"Would it be possible for me to speak to the Duke straight away? I have an important message for him."

He was now distinctly ill at ease, there was something going on around here that he didn't want to share with me. "The point is Freddy, that HRH has been waiting for a word from London for the last six months, and what have we heard? Nothing. Even when Winston flew over to meet Reynaud, two days ago, he never called round. And those two used to be thick as thieves."

"I can imagine it must be rotten for him, but frankly I'm not usually involved in that sort of thing. It's simply that I was in Paris on Air Ministry business when I discovered something that might affect the Duke directly."

"He's actually a bit pressed at the moment, so if you give me your message I'll make sure it gets to him, 'Fraid that's the best I can manage."

"I'm sorry Fruity but that simply won't do. I have information that the Duke's life could be in immediate danger, and I must speak to him personally - without delay."

"No can do old chap. London chose to leave him dangling in the wind, while the entire German army was heading straight for him at high speed, and that's simply not good enough, not good enough at all. He and the Duchess are now taking the necessary steps to secure their own safety. If London don't want to talk to him, then he don't want to talk to them. It cuts both ways, don't you see?"

That proved it, the talk of securing their own safety; Heidi wasn't just here, she had spun them some sort of story to persuade them to shelter her. Or even more outrageously, to accept a cock and bull offer in Hitler's name, for her to shelter them. She should win a medal for sheer damned effrontery. That's what he meant by us being too late. They hadn't taken the new King's shilling, they'd taken the Fuhrer's Reichsmark, or thought they had.

"The German woman's already here, isn't she? She's told the Duke that she's speaking on behalf of Hitler, and that she'll keep him safe. And then what - do they come back to London with a conquering German army, goosestepping their way back into Buckingham Palace - is that what you've got in mind Fruity? Because there's a name for siding with the enemy in time of war, it's called treason, or doesn't that bother you?"

I was incensed, and without meaning to I had grasped my walking stick half way down the shaft, as if I was going to hit him with it. He backed away, covered in embarrassment but still spluttering with self righteous denial.

"You've got no right, no bloody right at all, to come barging in here being high and mighty with us. Who the hell do you think you are, with your cheap accusations? David's done every single thing in his power to serve his country, and what has he got in return? Nothing but contempt. Well it just won't do, if you won't help us we shall have to help ourselves, and we'll take our friends where we find them."

"You damn fool, this isn't just treason, it's utter gullibility. The woman you think is from Hitler is a deranged assassin who has killed more than six people in the last three days alone. There is no message from Hitler, there is no offer of safe passage, the only person she wants to help is herself. Even her own people are chasing her. She had nowhere left to run, so she thought she could pull the wool over your eyes, and from the sound of it she's succeeding beyond her wildest dreams."

"You don't fool me for a second, you're just another one of the rabble who supported that humbug Baldwin and his chum the bloody Archbishop, Wallis was a positive Godsend to bigots like that. David was a true man of the people and the Establishment weren't just jealous of his popularity, they were frightened of it. They were determined to get rid of him at any cost, and if he hadn't met Wallis they would have found some other excuse to knife him in the back."

"For God's sake stop talking such absolute bilge, the man was put to the test and found wanting, he has the intellect and maturity of a backward child. He thought he could subordinate the interests of the Empire to his perverse sexual desires, and he was wrong. Now I suggest you stand aside, because I'm going to speak to him, with or without your permission." My outburst had been louder and gone much further than intended, but it had at least the virtue of truth, and Fruity's pig headed inflexibility had seriously provoked me.

I started to move towards the stairs, ready to barge the man out of my way, but before I could, I was stopped by a voice from above. However, on this occasion it wasn't God, but simply Heidi, who only thought she was God.

"Oh you boys, all this talk talk talk, and the pushing and the shoving, what are we going to do with you, heh?" In English she sounded like Marlene Dietrich, any minute now she would probably start singing 'Falling In Love Again', a song that Mary and I used to dance to. You should give it a try, it's in perfect waltz time.

She was standing on the first floor landing, looking down on us, unfortunately she was standing behind Martine and holding a pistol in her right hand, while her left hand had a length of Martine's black hair wrapped around it. She was holding the hair tightly enough to pull Martine's head back and make her wince. I stopped exactly where I was. Astonishingly, before any of us could do or say another thing, a door across the first floor landing from Heidi was thrown open and a woman I recognised as Wallis Simpson stormed out.

"You." She flung an accusatory arm in my direction. "You don't know a single damn thing, you upper class limey pervert, you're not fit to lick David's boots. Well you just take note buster, that when the time comes it's people like you that are right at the top of our list to be sorted out."

Before she could enlarge on any this, Heidi pointed the gun across the stairwell and fired, she can't have been aiming for Wallis, as she hit a picture on the wall behind her. There were a succession of noises, the gun shot, the glass breaking and the thud of the slug hitting the wall. All of which were quickly followed by the loud slamming of a door, as Wallis retreated. Heidi returned her attention the frozen scene in the hall.

"Not your typical Duchess, I think? Now you, Mr. Fruity, my friend and I are coming downstairs. If you or

301

anyone else does something to make me unhappy I will kill you first, even before I kill her." She pulled Martine's hair even tighter for a moment, which made her gasp slightly.

As the two of them made their way down the stairs, I turned to Fruity. "She means exactly what she says, if there's anybody likely to try any heroics, tell them not to."

"Nobody will do anything to stop her, just as long as His Royal Highness is safe."

"Oh he's safe," said Heidi, and then in a lower tone, "For what he's worth." The two of them had now joined us in the hall. I put my hand out to take Martine's, but Heidi used the pistol to gesture me back.

"It looks like the comedy is over round here. I had thought of taking him," she jerked her head upstairs, "As my hostage instead of Martine, but us girls have been getting along so well it would be a shame to lose her, and frankly he wasn't much of a talker."

"What are you going to do? You can't keep on running indefinitely, why not just release Martine, neither of us are the slightest threat to you. All I want to do is go home, empty handed, and Martine wants to go back to Chalons. You can go and do what you like for all we care, surely the game is over now, we've both failed to get the magnetron."

She looked at me, with a shrewd and calculating look on her face. "You know English, that was just about the conclusion I had reached, but now I'm not so sure. Just hearing it from your mouth makes me think it's a lie. Like the Duchess says so sweetly, you are an upper class limey pervert, and your sort are famous for telling lies. So whatever your agenda is, it can't possibly be what you just said. I think Martine and I might have to spend a little more time together."

I looked at Martine, she didn't look as rough as I would have expected from spending all this time as a hostage, in fact she looked, and probably smelled, cleaner than me and her hair had been washed recently. I was almost overwhelmed by the urge to hug and kiss her. The fact that I failed to do so can be variously ascribed to: the gun, the circumstances and an English awkwardness with public displays of affection. Whatever the reason, I should have simply done it.

What actually happened was that I said, rather weakly; "I'm so sorry, I know a lot of this is my fault, but I won't rest until your free."

"Thank you Freddy."

"Yes, thank you Freddy," said Heidi sarcastically. "That was very nice, but now we have to go." She pushed Martine towards a door at the far side of the hall. Jacques and I followed, it led through to a back hall, a surprised looking man stood there with his hands up as our procession made its way past him and through the next door, which led outside.

"Don't get too close, remember who gets it first."

I paused in the doorway as they walked slowly towards a line of cars parked there, Jacques was with me. I stopped just outside the door, I wanted to see which car they left in, hopefully without provoking a reaction. As Jacques and I stood watching, the heavy door slammed firmly shut behind us, and bolts could be heard slamming home. I should have thought of that.

At that moment a flashlight shone along the side of the building, from the pavement. It flicked briefly over Jacques and I before moving to, and settling on, Heidi. A German man's voice shouted out that she should stop moving and drop her gun. If he'd asked me I could have told him he was wasting his breath. Another flashlight came on from beyond the striped arm that acted as a traffic barrier. There appeared to be a group of at least four men spread out along the pavement, I thought I had seen a Gendarme manning the barrier when we arrived, but there was no sign of him now.

The German voice shouted out again, this time warning that if she didn't stop they would open fire. Jacques and I were stood between the men on the pavement and Heidi, so when the shooting started it wasn't just going to be Heidi that was in danger. It was a situation that called for some degree of rearrangement. I grabbed Jacques' arm and dragged him with me, sprinting down towards the line of cars; apart from two dustbins, they were the only cover round here.

As we arrived behind the cars, a fusillade of shots rang out, most of them hitting the French car on the end. The four of us were behind one of two identical Daimlers, which, being twice the size offered much better cover. Crouching there, I was aware of the uncomfortable lump of Jacques' pistol, digging into my side and ruining the cut of my jacket pocket. The thing was a damn nuisance, but one doesn't like to throw away another chap's property.

"Who are they?" I asked Heidi.

"The Gestapo, there seems to have been a misunderstanding."

"Misunderstanding?" I echoed, feeling the word didn't quite cover our circumstances, whilst wishing that my earlier misinformation could have taken effect on another occasion.

Then an unknown English voice spoke. "This has got nothing to do with me, do you think they'll let me go?"

Who the hell are you?"

"Hale, the butler sir, I was just fetching some items from the car."

304

"Have you got the keys to one of these Daimlers?"

"Yes sir."

"I sent Hale to shelter behind the next car in line, and then despite Heidi still holding her pistol, told her and Martine to get into the back of the nearest Daimler, while Jacques and I got in the front. Under the circumstances, it seemed perfectly natural that they did what they were told. Luckily, I was familiar with the controls, although this one was a Sports Saloon, my brother has a Straight Eight which is very similar, and so I was able to start the engine without any unnecessary delay. Neither Heidi's pistol, nor her hostage had impressed the group at the end of the drive, but one of us needed to take a grip of things and get this nonsense sorted out.

I looked over my shoulder. "Keep your heads down, this might be a little bumpy."

Chapter 20

Fraulein Heidi Fuchs
Paris, late evening, Friday May 17th. 1940

It had almost worked, in fact for a while I had begun to relax and think of my next move, but then I'd heard that Englishman's voice from downstairs. How he could possibly have followed me here I couldn't imagine, I certainly hadn't confided in von Strenglen about my earlier involvement in the abandoned plan to kidnap the Duke and Duchess. Unless perhaps he'd heard about it from service rumours, despite all precautions these things are never completely watertight. But ultimately, it didn't matter, my options had been closing down anyway, we were moving into the endgame now.

The only sanctuary I could realistically find in France was going to be on a very temporary basis. Even in enemy territory the Gestapo were successfully tracking me, and when the occupation of France was completed they would find that process very much easier. Was there still some way of me getting back to Berlin, to present my version of events? The trouble with that was that having failed to kill von Strenglen when I should, he would already have his story in place, with all the blame for our failure resting firmly on me. Going back to find I was out of work wouldn't have bothered me so much, I've had hard times before. The real risk was not losing my job, but losing my life. A cock up like this was going to require a fall guy, and it looked like my name would already be in place.

There might be opportunities for someone with my skills in a third country, but where? The two obvious choices were Spain and Italy, but I spoke neither of those languages and certainly wouldn't be safe in either one of them from the long and claw like reach of Heinrich Himmler. Heading for South America might be safe enough, but could I honestly bring myself to wear a sombrero and live amongst the gauchos? Now North America, that might be a possibility, I brightened up a little, that could bear thinking about.

After we had been herded into the Duke's big car, Sir Freddy had charged the barrier at full speed, ignoring the prospect of there being any passing traffic on the Boulevard, I wouldn't have thought he had the nerve. From the feel of it, we must have run over at least two of the attacking group, and serve them right. He had raced off at speed, but even so within less than a minute it was clear that we had a car following us. I was so dispirited that I couldn't even be bothered to point the gun at Martine, and even if I had she was pretty confident that I wasn't going to shoot her, and I agreed with her assessment.

It's not a feeling that I'm familiar with, but just for once I found the fact that someone other than me was taking the decisions a relief. I could always step back into to the driving seat when events dictated.

Martine's Sergeant, Jacques, had turned round in his seat and was looking between us, back through the small rear window.

"There are two cars following us now." He said. Sure enough, shortly after that the first bullet hit the back of our car. The British limousine was a lot heavier than most of the cars I was used to, and thus provided more protection, but even so it was not a good sign. They were sufficiently desperate to reach me that they were even prepared to engage in a running battle on the streets. That alone was sufficient evidence of the reception that was waiting for me.

"It's not us they're after is it?" Asked Martine, but I didn't think the question needed answering, and just looked at her, so she continued. "Even if Sir Freddy can somehow shake them off tonight, they'll be back tomorrow, and the next day, until they get you. Do you have any plan, or are you just going to shoot it out?"

She was either a world class actress or she was sympathetic, in the way you would be for a wounded dog, just before you shot it.

"You might as well put the gun down." She said. "You're not going to shoot any of us."

"Don't be too sure, your English friend is almost as much of a nuisance as von Strenglen, it wouldn't take much for me to put a bullet in him." Martine pursed her lips, and gave me a disbelieving look. I started to put the gun back in its shoulder holster, but she held out her hand for it. I thought about things for a moment and decided that she was right, they would trust me much more if they knew that I was unarmed. The fact that I was faster and more dangerous than any of them, wouldn't seem as important as me having surrendered my gun. So I smiled and handed it to her, situations like this were usually quite easily reversible.

"I'm sorry about grabbing your hair, but I had to make it look realistic or some idiot would have started shooting." She shrugged, which means it can't have hurt that much. But then I've always found pain and pleasure to be very close bedfellows. Another two bullets smacked into the bodywork behind us, but it was a heavy car and they didn't penetrate. I looked around me distractedly, with or without my gun it had been a long time since I'd been quite this deep in *der Schiesse*, but something would turn up, something always does.

For some reason the French still had their street lights on, they didn't seem to feel any need for a blackout. As the intermittent flashes of light from passing lamp posts, illuminated the interior, I saw that in the solid wooden bulkhead behind the front seats there was a drop down door. I stretched forward and pulled it down. A light came on inside the cocktail cabinet and the door locked into position as a small tabletop, stored inside were four flute glasses and two bottles of Pol Roger champagne. I passed Martine two of the glasses and set about removing the wire cork holder from one of the bottles.

The correct technique is to hold the neck in one hand and the cork in the other, you twist in opposite directions and then pull them apart, that way the cork comes out smoothly without any noise or spray. But it had been a long day and I couldn't be bothered, so I levered the cork out with my thumbs. There was an explosive pop and the cork sped forward, hitting the inside of the windscreen with a bang. Both Sir Freddy and the Sergeant reacted as though they'd been shot, jerking several centimetres in the air and swivelling their heads frantically to locate the enemy.

We had been travelling at a considerable speed and Freddy's momentary loss of control was enough to send the car into a spin. I hung on to the fat central arm rest with one hand, and the bottle with the other. Martine performed equally well with the glasses, you'd think we'd been trained for it.

Sir Freddy seemed to be coping well - this sort of driving was probably something that Military Intelligence taught all their agents. We came to a rest facing in the opposite direction, and with a quick thinking that reminded me of myself, he put his foot flat down. The car's powerful engine roared and we surged forwards. As our lurch forward had pushed me back in my seat, I couldn't see what he was aiming at, but his hunched forward position and his repeated jinking this way and that, made it clear that he had something in his sights.

There was a noisy impact, and I caught a glimpse of another car rolling past us as we carried on our way, Freddy was still hunched over the wheel and accelerating. He was going for the double. I pushed myself forward to get a better look. There was another car, which had been heading in our direction, but which was now turning hurriedly to one side, Sir Freddy swung the wheel to follow him. We struck his rear three quarter a violent blow, he was thrown to one side, but with our much greater weight we had sufficient momentum to keep moving in an almost straight line. By the time we had gone round another couple of corners it was clear we had lost them.

"Sorry about the cork." I said, without the slightest hint of regret. "But I thought you just weren't trying hard enough." The Englishman ignored me, he probably doesn't have a very high opinion of sarcastic German ex whores, but the Sergeant turned round and told me I should be more careful. As he was delivering this gem his face registered the fact that I was no longer waving my gun about the place, and he looked at Martine for explanation.

"It's alright Jacques, I have her gun and I'm back in charge, but I promise you can shoot her if she tries any more of her tricks."

He gave me a warning glare, and for lack of anything better to say I asked if either he or Sir Freddy would like a drink. They both declined, the only difference being that Freddy did it politely and called me My Dear. So in the hope that we would have no more collisions for a while, I poured Martine and I a glass each. I savoured the taste, Pol Roger has always been a favourite of mine, but it could have usefully been a few degrees cooler. I took another look through the back window, just to check. No, there was no sign of them - astonishing.

"Where are you taking us Sir Freddy?"

"Well Martine and I need to have a private conversation on that subject, and I imagine that Jacques would like to get back to Chalons, so the more immediate question might be; where are you going Miss Fuchs?"

"Am I under arrest?"

Martine answered for him. "If we shoot you, as you deserve, then we might have problem with your advancing forces. Even if the Gestapo are hunting you, they might object to us killing you before you've been questioned, and if we put you in prison, you'll be out in a couple of weeks. For the time being it seems that our hands are tied."

Jacques turned to stare at me, a hard unforgiving stare, if he had his way I'd be left dead in the nearest gutter. Well that's alright Jacques, you're just a country copper and I've handled experts trying to kill me, when the time comes you'll need to be one hell of a lot smarter than I think you are.

I stared out of the window while sipping my second glass of champagne and considering the possibilities. Was Sir Freddy really this much of a soft touch, or was he just keeping me quiet until we got to wherever we were going? He was the one to watch, and also the first one that would need killing.

Sir Freddy Villiers
Paris, early hours, Saturday morning,
May 18th. 1940

There was a satisfying directness in our departure from the Boulevard Suchet, the violence of smashing unstoppably through the barrier and scattering the gunmen, or more probably running straight over some of them, had thrilled me. Such emotions were a revelation, perhaps I had a long repressed talent for running people down. Although it's such a niche market, there can't be much of an outlet for the skill.

One doesn't wish to rush to judgement on other men's lives, but the rampant self interest and the complete absence of moral standards in that household had been shocking. A group of self obsessed and not very intelligent people flirting with treason, the greatest tragedy being their direct and unavoidable connections with the highest in our land. I was horrified, and glad to be out of there.

The British system of government, like most others, routinely throws up a mixture genius and idiocy, but only rarely can it ever have produced a man so pathetically self obsessed as our ex king, and his truly appalling wife. I shuddered; if they ever did climb into bed with the Nazis it would be difficult to decide which of them to feel more sorry for. Just as long as he never came anywhere near England again.

I had been disturbed to hear one of the Gestapo shouting out to Martine, by name, threatening her with retribution - they seemed to think that she and Heidi were in league. No doubt as a result of von Strenglen's lies. This could make it difficult for her to go on living

313

a normal life in occupied France. But as things stood now, we would all be lucky to have any further life to consider.

After I had brushed aside Heidi's request for more information on our destination, Jacques had quietly asked the same question. The size of the car made it possible for quiet remarks in the front to be unheard by those in the back.

"I'm not sure, freeing Martine was at the heart of everything, my only other intention was to get back to England." I told him that I had hoped to take the magnetron back with me, but that it was half way across town and we wouldn't stand a chance of staying undetected for that length of time. The Germans had got every agent they possessed out looking for us. I had decided there was no option but to abandon it and make a run for safety, dropping the two of them off wherever they wanted en route."

"And what about Heidi? I reckon we shoot the bitch and dump her in the river. She'll be trouble for as long as we leave her alive."

I made an indeterminate *mmm* noise, meaning that I still hadn't made my mind up on that one. Although it wasn't me who had somehow removed her gun and turned the tables on her, so strictly speaking she was Martine's prisoner, not mine.

Then I recognised where we were. We were coming up to the huge roundabout at the Porte Maillot, one of the principal western exits from Paris.

"Martine," I called over my shoulder. "We're nearly at the Porte Maillot, it's going to make sense for you and me to take the N13 out towards Evreux and then maybe Caen or St. Malo, as we'd originally planned. Basically, it's a case of anywhere to get us out of Paris." I turned to Jacques. "As they're not chasing you, do you want to get out here, and make your way back into town? Then you could check in at some convenient Gendarmerie, or just make your own way back to Chalons. What does anybody think?"

"That makes sense to me." Said Martine, and Jacques nodded his agreement. Heidi asked what I proposed to do about her. Not having any other ideas, I told her that she would be staying with Martine and I for the time being.

As we joined the massive circular road junction, one of the biggest in Paris, I was looking round for a Metro station or a bus stop at which to drop Jacques. It was past midnight by now, and the next four or five hours would be the only time of day when this place wasn't busy. Even if the Metro and the buses had stopped for the night, it was only half a mile or so the Arc de Triomphe, he would find an all night bar open somewhere.

The circle of the roundabout was so large that there was a park in the middle, I cruised slowly round, waiting for Jacques to pick a spot to be dropped off. But instead of spotting a bus stop, he spotted danger.

"We just passed a parked car, there were three or four men in it and as soon as they saw us they started up and moved out to follow us." He had swung round in his seat to watch. "It's got a radio aerial, they're using radio controlled cars, that will be how they knew which car to look for. Even while they're following us they will already have called in reinforcements."

"Heidi and Martine, change places." I instructed. "Martine get on the same side as Jacques, with your gun ready and the window wound down." We needed to do something about it, while we were still dealing with just the one follower.

I had them spotted in my mirror, and for the time being they seemed content simply to follow, rather than attack. That made it certain, they were waiting for assistance, to make quite sure that this time they stopped us once and for all. They were fifty yards back and matching our speed, making no move to overtake us.

"Hold on tight." I swung in a lane and slammed on the brakes, coming to a tyre smoking emergency stop. After a second's hesitation they did the same, but even as they were doing that I had the Daimler in reverse and was careering backwards at full speed. A small van that I had cut in front of, couldn't believe his eyes and failed to get out of the way in time, there was a glancing collision, but I kept going.

"Kill the driver, you have to kill the driver." I shouted. Then before the Germans could start to reverse out of our way, I had positioned us alongside them. Jacques and Martine were both shooting from the same side, directly at the other car's driver. After hearing four or five of their gunshots I re-engaged a forward gear and drove off, as fast as possible. The whole thing had taken less than fifteen seconds, and as we took the first exit I could see in the mirror that their car was unmoving, just where we'd left it.

We were on the N13, the road I had said we'd take, leading eventually out to Evreux and on to Brittany.

"We didn't kill them all." Said Martine. "Which means that they will already be on the radio, directing anyone in the area to follow us."

Jacques had swivelled round in his seat, to watch them disappear behind us. "They're out of sight now, turn left. They will assume that we'll be desperate to leave the area."

"I can't turn left, there's a central reservation."

"So much the better, they won't think we've done it. Drive over it and go down that road there. I know where we are."

I slowed us down, swung away to the right to give myself more room, and then swung hard back to the left and charged the raised central strip. We bounced stomach churningly in the air, and landed hard enough for parts of the underside to hit the tarmac. Then with sparks flying out behind us we disappeared down the small side road he had pointed at. We came to a T junction, there were trees ahead of us.

"Turn right." He said, I did so.

"Where are we?"

"Running alongside the northern end of the Bois de Boulogne. In another minute or so we'll be back at the entrance to the football pitches we were at earlier."

"And then?"

"Then, if the German plane is still there, we break in, hot wire it and you and Martine can fly your way out of here."

"I can't fly, I'm not a pilot."

"Martine told me that you had landed the aircraft at Condé Vraux."

"Yes, I somehow managed to get it onto the ground, but I had no choice. If I hadn't have done I would have been killed."

"And how exactly does that situation differ from this? At best we might have ten or fifteen minutes before they work out that we're not speeding down the N13, and at that moment it isn't going to take a genius to think of looking here. They might be Nazi swine, but they're not stupid."

"I agree with him." Said Martine from the back. "If we stay on the ground they'll find us. Even if you can only fly us twenty kilometres away, it will take us out

317

of their immediate search area, which could give us some sort of chance."

"It's stupid, the Germans have complete control of the air, I've already been shot down once, and that was with a professional pilot."

"Oh for God's sake Sir Freddy, don't be so bloody vet. That is correct - you say in English *vet,* ja?" The woman sounded increasingly like Marlene Dietrich every time she opened her mouth, I think she was doing it deliberately.

I was reluctant, but the more I thought about it, the more obvious it seemed. It was not so much that I had any great confidence in my aeronautical skills, it was more a weary resignation that my options were severely limited. The German network in Paris was large, well organised and extremely determined. The existing agents they had in place during the Phony War, would almost certainly have been strengthened by now, preparatory to the invasion. The group that Heidi and von Strenglen had been part of, would just have been one of several. They had tracked us this far and it wouldn't take them long to corner us, they had the manpower. The fact that we had already killed several of their men would only increase their determination to bring us to a very permanent stop. All of which brought us neatly back to my earlier thoughts about the inadvisability of poking large dogs with sharp sticks.

"You do realise," I said over my shoulder to Martine, "That there is every bit as much chance of crashing as managing to get airborne?"

I'd never planned to live for ever."

"Well in that case, we don't need to hot wire it, it was me that locked it up and I've still got the key in my pocket."

That pretty much seemed to settle the matter, all we had to do now was work out how to start an unknown aeroplane in the dark.

Directed by Jacques I turned down the track to the football pitches, One of the cars was still where we had left it, but the four bodies had been removed as had von Strenglen and the pilot. Whether they had been taken by the French or the Germans I had no idea.

The aircraft was also still where we'd left it, parked at the far corner of the open area, pointing optimistically in the direction of its proposed take off run. I drove over and parked alongside, so that our headlights lit it up.

Up close, the reality of our proposal began to seem more frightening, the aircraft looked like some ungainly and alien insect, flimsy and insecure on its unnaturally long legs. This sort of thing had to be the province of experts, my obituary writer would probably describe what was about to happen as a moment of insanity, with inevitable consequences.

I collected the French road map and torch from the car, and walked over. Standing next to the plane, the door was a long way off the ground, I unlocked it and swung it open. There was the pilot's seat and then another seat behind it, the second seat was sufficiently far back to allow at least the possibility of squeezing two people into the space. This opened up the prospect of taking Heidi back to England as our prisoner. Major Grand would be delighted to interrogate her, and it would be better than arriving back completely empty handed. This whole nonsense might just make some sort of sense.

Using the wing strut as a step, I climbed in. I was basing my hopes of starting it on the premise that an aircraft designed for single crew operation in enemy territory would almost certainly have an electric starter, rather than relying on hand swinging the propeller. In the light of the car's headlights I examined the dashboard.

RPM, Turn and Bank Indicator, Vertical Speed, Altimeter, Direction Indicator, Airspeed Indicator, so far so good, but where was the fuel gauge? I looked, but there wasn't one. There was a fuel tank selector, but no gauge. Then I remembered being taken for a ride in a Tiger Moth, that had a glass tube sticking out of the fuel tank in the middle of the top wing. The fuel level was shown by a cork floating in the tube, primitive but effective. I looked up, but there was just a Plexiglas cockpit roof above my head, through which I could see the stars. Finding nothing inside the cockpit, I looked outside, and found the answer. The wing on this aircraft was fixed to the top of the cockpit, and hanging down from underneath it, one on each side, was a Tiger Moth style glass tube. They each had a cork floating about two thirds of the way up. That would be enough to get us out of here.

Then I was struck by an awful thought, an insuperable obstacle, I jumped out of the plane to tell Martine and Jacques.

"Even if I can get this thing off the ground, I can't land it again until dawn. If you think about it, once I'm up in the air there isn't any way for me to determine where I can land. If I can see lights on the ground, it means there are buildings or lamp posts, and if there are no lights how can I tell which of the black areas are safe to land in?" I looked at my watch; it was just after one o'clock in the morning. "The tanks seem to be over half full, but I'm sure that won't be enough. We'll need to stay up for about three and a half hours, until there's enough light in the sky to find a field. Because otherwise, if the take off doesn't kill us, the landing certainly will."

"The car's got a full tank, they were planning to make an early start tomorrow."

"Today."

"Whatever, the point is we can siphon petrol out of there, even twenty or thirty litres might make a difference, but we'll need to move quickly."

We moved very quickly. There was a length of hose and an empty 25 litre can in the Daimler's boot. Jacques got the petrol moving, Martine watched Heidi and I took the flashlight to look in the changing hut for a step ladder, or anything else to stand on to reach the top of the wing and the fuel filler caps. I found a step ladder, and it was long enough, but as I picked it up I heard a scream from outside.

Chapter 21

Fraulein Heidi Fuchs
Paris, early hours, Saturday, May 18th. 1940

Handing over my gun to Martine had been one of my more inspired moves, they all relaxed and took it for granted that I had surrendered, given up, abandoned myself to their mercy. And pigs might fly. It also meant that I could leave all the worry about dodging the Gestapo to them. It was as if I had just hired an extremely well motivated chauffeur, with champagne provided.

Sir Freddy smashed his way majestically through the opposition, and I was seriously impressed. The stunt he pulled with the emergency braking at the Porte Maillot roundabout had been brilliant, I would have been proud of that move myself. Yet even so, the three of them still failed to tie me hand and foot, and gag me, which was a mistake, because frankly anything less wouldn't have helped. The one who came closest was Jacques, he never trusted me and his instinct all along had been to kill me. Which is exactly what I would have done to him, in similar circumstances.

I even liked the idea of flying the Storch out and fooling the Gestapo that way. For a while, I planned to go along with them, and then make a break for it when we got to wherever it was. In fact, I was seriously considering going with them all the way to England. At some stage, it would finally occur to Sir Freddy that what he ought to do was to suggest that Martine should come with him, she would breathe a sigh of relief that he had finally woken up to what was going on, and off they would go. If I manoeuvred the situation correctly, they would find themselves deciding to take me with them as a captive, a sort of consolation prize for not getting the magnetron thing. I would then find some way of moving myself from England to the USA, and with the number of naturalised Germans in Chicago and New York I could start a brand new life under a brand new name. I was quite excited by the prospect.

But then - then it had all changed. I heard Sir Freddy, thinking himself to be talking privately, tell Jacques that he knew exactly where the magnetron was. That was my ticket back to Berlin. He'd had me fooled before, but now I was sure that Freddy actually possessed this information, then hurting Martine would undoubtedly produce it. This was going to be a most enjoyable and successful way to conclude matters. Von Strenglen and his bullshit story about me trying to sell the device would evaporate like snow in August, if I could produce the blasted thing.

I relaxed for a moment into warm thoughts of Martine, I had grown quite close to her, even fond of her, and that is always the best way to inflict pain. Her sudden shock at seeing me in a different light would be quite moving, and if that didn't get Sir Freddy's stiff upper lip trembling then nothing would. I was cooperative, I was humble, I was pleasant, but most of all I watched and waited.

Jacques was messing about with the petrol at the back of the car, while Sir Freddy had gone off to look for something in the hut, which left Martine and I standing in the darkness, with her holding my gun. I had already looked around and I knew what I wanted, and now I was going to get it.

"I need a pee, can I go over there, where it's a bit darker."

Martine looked doubtful, she was looking for the trick, but couldn't see it.

"You've got my gun, and I'm not much danger to anyone with my knickers round my knees."

"Go on then."

I walked over to the slightly darker area, squatted down and had a pee. There was no mistaking what was going on, she could hear it. One woman having a pee in front of another is no big deal, but even so, she still looked away. People are so predictable, she should have watched, but she didn't like to. Lying on the ground next to me were six corner flag posts from the pitch, one and a half metre long wooden poles. When I stood up, I took one with me. Could I possibly get away with something as brazen as this?

As I walked back towards her, I held the post behind me with one hand, while I adjusted the waistband of my skirt with the other. I moved my shoulders around as if I was generally sorting out my clothing. She could see that my behaviour was perfectly normal after what I'd been doing and so she didn't stare. As well as watching me, she was also watching Jacques with half her attention. It was just one mistake after another.

Once I was close enough, I didn't hesitate, but swung the pole round in both hands. Her right hand, the one holding the gun, was hanging down to her side, ready for use but not pointing at anyone. The pole hit her right forearm hard and I heard the bone crack, I'd work on that later, it would produce all the pain I needed. More importantly the gun dropped to the ground.

While her mouth was still working on the first scream, I charged her using the pole as a spear. She went flying, just as the scream reached her mouth. I scooped up the gun, my gun, which she'd been keeping warm for me, and swung round to Jacques.

Alerted by the scream, he was turning to look for the cause, still holding the siphon tube in the neck of the fuel can. Not wasting any time on careful aiming I shot him, firing as he turned. He fell backwards, but I'd just winged him so I raised the pistol to line up the killer shot, I needed him permanently out of the way. But as I did so, I heard Sir Freddy behind me, and turned to take care of him first.

He was coming through the door of the hut carrying a two or three metre wooden step ladder. He showed all the classic signs of shock: coming to a standstill, eyes wide open, mouth gaping. Remembering that he had to live long enough to answer my questions, and that his sort might take quite a bit of persuading, I shot at his legs. He was unarmed, so all I had to do was stop him moving. But as I did, the top of the step ladder swung in front of him and the bullet hit that. Then, annoyingly and distractingly, there were two unexpected shots from over to my left.

I knew at once this meant that my fellow countrymen had arrived, ahead of schedule. I was impressed by the speed of their deductive process, but unhappy at their interference. I risked a quick glance but could see nothing in the darkness, until another muzzle flash showed their location. They were too far away to bother me, pistol shooting in combat is a close quarters game, the stupid bastards were more likely to hit a tree than me. I swung back to Sir Freddy.

Incredibly, he had rested the heavy wooden step ladder's feet on the ground and was holding it upright in front of himself. His face appeared round one side, as did his right hand, holding a gun. I had been sure he was unarmed, he carefully raised the gun and fired at me. More in astonishment and anger, than careful calculation, I stood my ground and fired two shots back at him. As my shots hit the step ladder, he fired again, and I realised that I'd been hit.

There was a silence, when nobody fired. I could feel two impact points, one in my thigh and one in my belly. Neither of them hurt, but I was feeling faint, slightly dizzy. I think I was swaying. Then without any sensation of falling I found that I was lying on my back, and staring up at the night sky. I was dying, I was astonished.

I had often wondered what this would feel like, this dying business, and the fact of the matter was that it didn't feel like very much at all. Was this how poor old Theo had felt, with that tent peg spike?

As I lay there, getting colder and colder, I could hear voices but couldn't make out what they were saying. And slowly I became aware of something else, some kind of familiar sensation. It was difficult to concentrate but eventually I realised that it was a smell - the smell of petrol.

Then there was a sudden bright flash of light.

Sir Freddy Villiers
Northern France, early hours, Saturday,
May 18th. 1940

Emerging from the hut, I was confronted with a lurid scene from Bedlam, lit only by reflections from the car's headlights on the aircraft. Jacques was by the car struggling to get up, Martine was on the ground, holding one arm and quietly gasping, somebody in the tree line was shooting - but at whom? And right in front of me stood our disarmed captive, pointing a gun straight at me and firing it.

There was the impact of a bullet striking the ladder, then as she glanced about her I stood the folded ladder in front of me, while I reached for Jacques' pistol. For the life of me, quite literally, I couldn't remember if the safety catch was on or off, and looking at it in the darkness gave me no clue. I peered round the edge of the ladder, pointed the damn thing at her and pulled the trigger. Surprisingly, it went off. She gave a slight stagger, but then fired her own gun back at me. So I pointed my gun and fired again. This time her gun arm dropped to her side. She stood there looking at me for a second, and then the gun fell from her hand. She took half a pace backwards and fell to the ground. I think I just killed someone.

This was a prime shambles, shoving the pistol back in my pocket I ran to Martine, but she waved me away.

"I'll be OK, it's just my arm, see to Jacques."

He had a bullet in one shoulder, and was already getting unsteadily to his feet, I helped him.

"Martine and I are getting in the plane, we could take three, do you want to come with us?"

"No, I've got a wife and child at home, they're going to need me more than ever now. But you two get in the plane and I'll give you some distraction on my way out of here.

"Will you be alright?"

"I've got friends nearby, and that lot," he looked in the direction of the other shooters, "don't know the area like I do. I can lose them on foot, through the trees. We don't have time for the petrol, you'll just have to go with what you've got. You get Martine to the plane, I'm going to turn the car round."

As I shepherded Martine to the aircraft, he swung the Daimler round, so that its lights pointed at the shooters, giving us some cover behind the glare.

Martine stood looking helplessly at the huge step she needed to take to reach the cockpit. Having an unusable right arm didn't help matters. I reached down, grasped the hem of her skirt in both hands and yanked it all the way up around her waist. She raised her eyebrows, but made no protest, I should have done this days ago. Then I turned her round, told her to reach up and grab the edge of the doorway with her left hand. Without the restriction of her skirt, she was able to lift one leg high enough to get a foot on the wing strut. Then with both my hands pushing her backside she was propelled into the cockpit.

One might have thought it impossible to be seized by lascivious thoughts in such a place, at such a moment, but with my hands on her firm round bottom, I found myself rising to the occasion.

Seeing her safely in, I followed. As I turned to shut the cockpit door, there was a flash of light from the far side of the car, no doubt Jacques had set light to the petrol, to create a further diversion. As I looked, I suddenly realised exactly what it was that was burning, a human form was writhing feebly in the flames. I turned away, sickened. There were going to be a lot more burning bodies around here before this war was over, and not all of them would have asked for it quite as insistently as her.

I used the flashlight to scan the panel methodically, whilst remaining aware of the oncoming gunmen, I had to avoid panicking. On the right was a switch marked *Magnetzunder* with three positions marked *Ein, Zwie* and *Beide*, or both, it was clearly the magneto. I set it to both. Below that was a large plunger, sticking out from under the edge of the dashboard. I moved it experimentally, it felt like a fuel primer - come back to that in a minute. Across the middle were the normal flight instruments that I'd looked at earlier.

On the left was a red button, with no label, that would be the starter. Below that was a key socket, I tried the key and it fitted. I turned it to the right and a small green light came on, this was progress. Attached to the under edge of the dash was a lever, marked *Benzin*, with positions; *Rechts, Links* and *Beide,* this was the fuel tank selector so I set it to both.

There seemed to be nothing else starter related on the panel, so I looked down the left side to the throttle levers. There were two unmarked levers, the larger would be the throttle, so thinking back to starting Sandy's motor launch at Hayling Island, I set it to fully closed, and the smaller one would be mixture, so I set that to fully forward.

I looked around there didn't seem to be much else to do, so I pressed the red button. For a moment nothing happened, but then I heard a bullet strike some part of our airframe, I didn't think the two events connected so I pressed the button a second time. Still nothing. I started looking round again.

There was a strange contraption on the left of the cockpit, whereby a pulley handle turned what looked like a bicycle chain, which disappeared upwards into the wing root. I gave it a trial turn and saw the flaps begin to twitch - not that. Behind it was an indicator needle - no idea, but it wasn't going to start the engine. I looked on the right side, and there, below the door, was a black box of electrical switches. Jackpot.

The labels were hand written and very small. The first one said *Zündung* and the second *Batterie,* I couldn't read the rest. I switched them all on, and a red light started to glow on the dashboard. Then I pressed the button again, this time it coughed but didn't start. Bugger, I hadn't primed it. I grasped the primer knob and pumped it vigorously half a dozen times. Then I pressed the button again, third time lucky?

This time the engine coughed a couple of times and then settled itself into a comfortable sounding roar. With a shuddering release I began to breathe normally again. Proper pilots go through all sorts of very sensible pre flight checks, to make sure all their bits are working, but I'm not a proper pilot and I'll find out if any of my bits aren't working when we hurtle uncontrollably to our doom.

There are moments in life which call for reasoned analysis and careful judgement, but then there was the smack of another bullet hitting us somewhere; I just opened throttle, all the way - it seemed to cut out the middle man.

The aircraft lurched forward, I put my hand on the stick nervously, unsure what to do with it. I held it loosely, more or less where I'd found it. The plane bounded forward, my way dimly lit by the car's headlights, which shone weakly on the distant tree line. The tail must have lifted from the ground almost as soon as I applied the power, because now we were moving I had a much better forward view. I was wondering when I should pull back for take off, when suddenly the bouncing stopped and everything became much smoother. I couldn't work out why, and then realised that I could see cars moving along the N13, which was now passing under our wheels.

I was wondering whether or not any of the stray ordnance passing our way had hit Martine, when her unbroken arm came round my neck and she started kissing the side of my face. I took that as a positive result to the passenger satisfaction survey. While I had her this close, I gave her the torch and told her what to do.

"You need to look at the atlas, and find somewhere we can land, somewhere that can be recognised in the dark. I'm guessing that we've got perhaps an hour and half's flying time. You concentrate on that, while I try and sort the plane out."

After she had sat back in her seat, I thought that I should have asked how her arm felt, but I was better employed trying to be a pilot.

First things first, I turned the flap wheel until it came to a stop and they were fully raised. Next I eased the throttle back just enough to reduce our RPM by about ten per cent, and then I brought the mixture lever slowly back, by small increments until the engine gave a hesitant cough. Then I edged it forward just a little, for smooth running. This was like driving one of the old Rolls Royces, one had to adjust their mixture controls for the best range, I assumed that aero engines worked on the same principle.

We had been slowly climbing as I fiddled around with things, the altimeter seemed to be in metres and was currently reading 450, which was about 1500 feet. That was plenty high enough, so I pushed the stick slightly forward to drop the nose, this required a constant pressure to hold it there, so I felt down the side of the seat for the trim wheel. With the lights of the western suburbs beneath us, it was relatively easy to maintain our straight and level attitude, by reference to the ground. What I didn't know was how I was going to maintain that when we were really in the dark.

The glass tubes showing the fuel contents were dimly visible in the reflected light from the ground, but the level of the indicators couldn't be seen. We would find out when the fuel was gone by the fact that the engine stopped.

A hand rested on my shoulder and I could smell her face near mine. "Head three zero zero degrees."

"Where will that get us?"

"The coast, near Caen, then we turn right and pick up the Seine estuary. When you've found that, Le Havre is on the corner of the north bank, and Le Havre airport is just to the north of town, and it's right on the coast."

I used one of my hands to take hers, I turned it over and slowly kissed her palm, it was all of her that I could reach.

The lights on the ground disappeared quite rapidly, and we droned on in our little bubble. The softly glowing array of professional instruments in front of me, making it look as if I knew what I was doing. In fact it was a constant struggle to avoid over compensating, I found that once I had the trim set properly, then the less I moved the stick the better we were. I had come to rely on the Vertical Speed Indicator to tell me if we were going up or down, and the vertical needle in the Turn and Bank Indicator to reassure me that the wings were level. What real pilots did, I had no idea. I felt as if I were standing on top of a flagpole, and that if I moved too much in any direction we would fall off.

I had the speed more or less constant on 160 kilometres per hour, which I guessed was about 90 miles an hour, I was too frightened of losing my balance to engage in mental arithmetic. We had been in this relatively stable situation for about twenty minutes, when I was aware of a black shape flying directly over the top of us, from straight ahead. We bounced up and down and rattled about. Our combined speed was so high that I saw little more than a fast moving piece of deeper darkness than the rest. My heart sank, this was going to be a re run of my arrival in France when a pair of Messerschmitts had jumped us.

"Look out for the flash of gunfire." I shouted back.

After only the briefest delay she tapped my shoulder urgently. "You've got the outside lights on."

I looked, and she was right. That had to be one of the switches down at the right. I started at the back, and switched one off, a glow that I hadn't noticed from one of the wings went out. That must have been our landing light, I hadn't even realised it was on. Then I switched off the next one and the red and green glows at the wing tips disappeared. I tried the third, and the instrument lights went out, so I switched that one back on again.

"I can see them shooting, they're off to the right."

I pulled the throttle fully back and pushed the nose down. In theory if I cut the power, but kept the speed the same, we should be going down like an express lift. Maybe operating the flaps would increased the effect, but I couldn't cope with that. I needed all three hands to control the plane as it was. The Airspeed Indicator had gone past 200 kilometres, I pulled the nose up slightly to stop it going any further. The Turn and Bank needle showed that I was falling over to the right, the direction I had been looking in.

I pulled back a little more and moved the stick slightly to the left. It wasn't enough, we were still accelerating and still tipping sideways. I pulled back more firmly, and moved the stick more positively to the left. We stopped accelerating and moved slightly back to a more level position. I moved the stick even further. The airspeed began to drop, too much so. I pushed the power back on. The altimeter was showing 150 metres, try and hold it at that. I was scanning feverishly from the Vertical Speed, which I wanted to be nil, to the

Turn and Bank needle which I wanted to be in the middle. The sweat was pouring off me, and I was gasping for breath.

The hand came on my shoulder again. "That was fantastic, I think we've lost him."

I wanted to shout that it didn't feel fantastic, but couldn't divert any attention from my balancing act. There was a suspicion that the slightest further disruption could make me vomit, either from air sickness or fear. After a few more minutes of racing heart and clammy hands I realised that I had lost all idea of heading. The business of turning us back onto three zero zero, helped stabilise my heart sufficiently to resume normal service.

The fact that I had been flying over a country at war, in an enemy aircraft, lit up like a Christmas tree, made our interception unsurprising. The surprise was our survival.

It was a starlit night, and half an hour later we saw the coast before we reached it. The Seine estuary was clear and the petrochemical works up river from the town could be seen pumping smoke into the sky. I swung out to sea to come back in to the coast just to the north of town. There was certainly a black area, where the airport should be. I dropped us down to 100 metres and slowed to 65 kilometres an hour. There was a gleam of reflected light from what I assumed to be a runway, but it came too late to be useful. I went a little further, turned round and came back on that line, there was enough starlight to land by. Though frankly it was neither neat nor particularly smooth, I was too tired for that. But unlike my last aeronautical escapade, at least the damn thing didn't explode.

Epilogue

Section D, Metropole Hotel,
London, Monday May 20th 1940

"Yes I agree, it would have been too dangerous to go back across town with the Hun at your heels, especially as it was only a duplicate. But where exactly is it now?"

"In the hen coop at the end of Tante Mimi's garden."

"In the hen coop?"

"Why not? Clearly you wouldn't have looked there, and neither will they. A little chicken shit won't hurt. If there's anyone left at the Embassy they can go and collect it - she'll probably give them some eggs as well."

Martine nodded her agreement. "She's nice like that."

The Major sighed, the heavy sigh of a man dealing with idiots.

"Moving on to your arrival here. So you flew straight in from Le Havre to Heston, that I understand, but that was two days ago. Where the hell have you been since then?

"In bed mostly."

"And where have you been staying Miss Dumont."

"Don't be so silly."

"I beg your pardon."

"I've been in bed too, with him."

"Oh, I see. But even so you can't just park an enemy aircraft at one of our airfields and walk away, without saying a word."

"I left the key in the ignition."

"Well perhaps, but it caused all sorts of ructions. Nobody had the slightest idea where it had come from."

"You're Military Intelligence, you should have worked it out. Anyway if you don't want it I'll take it away with me."

"That's not the point . . . "

The elderly lady in civilian clothes at the side table joined in."Oh Lawrence do shut up, you're giving us all a headache."

Then she turned to Martine. "What's he like, is he any good?"

Martine looked at me, considered the issue for a moment and then said. "Well we have to be careful with my arm." She glanced down at her right arm, in its sling. "But I suppose he's not too bad - considering." The two women pursed their lips and nodded thoughtfully, as they contemplated my attributes.

The bloody nerve of the woman.

Major Grand and I looked at each other and shrugged, there didn't seem to be much else to say.

###

Historical Note

Although Rendezvous in Paris is a work of fiction, many elements are completely factual. The arrival of Professeur Maurice Ponte at the GEC office in Wembley on May 8th. 1940, clutching a supposedly top secret magnetron in a cardboard box is what actually happened. Unfortunately, that particular model didn't turn out to be quite the great advance that everyone hoped at the time. Claude Roland and his duplicate device are just requirements of the plot.

Whilst it was useful for the cover blurb, the word 'radar' isn't mentioned in the book's text for the very good reason that the term wasn't invented until the following year. The Radio Direction Finding research centre at Bawdsey Manor, and its brilliant if somewhat prickly director Albert (Jimmy) Rowe, are accurately described. It was there that the first usable short wavelength ship and airborne radar installations were developed, which gave the British such a dramatic technical lead over both their enemies and their allies.

The two Air Ministers and their political affiliations are descriptions of real people, as is Major Grand of Military Intelligence Section D. The German Blitzkrieg, the collapse of the French army, the resultant political and civil chaos and Heydrich's use of Einsatzgruppen, in the way described, are historically correct. Even the presence, almost unbelievably, of neutral tourists in Paris at this time is factual. The Windsor's domestic arrangements, contemporary questions on her sexuality and the previous occupants of that address are well known facts, as is the Nazi plan mentioned to install them as puppet monarchs of an occupied Britain.

However, Sir Freddy, Martine and dear sweet Heidi are the products of my fevered imagination.

Finally, if anyone has been offended by my rudeness about the Swiss, the French, the British, the Germans, Joseph Kennedy, the Duke and Duchess of Windsor or Japanese tourists, then frankly they should get out more.

To all the rest of you, I thank you for reading and hope to see you again with the next book.

Best wishes
Ian Okell

About the author:

Ian was for many years a ship's chandler, part of the fourth generation in his family business, supplying merchant vessels around the UK and north west Europe. Deciding that too much of his time was spent travelling and looking for a job which allowed more time for a home life, he set up a local business of his own, a Registered Firearms Dealership.

However, although still fun, the gun shop has turned out to be much busier than originally envisaged, and is now run by son Mike, with Ian relegated to general dogsbody. He is also a commercially qualified pilot on medium sized twin engined aircraft.

Ian and his wife Margaret, another pilot, live in Cheshire, they have three grown up children and, so far, two grandchildren. For many years writing has been his hobby, resulting in about one book a year, although never with any thought of being published. It was only after taking part in an Arts Council literary criticism website that his books found their way into print.

If you enjoyed reading
'Rendezvous in Paris'
then you might also enjoy
some other books
by the same author -

Loose Cannon
Ian Okell

Harry Lyndon is a civilised and happy man, his world organised just the way he likes it. But then, out of the blue, someone tries to kill him - and he has no idea who or why.

The trouble is that when he tells the police it turns out they also want him dead. Something is horribly wrong, He's forced to run, with nothing but the clothes on his back. It isn't mistaken identity. His credit cards have been cancelled, his flat watched and his girlfriend disappeared. He is the named subject of a full scale terrorist alert - and they're going to shoot him on sight.

Only one thing might help - without his anti psychotic tablets he's getting more than a little unstable himself - dangerously so. Somebody, somewhere, thought he'd be a pushover . . .

'It isn't paranoid to think they're trying to kill you - not if it's true. Loose Cannon takes up where The 39 Steps and Rogue Male left off, but this time with a regular supply of sharp one liners to go with the mayhem.'

Sample Five Star Amazon Reviews - more onsite

- I used to think Lee Childs was as good as it got with fast paced thrillers - this is better (Matt D)

- The most satisfying book I've read in years (Pat R.)

- Just what I needed. I read this book on a 12 hour plane trip and didn't bother with the inflight movies.(Tim H.)

Published by - feedaread.com
**Available from Amazon and good book shops
and in Kindle, Apple, Sony, Kobo, Nook etc.**

Charlie Chaplin's Uncle
Ian Okell

London, December 1892 – A mist drifts in from the river – on the streets there are gas lamps and Hansom cabs. There are dirty doings at the music hall and even dirtier doings on the Royal Train.

The Prince of Wales has designs on another man's wife and visiting Royalty look like getting shot – one way or another somebody is going to come to a sticky, sticky end.

The Freemasons are in there somewhere, but what's their interest? Then things really begin to fall apart. The constabulary turn out to be no use at all – and meanwhile the body count is rising – inexorably.

Who's going to be the most help: young Charlie Chaplin, Sherlock Holmes, or Mr. Fowler the engine driver?

'A Victorian railway caper in a snowstorm, gripping, ruthless, and very funny. An absolutely brilliant book, fantastic fun. Just read it!'

Sample Five Star Amazon reviews - more onsite

- 'An original and unusual book – had me laughing quite helplessly. The sort of quality that should win prizes, but probably too much fun to be taken seriously in grand literary circles.' (Sam L.)

- 'The pace is fast and the plot fits together like expensive joinery. Beautifully crafted, enjoyed every bit of it.' (Bob S.)

- 'I loved it, loved it, loved it.' (Janet M.)

Published by - feedaread.com
Available from Amazon and good book shops and in Kindle, Apple, Sony, Kobo, Nook etc.

Rude Awakening

Ian Okell

"They were either going to install me as the Arch Druid, or they had something of a sacrificial nature in mind. Perhaps I should tell them I wasn't a virgin."

He already knew his cancer was terminal and lying in hospital, finally surrendering to the morphine, Michael accepts that he is dying. But suddenly it's all gone wrong - he's awake when he should be dead, and in a place he's never seen before.

Is this just the random sparking of failing brain cells before the last goodbye? Is this what death feels like? Out of place and out of time - even realising that he is still alive doesn't do him any good. He is at the wrong end of an impossible journey, in a society untouched by civilisation.

'Tangled and dangerous relationships in a sweeping saga of conflict, betrayal and discovery. As seen through the eyes of an entertaining and extremely devious observer.'

Sample Five Star Amazon Reviews - more onsite

- 'A magical mystery tour - had me laughing and crying. I'm still not sure if I've been reading an adventure, a history, a travelogue or a very moving love story. I'm going to have to read it again.'(Rosie B.)

- 'I've never read a book before narrated by a dead man, if that's what he is - kept me gripped right through to the end.' (Drumwilldrum)

- 'A seriously good book - I loved the self deprecating black humour and irony (Wildwildwest)

Published by - feedaread.com
Available from Amazon and good book shops and in Kindle, Apple, Sony, Kobo, Nook etc.

Lightning Source UK Ltd.
Milton Keynes UK
UKOW040635070513

210293UK00001B/2/P